NICHOLAS ROYLE has published five collections of short fiction, including *London Gothic* and *Manchester Uncanny* (both Confingo). He is also the author of seven novels, most recently *First Novel* (Vintage). He has edited more than two dozen anthologies, including fourteen earlier volumes of *Best British Short Stories*. He also runs Nightjar Press, which publishes original short stories as limited-edition chapbooks. His books-about-books, *White Spines: Confessions of a Book Collector* and *Shadow Lines: Searching For the Book Beyond the Shelf*, are published by Salt. Forthcoming are *Paris Fantastique* (Confingo) and *Finders, Keepers: The Secret History of Second-hand Books* (Salt).

BY THE SAME AUTHOR

NOVELS
Counterparts
Saxophone Dreams
The Matter of the Heart
The Director's Cut
Antwerp
Regicide
First Novel

NOVELLAS
The Appetite
The Enigma of Departure

SHORT STORIES
Mortality
In Camera (with David Gledhill)
Ornithology
The Dummy & Other Uncanny Stories
London Gothic
Manchester Uncanny

ANTHOLOGIES (as editor)
Darklands
Darklands 2
A Book of Two Halves
The Tiger Garden: A Book of Writers' Dreams
The Time Out Book of New York Short Stories
The Ex Files: New Stories About Old Flames
The Agony & the Ecstasy: New Writing for the World Cup
Neonlit: Time Out Book of New Writing
The Time Out Book of Paris Short Stories
Neonlit: Time Out Book of New Writing Volume 2
The Time Out Book of London Short Stories Volume 2
Dreams Never End
'68: New Stories From Children of the Revolution
The Best British Short Stories 2011
Murmurations: An Anthology of Uncanny Stories About Birds
The Best British Short Stories 2012-2024

NON-FICTION
White Spines: Confessions of a Book Collector
Shadow Lines: Searching for the Book Beyond the Shelf

BEST BRITISH SHORT STORIES 2025

SERIES EDITOR
NICHOLAS ROYLE

CROMER

PUBLISHED BY SALT PUBLISHING 2025

2 4 6 8 10 9 7 5 3 1

Selection and introduction © Nicholas Royle, 2025
Individual contributions © the contributors, 2025

Nicholas Royle has asserted his right under the Copyright, Designs and Patents Act 1988 to be identified as the editor of this work.

This book is sold subject to the condition that it shall not, by way of trade or otherwise, be lent, resold, hired out, or otherwise circulated without the publisher's prior consent in any form of binding or cover other than that in which it is published and without a similar condition including this condition being imposed on the subsequent publisher.

This book is a work of fiction. Any references to historical events, real people or real places are used fictitiously. Other names, characters, places and events are products of the author's imagination, and any resemblance to actual events or places or persons, living or dead, is entirely coincidental.

First published in Great Britain in 2025 by
Salt Publishing Ltd
12 Norwich Road, Cromer, Norfolk NR27 0AX United Kingdom

www.saltpublishing.com

Salt Publishing Limited Reg. No. 5293401

A CIP catalogue record for this book is available from the British Library

ISBN 978 1 78463 353 0 (Paperback edition)
ISBN 978 1 78463 354 7 (Electronic edition)

Typeset in Neacademia by Salt Publishing

Printed and bound in Great Britain by Clays Ltd, Elcograf S.p.A

CONTENTS

NICHOLAS ROYLE
Introduction — ix

CD ROSE
I'm in Love With a German Film Star — 1

LINDEN HIBBERT
Torsos — 7

WYL MENMUIR
The Incidents — 22

OKECHUKWU NZELU
The Headteacher — 30

CATRIN KEAN
Dŵr — 45

ELIZABETH STOTT
A Fictional Detective — 51

CHRISTOPHER BURNS
Junction — 57

IMOGEN REID
Fabrication — 70

NAOMI WOOD
Flatten the Curve — 77

ROGER LUCKHURST
You — 93

PIPPA GOLDSCHMIDT
Lord of the Fruit Flies — 100

MARK VALENTINE
Laughter Ever After — 106

DAVID BEVAN
Helium — 115

ROSE BIGGIN
The Ice Tigs — 121

BARET MAGARIAN
The Portal in Lisbon — 139

SIMON OKOTIE
When Viewed From the Head Rather Than the Foot — 146

HANNAH HOARE
Flight of the Albatross — 154

IAN CRITCHLEY
Ghost Walks — 163

IAIN SINCLAIR
Under the Flyover — 169

ALISON MOORE
The Junction — 196

Contributor Biographies — 213
Acknowledgements — 218

To the memory of Robert Coover (1932–2024)

NICHOLAS ROYLE

INTRODUCTION

THIS IS THE fifteenth volume of *Best British Short Stories*. To mark the occasion, here are fifteen lists that pertain, in one way or another, to the short story.

Fifteen UK publishers that aren't afraid of short stories
- British Library Publishing
- CB editions
- Comma Press
- Confingo Publishing
- Dead Ink Books
- Faber & Faber
- Fitzcarraldo Editions
- Fly on the Wall Press
- Galley Beggar Press
- Influx Press
- Jacaranda Books
- Nightjar Press
- Peepal Tree Press
- Salt Publishing
- Scratch Books

Fourteen UK print literary magazines that publish short stories
- *Confingo*
- *Extra Teeth*
- *Granta*
- *Gutter*
- *Lighthouse*
- *London Magazine*
- *New Welsh Review*
- *Open Pen*
- *Remains*
- *Seaside Gothic*
- *Shooter*
- *Stand*
- *Tears in the Fence*
- *Wasafiri*

Thirteen writers best known for their short fiction
- Robert Aickman
- Jorge Luis Borges
- Ray Bradbury
- Raymond Carver
- Julio Cortazar
- Roald Dahl
- Lydia Davis
- Shirley Jackson
- Franz Kafka
- Katherine Mansfield
- Alice Munro
- Edgar Allan Poe
- Saki

Twelve individuals who do a great deal to support the short story in the UK (with apologies to those people whose names will come to me only when it's too late)
- Jess Chandler, publisher Prototype Publishing
- Ailsa Cox, founder Edge Hill Prize
- Jonny Davidson, production editor British Library
- David Gaffney, author, deviser short fiction projects
- Cathy Galvin, founder Word Factory
- Jonathan Gibbs, author, creator *A Personal Anthology*
- Dominic Jaeckle, author, publisher
- Johnny Mains, anthologist, author, genre researcher
- Alberto Manguel, author, critic, anthologist
- Chris Power, short story writer, critic, broadcaster
- Amanda Saint, founder Retreat West
- Tony White, author, founder Piece of Paper Press

Eleven great films based on short stories
- *Don't Look Now*
- *Rear Window*
- *Blow-up*
- *2001: A Space Odyssey*
- *The Loneliness of the Long-Distance Runner*
- *They Live*
- *The Swimmer*

The Birds
Minority Report
Total Recall
Memento

Ten short story collections published by Picador, 1972-1999
    Alan Beard, *Taking Doreen Out of the Sky*
    Jorge Luis Borges, *The Aleph and Other Stories 1933-1969*
    Rebecca Brown, *The Terrible Girls*
    Robert Coover, *Pricksongs & Descants*
    MJ Fitzgerald, *Ropedancer*
    Ellen Gilchrist, *In the Land of Dreamy Dreams*
    Jamaica Kincaid, *At the Bottom of the River*
    Ian McEwan, *First Love, Last Rites*
    Bridget O'Connor, *Here Comes John*
    Bruno Schulz, *The Street of Crocodiles*

Nine short story anthologies published by Picador 1972-2001 with the caveat that some of these include novel extracts
    Dermot Bolger, *The Picador Book of Contemporary Irish Fiction*
    Amit Chaudhuri, *The Picador Book of Modern Indian Literature*
    Carolyn Choa & David Su Li-qun, *The Picador Book of Contemporary Chinese Fiction*
    Clifton Fadiman, *The World of the Short Story*
    Frederick R Karl & Leo Hamalian, *The Naked i*
    Patrick McGrath & Bradford Morrow, *The New Gothic*
    Peter Kravitz, *The Picador Book of Contemporary Scottish Fiction*
    George Lamming, *Cannon Shot and Glass Beads*
    Alberto Manguel, *Black Water*

Eight random notes
- Hats off to *Extra Teeth*, the only UK literary magazine, possibly the only literary magazine anywhere, to employ a vibe consultant. In fact, Nyla Ahmad is described on the *Extra Teeth* website as both 'vibe consultant' and 'vibes consultant'. So, which is correct? I asked the question. On social media, the response came back: 'Both are correct! Vibes is used when consulting on the multiple different vibes of a person, place or thing, whereas vibe relates to the general overall impression.' I'm now wondering if *Best British Short Stories* needs a vibe – or vibes – consultant and, if so, who it should be.
- Since the publication of *Best British Short Stories 2024*, three readers have contacted me, to say they liked my story reprinted in that volume. I explained to them that I was not the author of 'Strangers Meet We When' by Nicholas Royle, taken from *David Bowie, Enid Blyton and the Sun Machine*, by Nicholas Royle; that it was the work of the author I call the other Nicholas Royle; that he and I are two different authors; that he even suggested adding a note to his biographical note explaining all of this, but I decided against it, perhaps unwisely. What could or should I have done differently so that readers would not think that I had committed the ultimate act of vanity and narcissism, as an editor, by selecting a story of my own to be included in a book with the word 'best' in its title? Should I have included that explanatory line in Royle's biog note? Does anyone read biog notes? My thinking was that anyone who thought I had included a story of my own had only to read Royle-the-author's biog note and Royle-the-editor's biog note and they would see that these were two different writers. This was naïve of me and so I decided to write about the issue in this introduction for the record. What, then, should an editor

do? I felt that his story deserved to be picked. Should I have not picked it, simply because we write under the same name? Should the Writers Guild or the Society of Authors have a rule stipulating that there may not be two authors with the same name, that the newcomer should come up with a new name, as Equity demands of actors? Royle published his first book – *Telepathy and Literature: Essays on the Reading Mind* (1990) – before I published either the first anthology I edited, *Darklands* (1991), or my first novel, *Counterparts* (1993). How would I have reacted had I been obliged to come up with a different name? I would not have been pleased. And now that I think about it, I had been publishing short stories, in magazines and anthologies, under what I regarded as my own name, since 1984, some of which I forwarded, precociously, to Giles Gordon in the hope that he and David Hughes might select one of them for their series, *Best Short Stories*, which they never did. Indeed, as I have written in one of these introductions before, so I'm sorry to repeat myself, but it is a story told at my own expense, Gordon eventually wrote to ask me, in the gentlest, politest, but still quite a direct way, to desist. 'In truth your stories just don't appeal sufficiently to us,' he wrote. 'They are certainly most competent but they don't, for us, sing out with the necessary individuality and voice. I'd suggest that in future we contact you if we see a story of yours which appeals rather than your going to the trouble of sending stories to us.' My name did appear in the introduction to *Best Short Stories 1992*, when the editors acknowledged *Darklands*, from which they reprinted Stephen Gallagher's 'The Visitors' Book'. Gordon and Hughes wrote, 'Above all we congratulate Nicholas Royle, himself a prolific short-story writer, for editing and publishing the first of what he intends as a regular visitor to the scene, based on his belief that good writers of horror were missing out. We might easily, had space allowed, have fallen for more of his choices than Stephen Gallagher's restrained treat of a ghost story.' My stories since have been reprinted in anthologies containing the word 'best' in their title, but they were selected by the editors of those series (Karl Edward Wagner, Stephen Jones, Ellen Datlow and others), not by me. I do know of one editor of an anthology that, while it may not have included the word 'best' in its title, did have a cover line describing its featured authors as 'literary legends', who included one of his own stories, but generally it's considered just not done.

- I can't claim to read every new story published or broadcast by every British writer, but I read as many as I can. While it was still going, *Ambit* provided me with a complimentary subscription so that I could keep track of all the stories they were publishing. *Extra Teeth* and *Confingo* have done the same. Occasionally a publisher will send a new anthology or collection. Sometimes I request a book. Some authors send me their own stories, as I used to send mine to Giles Gordon and David Hughes. Sometimes I've picked one of those or, if they've sent me, say, the anthology in which their story appeared, I've ended up picking up a different story by a different author from the same anthology, and I can only imagine the look on their face when they discover that's what I've done. Think of someone sucking on a lemon. I don't necessarily privilege new writers over established writers, but if it came down to a straight fight between new author A and established author Z, and I genuinely thought each story as good as the other, I'd probably go for new author A. Or forgotten author B. Over established author Z, who doesn't need the exposure and more than likely will insist that all communications go through their agent.

- I sometimes wonder if there might be some readers who think I include too many stories by writers they have not heard of and too few stories by big names. In addition to the big names I have included, I could add, here, some other big names I have tried to include, but who for one reason or another either never replied or did reply, or had others reply on their behalf, and said no. Or asked for £900. Which is the same as saying no.
- I think a lot of people feel that the words 'anthology' and 'collection' are interchangeable. For clarity, I reserve 'anthology' for a book containing stories by different authors and 'collection' for a single-author volume. I'm not alone in this, but it's not like it's a rule or anything.
- I believe it's good practice, if you are editing an anthology, to acknowledge where a story was first published, rather than where you happened to come across it, if you saw it in a later work.
- I also think it's good practice, when assembling your own stories for a collection, to acknowledge where each story first appeared or was broadcast.
- I have sometimes picked stories that were published in the first instance by me. I don't do this in order to publicise my own publishing efforts, but because I believe those stories are among the best and don't deserve to be overlooked simply because they were published by me – or by Nightjar Press, in most cases. It is true, of course, that I see everything that Nightjar publishes, whereas I don't see everything that Cape or Faber or Penguin publish. I would be delighted if more writers encouraged their publishers to send me any anthologies or collections containing new work by British writers. It is not difficult to get in touch with me via social media or via Salt Publishing.

Seven much-missed literary magazines
  Adam
  Ambit
  Antaeus
  Hotel
  Panurge
  Transatlantic Review
  Warwick Review

Six great double acts in the world of the short story
  Livi Michael & Sonya Moor – Small Pleasures podcast
  Giles Gordon & David Hughes – Best Short Stories 1986–1995
  Stephen Jones & David Sutton – Dark Voices, Dark Terrors etc
  Ailsa Cox & Elizabeth Baines – Metropolitan magazine
  Robert Aickman & Elizabeth Jane Howard – We Are For the Dark
  Mark Valentine & John Howard – Secret Europe etc

Five short stories with the title, 'Snow'
  Ted Hughes, Wodwo
  James Lasdun, The Silver Age
  Jayne Anne Phillips, Black Tickets
  Miles Tripp, More Tales of Unease
  Marc Werner, Murmurations

Four random examples of disrespect towards the short story
- Reviewing Rupert Everett's short story collection The American No (Abacus) in the Sunday Times, Hadley Freeman wrote: '. . . his new book, The American No, which is described in the press release, rather untemptingly, as a short story collection.'
- Included in the blurb on the back of Cees Nooteboom's short story collection The Foxes Come at Night (MacLehose Press): 'Set in the cities and islands of the Mediterranean, the eight stories in The Foxes Come at Night read more like a novel, a meditation on memory, life and death.'
- Standfirst to Observer review by Lucy Scholes of Saba Sams' novel Gunk (Bloomsbury): 'Saba Sams, one of Granta's best

young novelists, paints a complex picture of motherhood in her first full-length book.' Saba Sams' first book, as the review points out, was her short story collection, *Send Nudes*, but according to the standfirst, which would normally be written by a sub-editor, if they still employ subs at the new Tortoise-owned *Observer*, that was not a full-length book. *Send Nudes* is 210 pages long.

- Jamaica Kincaid's first book, published in the US in 1983 and in the UK by Picador in 1984, was *At the Bottom of the River*. Barely eighty pages, it is a wonderful collection, but you wouldn't know that if you picked up the latest edition reissued in Picador Collection. The front cover has the title, the author's name and the publisher's logo, and a detail from a painting by Hughie Lee-Smith. On the back cover Derek Walcott's warm endorsement is followed by a blurb that mentions 'pieces' and 'works', but the dreaded words 'short stories' do not appear anywhere on the cover.

Three publications that *occasionally* publish short stories
  Guardian
  New Statesman
  Prospect

Two books that are either novels or short story collections depending on who you talk to
  Samuel Beckett, *More Pricks Than Kicks*
  Claire-Louise Bennett, *Pond*

One brilliant idea
Every Friday morning I look forward to the email due to arrive that afternoon with the latest addition to Jonathan Gibbs's ingenious online project, *A Personal Anthology*. Writers and readers imagine themselves in a world in which they have at their finger tips all the

short stories that have ever been published and they are free to select whatever they want to create their Personal Anthology. They 'dream-edit' it, in Gibbs's words, and then tell us what they have chosen and write a few lines about each story. There are no copyright issues, because there are no stories (although, if they're available online, Gibbs links to them), just these pithy paragraphs about the stories they've chosen. But - and for me it's a big but and getting bigger - some contributors' interpretations of what is a short story are broader than the spine width on JG Ballard's *The Complete Short Stories* (Flamingo - so broad the paperback edition was split between two volumes). Gibbs, for whom I have the greatest respect and admiration, not only allows such flouting of the rules, he seems actively to encourage it. Indeed, it would seem, there *are* no rules. (You know where you are with rules.) A recent selection, posted while I was concocting this introduction, included an essay, a novella, a novel, and a song. What next? An encyclopaedia? A sandwich? An ironing board? This minor gripe aside, *A Personal Anthology* - sustainable, infinite, inspiring - remains one of the most exciting and positive additions in recent years to what Clifton Fadiman called 'the world of the short story', but it takes its name from another book published by Picador - Jorge Luis Borges's *A Personal Anthology*, which of course was a collection rather than an anthology, but let's not get into that. Gibbs launched his *A Personal Anthology* in 2017 and from time to time it has gone on a break, but I always worry when it does, in case, like a favourite bar closing down, it doesn't come back. I always think favourite bars, favourite cafés, favourite second-hand bookshops, shouldn't be allowed to close down. Similarly, if Gibbs ever threatens to pull down the shutters permanently, he must be talked out of it. If you don't know *A Personal Anthology*, sign up now at apersonalanthology.com.

NICHOLAS ROYLE
Manchester, May 2025

CD ROSE

I'M IN LOVE WITH A GERMAN FILM STAR

THE PASSIONS – 'I'M IN LOVE WITH A
GERMAN FILM STAR' (POLYDOR 7", 1981)
FOUR SLOW NOTES of shiver, blush, echoplex, and delay, then a tiny cascade, a shimmer, and a drop. A perfectly distracted rhythm section. A cold glow of voice. Not the first record I ever bought, but the first time I ever *heard* music.

It hadn't been a glamorous world, but now it was.

THE CURE – 'ALL CATS ARE GREY'
(FROM *FAITH*, FICTION, 1981)
I lay on the threadbare carpet in my room and watched the lights from passing cars throw abstract movies across the walls. I'd put this on and the room became a cathedral of shadow and smoke. It's the last track on side one and the tone arm on my record player didn't work properly so the music faded into the hiss and scratch of the runout groove. Even then, I knew that somewhere out there, Magda was listening to this, too.

LA DÜSSELDORF – 'SILVER CLOUD' (TELDEC 7", 1976)
I wouldn't hear this until much later, but when I did I knew that Magda had spent the long summer of 1976 dancing to it with a boy called Andreas or Jürgen or Max who was not worthy of her.

BERNTHØLER – 'MY SUITOR' (BLANCO Y NEGRO 7", 1984)
A video shop had opened between the chippy and the florist and as if by accident or magic they had a small section of the titles I only ever saw namechecked in the NME or showing at the Aaben in Hulme. The owner didn't seem to know what certificate they were and didn't blink when I checked out *Herzen und Knochen*. It isn't her best film, but it was enough.

Magda's luminous face appears fifteen minutes in. Her first word – *zwischen* – is a mere preposition that becomes a jouissant epiphany as she says it. All my future lay in those five phonemes.

John Peel played this record around the same time, but I couldn't get hold of it until it received a UK release nearly a year later. For some reason I became convinced that Magda was the singer, even though I knew it wasn't her. I could hear her, I thought, singing to me through it. The last scene of the film would have been so much better had this been its soundtrack.

THE DURUTTI COLUMN – 'SKETCH FOR DAWN (II)' (FROM LC, FACTORY, 1982)

An example of how music can go beyond evocation to become the thing itself. The bass is a long narrow avenue somewhere in Europe, the piano the high windows of a slightly shabby late-nineteenth-century apartment building, its echo the footsteps in their stairwells. There are trees, it is late summer or early autumn. The guitar is the touch of mist in the air.

Vini Reilly (who *is* the Durutti Column) recorded this in a damp flat in Chorlton, but several years later I would find myself buying then living in the place he had brought into being in this song, on the street that had been one of the principal locations for *Die Flammende Haut*. Reilly mutters the song's few words, but there's something in there about a late night or early morning cigarette burning dreams away, and I'm not sure if it was this line or the way Magda held a cigarette in *Herzen und Knochen* that made me take up smoking. I blame neither of them for it.

ASSOCIATES - 'WHITE CAR IN GERMANY'
(SITUATION TWO 12", 1981)

I'm listing the twelve-inch here, but it is also track one side one of the duo's *Fourth Drawer Down* LP, which I listened to obsessively on a Walkman throughout 1982 as I took the bus to school, already seeing myself on the open autobahn, speeding past cities, through forests, and over bridges in a vintage Porsche 911 convertible, a scene that would form the title sequence of *Tränen sind im Regen unsichtbar*, Magda's only venture into romantic comedy, and still much underappreciated.

WIM MERTENS - 'STRUGGLE FOR PLEASURE'
(ARIOLA/LES DISQUES DU CRÉPUSCULE 12", 1983)

It's been used everywhere (phone adverts, a Peter Greenaway film, some godawful Café del Mar chill-out compilation) and at first I thought I'd leave it out, but I'm certain I remember hearing it over the tannoy in Brussel-Zuid, or perhaps it was Köln Hauptbahnhof, or maybe Amsterdam Centraal, that first time I boarded a train to the Continent. On one long leg of the journey I met a girl called Claudia, who was interested in me because I was pretending to read Kafka, and who I was interested in because I told myself she looked like Magda. She fell asleep on my shoulder and woke up when we got to Hannover, or Hamburg, or somewhere, then got off, leaving me her name and address written on a slip of paper that I put between the leaves of the Penguin Modern Classic and forgot about, until now, when I listen to this piece of music again.

ROBERT GÖRL - 'MIT DIR' (MUTE 12", 1983)

Find the video for this and at three minutes forty seconds in, watch very carefully to see Magda appear as one of the faces in the slowly dancing crowd. The camera closes in on her and then, as if almost afraid of so much beauty, rapidly cuts away.

GRAUZONE - 'EISBÄR' (EMI ELECTROLA 7", 1981)
In a small feature in *Kino* magazine (Sept '83), Magda lists this as one of her favourite records.

CLOCK DVA - 'FOUR HOURS' (FETISH 7", 1981)
Many years later I got a rare chance to see *Mein Herz ist eine Bombe, mein Kopf ist ein Gedicht* while sitting on an upturned beer crate in a Kreuzberg basement. An experimental short made while Magda was still a drama student, it's not part of her official filmography (as much as one exists at all), but essential viewing for anyone seriously interested.

As the Super 8 projector spooled and whirred and the image on the screen flickered, I knew that the director of the film and Magda had been fucking while listening to this record.

NEU - 'SEELAND' (FROM *NEU 75*, UNITED ARTISTS, 1975)
This is the music in the closing scenes of *Die Flammende Haut*, where we see Magda walking for hours through the deserted city, alone, as dawn slowly breaks and she eventually reaches the sea. I knew the song long before I got to see the film and when I saw it, it felt like a homecoming. There is no more poignant scene in the history of cinema.

The film is currently unavailable on streaming, DVD, or even VHS, so I have instead played my copy of the record so often I can no longer tell where the rain effect ends and the surface noise of the worn vinyl begins.

DAVID BOWIE - 'HELDEN' (RCA 7", 1977)
Via the address of the production company listed at the end of *Haut*, I wrote to Magda asking what this song meant to her, or

even – I hoped! – if she would record herself singing it. I never received a reply, and suspect that this is because while Bowie himself remained tight-lipped on the subject, the two must have run into each other during his time in Berlin. There is one line in the song which can only refer to Magda. His decision to record this version of his most bleakly yearning and melancholically ecstatic song *auf Deutsch* was surely an indirect message to her.

BLONDIE – 'ATOMIC' (CHRYSALIS 7", 1980)

Silbernes Feuer, Magda's last film, was famously troubled. On-set tensions, three directors, and a production company going bust meant it was never properly finished, and despite the existence of several dubious 'final' cuts it has never received an official release. This song was supposed to accompany the climactic scene in which Magda leads revellers from a nightclub onto the streets of a collapsing city, but licensing issues rendered it unavailable. It was replaced with a cover version by legendary DDR punk band Zwitschermaschine, which I have sadly been unable to track down.

TONNETZ – 'MAGDA' (CHAIN REACTION 12", 1997)

All glitch and sparkle, this immersive piece of low-slung minimal techno I found via a recommendation on a discussion board dedicated to German cinema. The site told me many things: that she had married four times; that she was living in Los Angeles and working on a new film; that she had undergone extensive cosmetic surgery in order never to be recognised again; that she still loved clubbing; that she had been a Stasi agent; that 'Magda' was only ever a pseudonym used to cover her real identity; that she had made several other films that had gone straight to streaming; that she was living in Prestwich; that she had never really existed at all. I knew that most of these theories were nonsense.

Alva Noto – 'A Forest' (Noton DL, 2020)

The famous Cure song stripped to vapour traces, murmurs, and distant sighs. This was playing out in Berghain when I saw her again. Despite the darkness I recognised her immediately but did not approach as I had been taking some very strong painkillers while recovering from the high-speed accident that had written off the Porsche. She was dancing, of course, incredibly slowly, alone, and unselfconscious. I wanted to leave her that way.

This is the only Magda song that I do not possess as an object (its only physical form is an extremely expensive limited edition etched disc that I can no longer afford), and I rue this absence, as I fear my memories and dreams will vanish as quickly as a single spoken word or the vision of a face on a screen if I cannot touch them.

LINDEN HIBBERT

TORSOS

THE POLICE WERE called to the scene at the museum. The message was simple: a foot had been found. The note was passed to an inspector at his desk, who took pleasure in reading these five words aloud to himself. The case had pleasing potential, he thought, rising to fetch his coat.

Arriving at the museum the inspector was ushered around to the side entrance of the building. Inside, he found the curator waiting for him beside an audio point, signalled by a large graphic of an ear.

He knew nothing of curators; she was the first of her kind he had met, and he suspected the situation was mutual. He sniffed at her, expecting the earthy scent of a digger but she gave off a peculiar hint of rare elements and death. Startled, he reminded himself to assume nothing. He was here to ask questions, and yet there was a great deal that even an inspector could not ask.

Withdrawing his notebook from his top pocket, he turned to a blank page and licked his pencil, fighting the compulsion to sniff its new-sharpened point. He began.

It was you who reported the incident?
She nodded.
And discovered it also?
She hesitated.
You can nod.
She nodded.

His pencil awaited an elaboration, but when none was forthcoming, he offered her a way in.

A foot, I believe?

She nodded again, her expression distressed. He could hear her pulse quickening over what he could only assume was the sound of a clock ticking, which of course was impossible.

Perhaps I could see for myself?

Of course.

The whole conversation possessed an underlying tension. It was some moments yet before the inspector understood that some of that tension was arising from him. As he put it to himself later, he felt on the other side of things here, in this place of former worlds. Closing the notepad, he nodded at her rather formally, and suggested she lead the way. She walked ahead of him, noiselessly, he noted. His own shoes squeaked against the tiles, and his breathing was magnified by the otherwise total lack of sound, which he experienced as pressure against his eardrums. The light everywhere was constant and brilliant. The walls and floor a strangely indescribable neutral colour that was yet dazzling. The curator finally paused at an area that had been roped off and used the iris scanner to open the doors. He followed her into the first of a series of interconnected galleries. As he entered, he inhaled deeply. Ah, he thought to himself, *this* is the scent of antiquity!

The smells that greeted him were complex and overwhelming. His nose reddened and his eyes watered. Withdrawing his standard issue cambric handkerchief, he started swabbing. The scent was strongest, he observed, in the centre of all this whiteness. He followed it to its source. Something human appeared to be suspended in air.

Is that—

He moved closer. Three torsos were apparently levitating in the centre of the room, though he very quickly spotted the near invisible wires on which they were suspended.

As a professional man who made every effort not to express shock at crime scenes, nevertheless, he understood that shock was the desired response, indeed the very intention of the exhibition's design. The curator seemed content with him until he withdrew his notebook again and waved the pencil at her unspoken criticism. Police protocol, he assured her. It's perfectly safe. She looked unconvinced. No hacking this way either, he added. She stared back at him.

Trying to put the awkwardness of the moment behind him, he set to work jotting down all that he saw and smelled and heard. He was particularly partial to sketching evidence. It made him notice things he might otherwise overlook. There were three suspended torsos and one lying on its back on the pure white floor. The wires and rig that had held it suspended from the ceiling were neatly folded in a pile.

His sketch carefully noted differences among the three hanging torsos and, despite the damage, the fourth on the ground. The furthest left torso, he noticed as he captured it with his pencil, and the most complete of the four, was the torso of a man, from chin and neck down to the right hip, the left side being slightly truncated at both ends. He had the remains of both shoulders, but nothing beyond the deltoid. He might, once, have been carrying something, for the finely wrought muscles of his chest and belly seemed tighter on one side, and the other side subtly elongated. The torsos to the right down to the one on the floor were each slightly less complete, the first having only one shoulder, the third beginning at the pectoral muscles and ending at the belly. Still, the inspector noted, it was possible for him to know the whole from the fragment. The only individual sense from one to the other was the potential attitude each might have held. That was the only aspect requiring a degree of conjecture.

Lastly, he started to note the damage to the torso lying on the floor. Sketching also avoided the use of language, he noted, words like damage or the word wound, which was hovering in his head. Images simply showed evidence without implying opinion, which was, in his position, far safer ground. All the time he was sketching the curator continued observing him, as though he were somehow under suspicion rather than the other way round. What stuck him when he came to stand over the torso very carefully, so as not to affect the spatter pattern on the ground around it, was the shape of the mutilation of the belly. The damage appeared to be blunt force trauma from below, and from the side, such as the prison stompings he had seen early in his career. He squatted down and craned his neck to see as low as he could. Certainly, some damage had been inflicted from below in an upwards motion, like an upper cut or a kick. There was no damage from dropping it all the way from suspension to the floor, that kind of impact on the diaphragm area would be notably different. He turned his attention to the spatter evidence from the different blows. The material was quite well distributed across the floor, a fine dust. Licking the tip of one finger he pressed it into the dust and tasted it. He heard the curator's shudder of disgust.

Mmmm, he said aloud. Interesting.

It was more than interesting. For his palette possessed a capacity for history that his brain lacked, recognising the musk of long dead beasts, the barest hint of the east wind, the rains that had scoured the land when this torso was first created; he felt the hum of half-life from a hint of granite, tasted lime, calcium, potassium, and underlying carbon.

Still squatted down amid the spatter of dust, he gestured to the torsos. Tell me about them.

The curator, who had drifted away slightly, turned back to him. What would you like to know?

The way she said it was quite clearly a rebuttal and at odds from the words of her arrival when she had still been in shock. Then he had felt her silence as an inability to find the words. Now she was digging in her heels and resisting, which could slow things down. He cleared his throat.

For example, are they copies or originals?

Her eyebrows rose and fell in what appeared to him to be genuine shock at his ignorance. Then she said, I can't believe you really have to ask? I thought they had sent me an inspector. No museum of our calibre would display *copies*.

Over the spiral spine of his notebook, he noted her disgust in the margin as an observation, nothing more. He could get in serious trouble for noting down certain kinds of things, he knew.

He felt he needed to explain in case she made things unpleasant for him later. Someone like her could. A quiet word, no more, and his career would be over.

The thing is, he began and then stopped himself. The planets, the stratosphere felt closer to him than history. This whole conversation made him feel like he was floating, unmoored. It wasn't as if this kind of thing had been taught at his school. Not history this ancient anyway. He'd learned exactly what he needed to know and nothing more. His sense of a period beyond his own lifetime was hazy.

So, originals? He felt the need to be explicit.

Yes!

Rare?

Priceless.

This was not entirely what he had meant but he recorded the comment anyway. He had the strange sensation that the more he asked the further away from the details of the crime he was travelling.

He sketched out the spatter pattern and scribbled notes about scent and texture and colour in the margin. He had by now a shorthand which he had to practise regularly since crimes of any sort were so rare these days. He took his time, though she started to pace and circle around him. He felt her agitation was merely fuelled by a discomfort of his craft. He possessed the ability to smell and taste her loneliness, which her agitated state only seemed to heighten, and what he smelled and tasted of her brought out his compassion for her hard edges: how difficult it must be to possess all this knowledge that no one can share.

They are so fine, he mused, so beautiful, he continued, staring down at the damaged torso.

Is that a rhetorical question?

What? No. I was just thinking.

She consulted a small display near her wrist.

You don't need to stay here, if you have something pressing, he said. I can find you if I have any other questions.

This really isn't somewhere you can just wander around.

Her words hurt him and as a result the hurt cut free a question that he had been pondering but knew better than to ask.

How did they get here anyway?

She restarted pacing again in a rather stressful manner.

Everything is documented, she said, and all documentation is in order, if that is what you are suggesting.

He frowned. He felt he was stumbling around mines not knowing which might erupt in his face. I just meant, he began, if they are so rare, so very old, how long they have been here? What has been done to preserve them?

She tapped her finger against her hand, as though she were counting down to one in her head to calm herself.

We've had them since their rediscovery. They were removed here for their protection and held here ever since.

Removed from where?

You know I cannot tell you.

He was meant to look away at this point, to act subservient. That was the drill with these types. They didn't like being required to explain themselves to people like him. They resented it. Before he could say anything aloud, she was talking again in a curt voice, as though he were the one who needed reminding of the law.

It is for me to know what is and isn't relevant, she said. What *you* should be considering, the question you should concern yourself with, is the crime itself.

Which is?

Category violation.

He stood up too quickly feeling pins and needles in his legs from having been squatted down taking evidence for so long. Aware of her power over him, he dropped his head to his chest as though in apology, and took a step back, stumbling backwards over something unseen. Winded at first, he spun himself round by the arms to see what he had tripped over and found the foot!

Of course, he said aloud, for he had forgotten all about it.

It was almost the same colour as the interior of the museum. It would have been difficult if not almost impossible to detect from a distance. There was something lonely-looking and vulnerable about it lying there on its side which tugged on his heart. He estimated it was about three times the scale and size of the torsos, which were life-sized, and although, when he first saw it, he had been certain it was lying lying down, now, as he sketched it, it stood upright, the flat of its sole pressed to the floor. Getting back onto his feet he circled it. It had the air of something quivering with the effort of staying still, about to take flight. Such a fine ankle, showing just a hint of shin and calf. The foot was balanced perfectly on a sinewy arch, its toes splayed, as though it had never known the restriction of boots. It was the most beautiful foot he had ever seen. He fought an urge to lift his trouser leg, remove his shoe and sock and regard his own foot.

He came and stood behind the heel and looked in the direction in which its toes were pointing.

Hmm, he said, following the direction of the centre metatarsal with difficulty because of the flat colour of the walls into which it merged. Over there, he said firmly. It's pointed over there. Where does that direction lead?

Though he didn't expect an answer, the curator wearily walked in the direction he had indicated. As she neared the wall, he saw something.

Is that a door? he asked, excitedly, pointing beyond her as the curator leaned towards a scanner to get the door. The inspector hurried over. The door silently opened.

Where does it go?

Gallery four, she explained. She held the door for him.

Gallery four?

Legs.

Legs. He smiled but she did not. Well, worth a look, I should think.

He hurried into the room in case the doors suddenly shut him out, and yet for all this rushing and excitement to explore the museum, he felt part of him remained in the first gallery beside the foot. It was a curious thing how much it moved him. Without intending to he had slowed down and now lagged some distance behind the curator. Doubtless he would lag still further as there was so much to take in, so many pairs of legs - hundreds and hundreds - in cabinets lining the walls of this narrow space, floor to ceiling. Most were behind glass though not all. He couldn't grasp the basis on which some were protected while others were not. A small number were evidently still in pairs, but many more were lined by their original side of the pairing, with left legs on one side and the right on the other.

Legs seem more common than torsos, he called after the curator.

He walked slowly, observing the similarity of display here with that of the torsos, each ranked in order of completeness, starting, where he had first entered this gallery nearest the torso exhibition, with legs that were in a few cases whole, or in larger parts, preserved, with less visible joins. All stood upright. Progressing down the room, they shortened and there were visible differences in quality, but the presiding factor remained height. About mid-way he reached the legs cut off at the knee, and beyond that they were fragments of kneecap, and then fragments of what he took to be shins.

How he wished he could just linger, take it all in. He made a note to himself to return, but it seemed their intended destination was in yet another, more distant gallery. The curator had long since exited and so he was forced to continue. When at last he spied the curator waiting for him, he asked, Is this how they *want* to be catalogued?

She scissored her jaws looking annoyed.

Again, you are missing the point, inspector. We curate. That does not mean we consult. That is not how curation works. They are grouped by their aesthetic significance, their contribution to aesthetics.

And who decides that?

He regretted the question. It was the foot, he realised, it had made him a little daring.

Do you really want to be thrown off this case?

You could explain, couldn't you, but you won't.

You don't need to know!

It was odd because one of the central tenets of the police corps was that all policemen were the same. That rank did not duly matter. Rank was more connected with age and pension criteria. Long service. Lose a policeman and he can always be replaced. One is the same as the other. He muttered something along those lines and the curator, hearing him, finally made a sound of approval.

Exactly.

A head is a head, he said, quoting without remembering where he had read it. A leg is a leg.

At last she seemed to be pleased with him. For someone like you, inspector, she concurred, A head *is* a head, a leg is a leg. But heads are not legs. Not the same value, you understand. As you see we have many legs but, alas, scant few heads.

It was true. He had yet to see a single head.

Why is that? he asked.

I would have thought it was obvious.

Apparently not, he thought, looking at her enquiringly in the hope she would enlighten him. Surprisingly, she did.

Because we destroyed them, she said looking strangely pleased. Before we brought them here to be conserved.

You destroyed them in order to conserve them?

The idea was far from absurd. With population as it was, with so many more arms and legs able to work than were necessary, it was difficult to occupy them all. Sometimes a hole was dug only to be filled in, a disease manufactured only to be cured.

Not exactly, she replied. You know nothing of history. If you did, you'd appreciate the natural way of things. Every great civilisation including ours is necessarily built in the desecration of an older one. No civilisation believes itself defeated while their gods still smile and the glories of their civilisation, their art and so on, still exist. A civilisation only knows itself to be defeated, truly, when its achievements are crushed, its art is destroyed, its gods decapitated, their genitals cut off. Their hands too. Hands signify so much of what a people can achieve.

And their feet?

Pardon?

You must cut off their feet? he suggested. There are no feet.

Not here, no, she said, in the foot gallery, just through here.

Oh, he said. Well lead on.

I fear you learn nothing, she said as they entered gallery five: feet. It's not at all the same with feet, she continued. Anatomically, feet are just lower and therefore easier to reach. Feet are nothing, she said firmly. They are cultural barbarians. As you just witnessed. Only able to stamp and crush and pursue.

And dance, and run, he wanted to add, but did not, and still her words affected him deeply. By the time he could shake off the mood her words had brought down on him, she had moved on to talking about security, something he had neglected to ask about.

We should have foreseen such vandalism!

Vandalism? he queried. Is that what you consider has happened here?

Immediately her gaze dropped to his employee number on his inspector's badge.

Civilisation requires order and classification. But sometimes it needs to be imposed. We can't expect that everyone will understand even though it's for the benefit of the whole system. I would have thought you, inspector, would appreciate that part.

They had come to the end of a long line of left feet, where an empty case with broken glass around it drew the inspector's attention. Presumably the foot had smashed its way out. The bulk of the glass had been pushed out and remained where it had fallen on the floor, though glass was still wedged in the join between the plinth holding the box and the ceramic tiled floor. He took a sample and pocketed it before noting something further.

I think we are finished, the curator said from the far end of the gallery. Fill out your report, file it, you know the procedure.

Of course. Consider it done. As he walked towards her, it occurred to him to ask what happened next. What will you do with the—

He had been about to say *foot*, but the curator interrupted him on the presumption he had been about to say torsos. She explained, and as she spoke, a reinforced gurney appeared in the corridor behind her heading through the foot and leg galleries back towards the torsos.

It will be taken to the lab and repaired, she said. We are experts in restoration of course.

Yes. Of course, he said politely. Can I just—, he asked, gesturing that he would like to follow the gurney which was just then vanishing through the door.

Of course, she replied with evident disapproval. We have said we will cooperate fully.

He nodded and hurried after the gurney, arriving just in time to see the damaged torso being lifted off the floor and wheeled away. A large machine appeared from another door hovering a few millimetres off the floor. It was controlled remotely by an attendant also in silent shoes. It cleaned the spatter-dust into a museum grade filter ready to be inspected and potentially reused. The room was back to how it had been, the remaining torsos virtually invisible against their backdrop. The inspector's eyes started watering again. The foot, he noticed, must already have been removed for it was gone.

He set off for the entrance, and arriving there to find it empty, pushed his way out of the gallery's revolving doors. He thought he saw the foot reflected in the glass, as though it were standing behind him. He turned round, but it was nowhere to be seen.

Back at the station, the inspector completed his report, had it triple stamped and saw it dropped into its appointed pigeonhole, where it would sit for the necessary number of years before being destroyed. At his desk, alone, pondering the case, he felt the beginnings of a yawn. Everyone else had turned down for the night. He pulled his standard issue cot out of the knee hole of his desk, and had retired for the night, when a message came through. It was the exchange. He was needed back at the museum.

Hurrying back to the underground, the otherwise empty carriage moved him at double speed to the area of antiquities. The street of the museum was silent. At the museum entrance, he was asked to show his security pass and he stood waiting for clearance, mulling over the statistical unlikelihood of a first crime let alone a second.

The night porter let him in. The lighting in the halls had been dimmed. A smaller, older model of the curator met him, since the museum was closed.

You'd better come, was all she said, before leading him through the museum back to the gallery of the torsos. There, on the floor, in the centre of the room, two of the remaining three torsos had been removed and laid on their sides, their ribs dented with what appeared to be the same blunt force. The hint of a neck in the larger of the two torsos had snapped clean off from the blow so that despite their original differences, they resembled the earlier torso almost perfectly.

The inspector searched for signs of the foot and found a trail of dusty footprints leading towards the leg room. The curator hung back, he noticed. Have you inspected where these prints lead? he asked.

She shook her head.

He felt slightly buoyed up by the fact that her presence proved older types still had their place.

If you have access to an office, I suggest you stay there, he said, and I'll come find you when I'm done. As he ushered her back towards the cordons, he was aware of his keenness to get on and use his skills to hunt and seek. His phenomenal nose led him forward, his eyes trained on the faint markings of dust prints. Even for a foot of its size, the gap between each print was significant, requiring, he estimated, a considerable will to achieve in addition to great litheness of form. His left leg, always the eager one, quivered with anticipation. The door to the leg gallery was open. Letting his nose lead, sniffing deeply, he hurried towards the foot room negotiating a much more sparsely populated display case on his right, and an empty case on his left. He circled the empty case, the tip of his nose twitching. The scent indicated that the foot had lingered by its old case. What had it been thinking, he wondered; did it feel fear at leaving its glass cage? His compulsion to find the foot was overwhelming. He reached the door, only to discover it led to an emergency exit. The realisation was a powerful disappointment, and he pounded the walls with his fists. The scent of the foot was everywhere at the door. He sniffed the locking mechanism, the bar, the artificial eye, and came away with powder on his nose. Doubling back, he hunted for a window that looked outwards in the direction of the emergency exit. He found one, and saw beyond a courtyard, illuminated with security lights, and then a wall. He knew the foot was out there, somewhere beyond the perimeter.

Before he could investigate outside, he must let the curator know. On his way to her office, he spoke to security. Just a few questions, he explained. Had they checked the emergency exits, the windows, the sensors? Had they evaluated whether there had been any breach?

Yes, he was assured. Everything had been checked. The place was locked tight, alarmed, no sensors had been tripped.

Have you walked the perimeter? he asked urgently. Outside?

Nothing can breach our system, he was told.

But what about something in here trying to get out?

Their blank stares answered him and he hurried to inform the curator that he needed to widen the search, and then asked to be let out.

He had never, he realised, standing in the unlit back road, possessed the leisure to walk the streets for no purpose, day or night. Turning west, he followed the museum perimeter until he reached the part of the wall with the courtyard on the other side. On his approach, his nose began to twitch, his eyes to stream. He did not even need to inhale; he could taste the foot on the pad of his tongue, the arch of his tonsils. The scent was focused acutely on a spot about five metres from the pavement where the foot had landed. Standing on that same spot he felt rooted by a connection to the foot that was far more than this shared location. He felt exhilarated, as if he were trapped in mid-chase while standing still. Lifted by it – made younger even. Immediately he scoffed at himself. Surely this was evidence of nothing more than age and senility, and would lose him his job.

Engrossed in thought he didn't sense movement until the air rushing past seemed to knock him backwards. At best he had a fraction of a second's warning in his peripheral vision, no scent at all. He felt violently displaced though nothing had directly touched him. It took him precious seconds to regain his balance.

The sigh that came out of his mouth made him sound like he was deflating.

There, in the hazy moonlight, was the foot, magnificently drawn upwards, balancing on the toes and metatarsals.

Wait, he called, fearing the foot was about to go. Please.

The foot swivelled slightly on its toes to face him. Its simple beauty made him believe that the curator was wrong: a foot was not nothing.

I should, he began without conviction, I should, by rights have you destroyed.

The foot made a slight bow. Of course. It replied. What cannot be categorised . . . you know how it goes.

And he did. Of course he did. He had worked on little else but miscategorisations throughout his career. The foot hesitated as though it might say more, or at least the inspector hoped it might, but then it pivoted on the ball of its big toe and bounded away, leaving the inspector sniffing the empty air. It was there again, he acknowledged, that scent, that feeling he had first encountered outside the foot's shattered cage, only now more acute, and yet still imprecise and indefinable as ever. A sort of yearning, he decided, drawing down a deep breath; craving an outcome that could not happen. Like taking a stroll in the evening, he thought. Like wanting a child of your own. Or falling in love.

WYL MENMUIR

THE INCIDENTS

AFTER IT HAPPENED the first time, Blue Adderleigh's mother had laughed. It was a shaky laugh. A we-dodged-a-bullet-there laugh. Over the next few days though the laugh evolved into one that felt like the kind that would be appropriate to accompany an after-dinner story.

If I hadn't seen it, I wouldn't have believed it either, Emmaline Adderleigh said to her assembled guests the following week, employing said laugh. It's not something I'll forget in a hurry.

The story went that the proud parents had been out walking their charge and stopped at The Green Man at Hurst for a light lunch, leaving the child asleep in the pram outside. They emerged some two hours later to find a crowd of locals gathered around a pram that looked very much like theirs, only this one was filled entirely with bees, as though someone had turned on a hose and filled the basket to the brim with them. At first, she and her husband had joined the gawping crowd, amazed at the spectacle of it. When they looked for the pram with their child in it though, they could not see it anywhere and it dawned on them that this was their pram and that their daughter was, most likely, buried somewhere deep within the darkly buzzing swarm that had, until just then, held only fascination for them.

Emmaline shouted for her husband to do something about it and – this featured in the story, too – he called for a gun with which to scare the bees off, so it was left to Emmaline to call for someone, anyone, to stop standing around staring and find a damned beekeeper.

Messengers were dispatched in search of the beekeeper and a barman took charge of the gun Thomas Adderleigh had requisitioned, though which he had not yet managed to discharge. A short while later the village beekeeper arrived, an elderly man who calmly set about searching for the hairless queen, while Emmaline screamed, and Thomas demanded that he should be given the gun back in case the beekeeper failed. The gun was never needed, as the beekeeper eventually located the queen at the very heart of the swarm, tucked in one of the baby's palms. As he drew the bees away, carrying the queen aloft, it became clear that the child was unharmed and, further, that she was still asleep. The only sign that anything had happened was the gentle opening and closing of the hand in which Blue had held the queen, as though she were searching for it again in the midst of her dream.

They resolved to keep a closer eye on Blue after that. And though the story drew the best response from the room, Emmaline stopped telling it at some point around the second of what she began to refer to as *the incidents*. Blue was toddling by this point and had taken to exploring the gardens. One morning in early summer, while her parents sat on reclining chairs on the lawn beneath parasols, reading impractically large newspapers, she wandered off the manicured lawns into the rough. When she emerged, her legs and dress green with grass slicks, she held in one of her hands the neck of a mottled snake perhaps twenty inches long. She proceeded to wrap it around her neck as though it were one of her mother's winter stoles. Again, her father called loudly for a gun and Emmaline screamed at the sight of a snake so close to the house. Eventually, after Blue had twirled on the lawn with the snake for a while as she had seen her mother do with scarves in front of the mirror, it dropped to the ground and returned to the rough.

Later that evening, her father, having rehearsed the story in his head all afternoon, told it over dinner and was surprised when Emmaline stood abruptly, upsetting her plate, and snapped at him – Jesus, Thomas, could you show some goddam sensitivity – and left him to deal with their guests without any clue as to what he had done wrong.

The stories of Blue's way with animals – or, rather, their way with her – were shelved and the other *incidents* were not spoken of at all, not even between Emmaline and Thomas. They did not discuss her near smothering by a clowder of cats that appeared one morning like a sudden plague and that disappeared so quickly it was difficult to imagine they had been there at all. Nor the fledgling Emmaline discovered nesting in her daughter's hair and which had, by the advanced state of the nest, clearly been there for some time. Nor, in the last light of day, the deer that had emerged from the woods behind the house and which leapt directly over the child's head, the fur of its brush grazing the top of her head.

Eventually though, Emmaline took Blue to a psychotherapist who was unable to uncover the root trauma that had led to these events occurring. He was, however, glad of the business and suggested they should continue with the sessions until this trauma surfaced which he said it would, inevitably, given time.

In the winter of Blue's fifteenth year, Thomas Adderleigh died. It was an unremarkable death and did not make a good story. With her newfound freedom Emmaline bought a motorcar, the first she had owned. In a rare show of parental engagement, she asked Blue to choose the location of the holiday they would take in it and Blue chose the town of Fowey in Cornwall, where she dreamt of making the acquaintance of Daphne du Maurier, whose stories she admired and who she regularly imagined meeting, in passing and to the genuine delight of both parties. She was sure they would fall into a kind of easy conversation that would result in an invitation to stay, would later grow to correspondence, and from there to an inevitable and lifelong friendship.

Blue was surprised when her mother agreed to the suggestion. Her mother considered du Maurier's books to be little more than potboilers. Emmaline had friends in the area, though, and wrote to arrange to visit at their large house nearby at Lansallos, where they would be – Emmaline was assured – awaited with concern and sympathy. On the long car journey west, Blue's mother described their host, David Moat, as a friend from college, though it was clear even then that there was more to it than that. When Blue pressed her mother for details, she changed the subject of the conversation to the various rules she was imposing on her daughter for the visit. Blue was, firstly, not to ask the Moats if they were acquainted with Ms. du Maurier nor, if it came up in conversation that they were, was she to ask for an introduction under any circumstances. She was not to encourage the attention of any animals nor make a nuisance of herself in any way. Neither was she to encourage the attention of the two Moat sons, whatever that meant and no, Emmaline did not want to go into any further detail on that and would Blue desist from calling her Mother, it made her sound old.

The Moat house sat in a dip in the rolling hills, just out of sight of the sea and on arrival, David Moat announced that once they had settled in they would walk to the beach where he had arranged a picnic. His wife would not be joining them, he explained, though his sons would. Blue tried to make conversation with the Moat boys though they seemed incapable of it, and instead looked from her to one another and snickering each time she spoke to them.

David strode along ahead of the group, down the driveway and out through the gates, acting the tour guide and before they left the village he paused at the gate of the church. The Moats were responsible for the upkeep of the chancel, he said proprietorially, as though this explained everything, and Blue's mother nodded, clearly impressed. And here, in this very graveyard, were the graves of two notorious smugglers. He gestured to two thin gravestones the writing on which could have said anything really, before sweeping

Emmaline into the church. Blue held back and wandered in the churchyard. After a while though, she could feel the two boys' eyes on her between the gravestones, and she retreated into the church.

They are beautiful, are they not? Fifteenth century, David Moat was saying. He was waving his cigarette in the direction of the carvings on the pews. I offered to buy them, money in the church's pocket and all that, though no joy.

How ungrateful, she heard her mother murmur.

The couple, for that is what they seemed to Blue, wafted around the church. David's cigarette smoke and his loud and not always terribly well-informed opinions filled the small chapel. Blue knelt at one of the carved pew ends. The wood was dark and shone dully but as her eyes accustomed to the darkness, she made out griffins and flowers, snakes, cats and bees and, on the end of one, a carved face or, rather, three carved faces on the same head. One face looked forward and the other two, each of which shared one of the eyes of the first, looked out to either side. The faces were fringed with foliage which seemed to emerge from their mouths, making them beards of greenery, and their hair too was leaflike. The faces were serious and peaceful, or maybe disturbing, she couldn't tell which. Inscrutable would be the better word, perhaps, she thought. Though they had the features of men, they seemed to her more like the faces of animals. Though the eyes on all three faces were closed she imagined these figures were looking at her or, rather, seeing her across the centuries. When she looked up again, the church was silent. David's monologue had ceased and she could tell by the settling of dust motes in the air lit by shafts of light through the stained glass that they had left the building and she had drifted. She could stay here for a while, in the dark and the cool, she thought, though, as she was thinking this, from somewhere far away she heard her mother's voice shrilling. She rose, and before she left she stooped and touched the tip of an index finger to the forehead of the carved figure that faced outward from the bench.

The Moats were waiting for her on the road, impatient and hot. Emmaline gave her *that* look, the one she knew was meant to remind her of the instructions she had given in the car. Beyond the church they left the road, stepping over a stile through trees and suddenly there was the ocean, unrealistically blue against the green of the fields that folded down towards it. David Moat, leaning against a gate, pointed out a shack in the distance, built there, he said, by customs men to stem the flow of smuggled goods. It was owned by a writer now, he said. It was the shed from which she penned books for which he didn't have much time himself.

The sun was hot on their backs now and David announced that it would be cooler on the valley path, under the trees. If anything though, it was hotter beneath the thick canopy. The greens seemed to Blue oppressively bright, and everything felt sharpened by the sensation of sweat pooling on her neck and dripping down her back. The Moat boys were barking now, pushing and butting up against each other, and Blue was glad when they emerged from the tree tunnel and the sea came back into view and she felt the faintest of sea breezes as they crossed the last of the fields before the beach. There were gulls on the cliffs and standing around on the grass too, a huge host of large white gulls that did not move as the party approached and through which they had to pick their way. The gulls seemed unperturbed when the Moat boys kicked at them. Blue could see orchids in the grass, intricate towers, though David was back onto the subject of smugglers and Blue did not feel she could interrupt. Down there, David was saying, was where they'd drag the kegs off the beach, up through the cut they dug out of the rock. He did not approve of smugglers, of course. Thieves were thieves, though there was a certain thrill to the idea of getting one past the taxman who, after all, was just another sort of thief. They stepped down into the cleft and as they came out onto the beach Emmaline made a show of gasping at the wicker baskets and blankets set out on the sand. The Moat boys snickered at her and punched each other in the ribs.

Emmaline and David sat by one of the baskets and Blue, who was used to sitting at the children's table, even as an only child, sat at the other, which was some way off, kicking off her shoes as she settled on the blanket. The Moat boys did not sit, but stripped to their waists, not far from Blue's blanket, and fell to wrestling in front of her. Blue took a sandwich from the basket and her book from her satchel and tried to ignore the flying sand and the boys' grunts and exertions.

The first gull that swooped in missed Blue's head by centimetres, though she felt its wings against her face as it flew over her shoulder, after her sandwich. The second one that dived in caught the crust and ripped a chunk out of it and by the time she had gathered her thoughts, the first had wheeled round and dived again, this time more successfully. Blue looked round to see if anyone was going to come to her rescue but the boys were entangled with one another – the arms and legs of one folded around those of the other in a complex knot. If I let you go, you've got to promise not to hurt me, right? one was saying to the other, somewhat breathlessly.

Behind Blue, Emmaline was laughing at some story of David's. Bothered more by the fighting and the flirting than the birds, Blue lifted the lid of the hamper and spread out the remaining sandwiches for the gulls. She rose and walked down to the shoreline, to the mica-green sea, and paddled her feet. The water was cool and fresh and she waded in a little further. There were small fish in the shallows that gathered to her and brushed against her ankles and which, when she took a couple more steps, nibbled and tugged gently at the hem of her dress. She could see there were larger fish too, just further out in the darker, deeper blue, waiting for her, starfish and pipefish and sunfish too in huge numbers, gathered there for her. She waded in further still, the small fish and the larger ones now circling her feet and calves and urging her on, and as she got deeper, her dress floating up around her, she could sense, in the waters beyond, the ponderous whales whose deep reverberations called to her among those of the profound multitudes of the deep and their calls sounded like home.

The boys on the beach finished their wrestling, though by the time they wore themselves out and fell into a wary truce, they had forgotten what they were fighting about. They shooed off the gulls which had, by then, eaten what remained of the picnic. They were arguing again as they left the beach, about who had left the hamper open, and David and Emmaline were laughing at a joke they had first shared some twenty years earlier.

OKECHUKWU NZELU

THE HEADTEACHER

FOOD ALWAYS TASTES better stolen. The thought went back and forth in Jeremy's mind as he watched the sausage rolls, as keenly as if they might somehow move or transmute. Hiding in the spare room while the party carried on downstairs, he ran through myths about food and calories. Party food doesn't count. Nobody would see him eat them, so it wouldn't count. But he would know. And when his stomach started to swell, his husband would know. When his arse sagged, and his chest drooped. He should never have accepted them from that man at the door. What was his name? Nathan? Something like that.

Jeremy had been in such a good mood just before he let Nathan in, too. Even after he saw the plate of what was probably leftovers in the young man's hand, he'd tried to smile. He'd even said he would hand the sausage rolls round at the party. But then Nathan had made that bizarre joke about bringing sausages to a party hosted by two gay men, and he'd laughed that braying laugh and showed his uneven little teeth, and something had snapped, or slipped in Jeremy's mind, and that was that. He'd grabbed them, made his excuses, and now he was here, staring down a plate of sausage rolls while people ate and drank downstairs.

Why would anybody bring sausage rolls to a party at a house like theirs, in a neighbourhood like this? Hadn't Nathan seen the brand-new paint on the door, sixty quid a tin? Hadn't he seen the plantation shutters? Granted, it had only been a few weeks since Jeremy and Matthew had moved to Altrincham. And Matthew did like to point out that it was the smallest house on the street, dwarfed on either side by properties with more bedrooms than leaves of neatly mown grass. But all the same, this was a step up the ladder. There was a barrister two doors down. Across the road, someone from a Netflix drama. Jeremy looked at the sausages. What would the neighbours think if they saw him eating these? Did the people on Cameron Street even go to bakery chains? It seemed unlikely.

He should have got rid of them immediately. He had thought about throwing them away, or pretending to trip over and tipping them artfully to the floor. But what if Matthew saw them in the bin? What if they stuck to the plate when Jeremy faked falling over, and he had to shake them off? Besides, it would be fun to say something almost kind about the ways in which they didn't quite pass muster. He tried to remember the details of the offending remark, but Nathan had fumbled it halfway through and it hadn't all been audible. He'd clearly been expecting Matthew to open the door. Matthew would have been much more hospitable than his husband to that tawdry little attempt at humour, especially from an ex-pupil. Jeremy had just given him a look and told him where to hang his coat.

In the spare room, he rolled his eyes and wiped his mouth. Sex-starved straight men have a way of bringing this sort of smut into every context where it is least welcome. And they always seem to think their gay jokes are *original*, the first and best that have ever been made. Jeremy thought what it would be like to bite down hard and feel himself symbolically avenged.

Yes, that was enough. Just the thought of it was almost as good. He would have to leave the spare room soon, anyway. In a minute, he'd have to go down to the party and take the sausage rolls with him. Nathan would still be standing around with the other ex-pupils, and the other teachers. Jeremy groaned inwardly. Public sector workers are fine in small numbers, and some are even good conversation – civil servants, for example, who tend to either have gossip on cabinet ministers, or stay quiet because they already know that nobody cares what they do with bins all day. Doctors you can talk to, as they often have more than a hint of a desire to privatise the whole thing. Teachers, however – overworked, underpaid, undersexed – are the worst. All of them so tightly wrapped up in their little worlds that they can't think of anything interesting to say. Like nurses, with their tired, over-washed uniforms and near-identical anecdotes about their sad little staycations.

Jeremy had measured out his life in *mmms* and tight, grudging smiles. Teachers always had another anecdote, another in-joke that only *those* staff at *that* school would ever understand. Funny how every teacher is the hero of their own story. Even if they seem like they're making fun of themselves, they're really trying to tell everyone how cute and funny and humble they are. None of them are talking about the fact they failed in every other job but this one, or how they saw Mr Peters fondling little Jimmy after PE and didn't say a word.

Jeremy took a quick look in the mirror. He practised the expression – bland, unconcerned – that he would present to the room when he came downstairs with a tray of baked goods that was every bit as full as it had been when Nathan had arrived. He would make up some excuse and smile as though he hadn't even thought about eating them all, one by one or all at once. He should have been an actor.

He'd had enough practice. He'd played the therapist when, years ago, Matthew told him the school trip budget had been cut again. He'd pretended not to mind about Matthew's late nights, his early mornings, the pay so low it barely reached ankle height on Jeremy's. He'd listened gently to Matthew's accounts of the abuse – verbal and, once every couple of years, physical – that Matthew received from students, and occasionally parents too. He'd smiled at all the work Matthew did during his 'vacations'. He'd been a consummate mime when Matthew told him the board had appointed that bald little oaf Karl Moore to be the Head, despite multiple rumours that he'd tried it on with half the women in the staffroom, bad toupee apparently notwithstanding.

Acting wasn't the hard part. That was mostly just listening. The difficult thing was being married to someone who cared enough about ordinary children that he cried when they couldn't go on school trips because the Head had spent the money on a hotel room for his mistress. What kind of man cared so much about people who weren't family, weren't even colleagues, really? Matthew had been like that when they first met, but Jeremy had never thought it would last. It had lasted their whole marriage, Matthew beloved of everyone and Jeremy, not quite as handsome, nowhere near as kind.

It only got worse with time. Twenty years ago, Karl was finally sacked. Jeremy wished he could have been there to see the little pig in a wig escorted off the premises, but he'd been at home at his computer when Matthew came back with the news. Jeremy had listened patiently. And then he'd had an idea.

'Maybe it's time for you to leave too,' he'd said.

Matthew'd scrunched his face up. 'What? Why?'

'That Academy's a bit of a sinking ship, isn't it? Even before Karl, there was that budget problem, and the Ofsted reports, and all those staff leaving every year. Now this.'

Matthew gave a tiny nod. Jeremy pressed his advantage.

'What's the point wasting more of your career in a place like that? There are other jobs.'

'Nice to know you think I've been wasting my career,' Matthew said, quietly.

'Teachers leave schools all the time. Most people in your position would have left years ago. And you could do anything you want.'

'I'm thirty-five,' Matthew'd said. But he'd said it in the way all men say it when they approach middle age: part statement, part question.

'Thirty-five is young,' Jeremy responded. 'There are other things you could be doing. Maybe Karl getting sacked is a sign from the universe.'

Matthew'd actually seemed to think about that one for a moment, but when he eventually spoke he declined the idea. 'I can't leave now. If I handed in my notice right after Karl got sacked it'd look like I support him and I'd never get a decent reference. Let me think about it.'

Jeremy had let the matter drop. He'd made his point. He assumed that further thought on Matthew's part would lead him to a more sensible course of action, not less. What was Matthew doing in a school like that, anyway? Granted, Matthew hadn't had as much money as Jeremy, growing up. He'd only gone to a mid-table private school in Cheshire, not even boarded like Jeremy had, down in Oxfordshire. Still, that life had never been right for Matthew. He'd never known anything like these children's lives, no heating in the home, parents working all hours for no money, every other child on free school meals. When Karl was sacked, Jeremy had thought Matthew would finally come to his senses.

But then Matthew applied for Acting Head in a matter of days. And once that school had gotten their claws into him, they were never going to let him go without a fight.

Jeremy grabbed the tray of sausage rolls, opened the bedroom door and stuck his head out, sampling the noise from the party before he committed himself to re-entering it. The sounds of conversation bubbled up the stairs to him, with the occasional voice identifying itself. There must be nearly a hundred people in the lounge, treading their biscuit crumbs into the carpet. And Jeremy had agreed to put up with it, for Matthew's sake of course. Jeremy understood the need for a state school system, and he looked on with some sympathy on at Matthew's desire to be a part of it. He had, however, expressed some reservations about inviting their education system, seemingly in its entirety, into their house for drinks.

The only reason Jeremy consented to hosting Matthew's colleagues and some of his former students from the Academy – and consented to it taking place in their own home, where the LVT had just been laid down in the hallway – was because this was the last time he would have to see any of them. After thirty-five years spent working in that school and thirty-four years of Jeremy wishing he would get another job, his husband was retiring. It had been tough convincing Matthew to leave while he was fifty-five and still had some life in him. He'd only just turned the school around. If it hadn't been for the rental income from the new flats in town, he'd probably have stayed until he was sixty.

The party had been going for a full hour and the guests had swarmed through, into the dining room and the conservatory. Someone had taken over the smart speakers, ousted Jeremy's calming classical-contemporary playlist and replaced it with their own choice of music. As he descended the staircase, someone was whining about a wonder wall.

He stood in the hallway behind the glass doors to the lounge. He took a deep breath and opened it.

On the other side of the door, a woman with green eyeshadow turned to him. There was a kind of default smile on her face that faded momentarily as she recognised him and walked over.

'Jeremy,' she said. 'So good to see you.'

'Mrs Parkinson,' he smiled. 'So glad you could make it.'

'Call me Susan,' she said. Jeremy nodded and made a mental note not to. Once, he'd called her 'Parkers', which she'd hated because she said it made her sound like someone who went beagling. He'd blinked at her a couple of times before he realised that this was an insult, but by then the conversation had already moved on.

'Where's Matthew?' he asked her.

'Don't know,' she said, blithely making no effort to look for him. 'Probably off somewhere being adored. You want a drink with those?' She nodded to the tray of sausage rolls that Jeremy had forgotten he was holding. Reddening slightly, he set them down on a nearby table and picked up a glass of the ice-cold, bone-dry Pecorino he'd had recommended by last week's wine guide. He would mention it to Mrs P at some point, knowing she'd have no idea what it was. And she'd keep her face frozen still, determined not to admit any ignorance in front of him.

'Much better,' she said, a little too kindly, as though she'd just supervised the de-lousing of a child. 'Alright, then. What shall we drink to?'

'I'd like to drink to *you*,' said Jeremy, watching her carefully. But she barely raised an eyebrow.

'Me?'

'Absolutely. Nobody has been more supportive of my husband than you.'

She eyed him for a moment. 'That's true.' She raised her glass, took an approving sip and, making no excuses, went off in search of better company.

Jeremy was not terribly sorry to miss out on more conversation with her. He knew all about Mrs P. She'd been the one to get her claws into Matthew first, making him practise his Teacher Voice until it was perfect. She'd shown him how many slides he could cut out of his PowerPoints in order to make the best use of lesson time. She told him which members of the leadership team to steer clear of after the weekly meetings, and which extracurriculars to avoid if he wanted to keep his Saturday mornings free. Such a lot of energy to expend on someone totally unrelated to her. The truth is, she'd groomed him for leadership from the start. She told him how to keep the difficult staff on side; how to handle Mr Green's moody outbursts after the awful year nine class he always taught last thing on a Monday; what to buy Mrs Jones for Christmas so she'd lend a hand with classroom displays all year; which seat in the staffroom was only for the Head. It amounted to a kind of informal internship. It must have added hours to her working week.

Jeremy hadn't minded so much at first. It meant more money. They'd gone to Rome with his Head of Department raise. That hotel with two sinks in the bathroom. And on those first few mornings in the role, Jeremy had felt a kind of pride watching his husband set off for work, his suit pressed, his shirts starched, his hair gelled, ready to educate the community (not *their* community, of course). He'd still felt Matthew was his, then, however long he stayed away. But it didn't last. It was Mrs P who had convinced Matthew to apply for promotion after promotion.

What kind of person did that? Surely, she must have been a tiny bit jealous when he got the Head of Key Stage 4 job. Or when he applied for the deputy head role, three years later. Or when, five years after that, Matthew applied for the Headship. Or when the board appointed Matthew CEO of the Academy Trust, on a salary that rivalled even Jeremy's. But as Jeremy watched her now, beavering through the cheese and crackers, he didn't see the monster he'd built up in his mind.

It was hard not to find some sort of appreciation for the person who'd first seen Matthew's potential, the young teacher who'd gone to his pupils' football games, caught them in tiny acts of kindness or diligence and praised them, called parents to pass on any last bit of good news to curry favour at home. She'd taken his husband and refined him until he was barely recognisable, given him authority and confidence. And it shouldn't matter if Jeremy couldn't give him those things himself.

In the lounge, Jeremy found himself on the edges of a conversation with some of the staff, all talking with their mouths full, none of them using napkins. He tried to remember their names. There was old Elizabeth Something, who had been Head ten years ago, and had retired after only two years in the role because of her 'health'. Along the corridors of the Academy, there was an uneasy whisper that Elizabeth's 'health' was a matter of *mental* health. Nobody asked her about it publicly but among a few in the staffroom there remained an air of fear and pity when she was discussed, as though she were an unexploded bomb or a learner driver who'd wandered onto the motorway.

There was the eagle-eyed head of HR, apparently still in the role, who certainly knew what had led Elizabeth to seek early retirement. At the moment she was talking about *Coronation Street* in Jeremy's house, but she looked like the sort to enjoy a good gossip given half the chance. In his mind, Jeremy groped for her name. Thea Somebody. That Nathan man was talking to a smattering of the other former students, some in their early twenties now, some older, some just out of sixth form; Matthew had insisted on teaching one class every single year as Head, right up until he got promoted again. How wonderful that Matthew had had such a positive impact on them that they would still, years later, read an email invitation in his name. And now they were in his home. Jeremy tapped his back pocket and the keys to the BMW jangled reassuringly.

A few of them, the former students, looked rather uncomfortable being here. A little wary, as though they had been lured here under false pretences. Jeremy watched them speak to one another in hushed tones, the children who had been allowed to stay up for their parents' party but who didn't know how to dance to the music. Too old to be the darling child on display, too young to interact with the retired and semi-retired crowd in which they found themselves. They sipped their wine cautiously, afraid to get drunk in front of people who had watched them grow up from behind a desk. Perhaps their clothes made them seem more awkward, too, the too-formal shirts and ankle-length skirts, chosen as if this were a job interview or a visit to grandmother's house. Which, Jeremy reflected, were probably the only other occasions on which people so young would ever meet people so . . . his and Matthew's age.

Someone turned to him, startling him out of his reverie. 'Sorry, Jeremy, this must be boring for you.'

He became an actor again, made the usual polite noises, smiled.

'Your line of work must be much more interesting.' The man who was speaking was about ten years younger than Jeremy, and perhaps looking for a way out of a life of Saturday afternoons spent correcting spellings.

'I don't know about that,' said Jeremy. 'All jobs have their ups and downs, don't they?'

'What do you do?' said the man.

Jeremy mumbled something about tax law. The man nodded a little sadly, and the conversation went back to teaching, to what was said by whom in the all-staff meeting that morning. Something in Jeremy's mind sat down heavily as he realised that this was a world that simply did not stop. No matter who came or who left, no matter what had been achieved or sacrificed, there was always another cohort of children to be taught and fed and cared for, and none of them cared what happened outside their own tiny little worlds. And invariably the teachers were no better. He caught Mrs P's eye again from across the room. Was that her third glass, now? Did she even bring anything?

He went around the room with the wine, topping up glasses here and there, picking up bits of conversation as he went. Every so often he glimpsed the sausage rolls and had a thought, then set it aside. Maybe he and Matthew would have sex tonight. It'd been such a long time.

There was a gaggle of teachers in front of him, talking sceptically about the new skyscrapers in town. Jeremy forced himself to pour wine for them in no less generous quantities. He didn't particularly see where there was room for scepticism. The skyscrapers weren't some theory, or a figment of someone's imagination. And if investors were buying up the flats, so what? Renters needed landlords, and landlords need money just like everyone else. Wasn't this the city of the Industrial Revolution? When did everyone start getting so suspicious of the rich? His and Matthew's own investments were in one of the converted mills, where the modern Manchester had been born two hundred years ago. Beautiful flats, with so much exposed brick. Some people just couldn't control their jealousy. Jeremy smiled his bland, unconcerned smile and moved on, weaving through the crowd.

And there, like a sunset at the end of a long uphill walk, was Matthew himself. His husband, finally his again. Or he would be soon. Matthew was in the middle of a gaggle of slightly younger people. Jeremy recognised a couple of them as deputy heads, but Mrs P was in there too, and Nathan. Matthew, six foot three and still as handsome as he'd been in his thirties, made them all look up to him as they smiled and chattered on. He listened quietly and cheerfully – that was his way – and it gave him the appearance of being held aloft by them all. They were holding onto their wine glasses or their canapés, but it was hard not to see their hands all over him, owning him, claiming him.

But they'd have a good retirement. They'd both inherit soon. And the flats would make good money. One of them had a shower that needed fixing, as soon as enough rent revenue built up for it to be worthwhile. They'd get to it. And in the meantime, the income would help feather the nest.

As Jeremy got closer to Matthew, he began to hear them talking about the young man's job. He hoped to eavesdrop for a moment before being detected but Matthew spotted him and waved him into the conversation.

'There you are,' he said, kissing him on the cheek. 'Where've you been hiding?'

Jeremy shrugged. 'Around.' He said hello to Nathan again.

'This is my husband,' said Matthew.

'We met before,' said Jeremy.

'Oh. Did you know I taught Nathan when he was in year seven?' His glass was full, but he had a lot of a kind of energy.

'I actually remember you from before today,' said Nathan. He was looking at Jeremy. Jeremy glanced at Matthew with a hint of alarm.

'Mr Brown used to talk about you sometimes.'

'Call me Matthew, please. I think it's been long enough, now. And I'm not even a teacher anymore, after today. Haven't been for a while, really.'

'You used to talk about me, back then?' Jeremy did the maths in his head quickly. That was years before the repeal of Section 28. He couldn't think of anyone who'd ever lost their job for mentioning a same-sex partner in a school, but then he couldn't think of anyone who'd ever mentioned them in the first place.

'Never in class, never in front of everyone,' said Nathan. 'Just every now and then, with a few of us in Drama Club.'

'Oh,' said Jeremy. 'Even I know about Drama Club.' Truth be told, he mostly remembered Matthew's working late, running rehearsals and performances. But every generation of kids had some variation of Drama Club, where the artsy ones and the loud ones, and the ones who liked dressing up in clothes not given for them, could get together under the guise (occasionally sincere) of actually wanting to spend time outside of lessons committing Shakespeare to memory.

'I might have been to one of your performances,' said Jeremy. 'What were you in?'

Matthew faltered for a second, but Nathan remembered. He, after all, had only had one Mr Brown. 'It was *A Midsummer Night's Dream*,' he said.

His eyes widened. The tiny boy. Such a big voice. *I am that merry wanderer.* How had he not known, before?

'I remember,' he said. He would have said it even if he hadn't, but he did. It was the last play Matthew had directed as a classroom teacher, the last before he became Head of Department, after which he went from one play a year to one every three years. It was probably the play that convinced his Headteacher that he could handle responsibility, manage other staff effectively, think strategically. And afterwards, when Jeremy had told him it was a good production, he'd meant it. Matthew completely understood the magic of schools, the excitement of children on stage, knowing how to parlay that with music and costume, how to winnow it down to performance after hours spent cutting down the lines, explaining, rehearsing. Matthew had done that, and for this boy, who still remembered him now that he was a man.

'I played Puck,' said Nathan. Jeremy nodded, silently. In his mind, Nathan stepped out of one box, and into something else.

'And you were brilliant,' said Matthew. Nathan, who had clearly seen that Matthew did not remember this properly, blushed nevertheless. How old must Nathan be, now? Thirty-four? Thirty-five? And Matthew, giddy as he was on wine, was looking at him utterly steadily. He threaded his arm through his husband's and squeezed, but Matthew only shifted his weight slightly and smiled wider.

'You were such a good teacher,' said Nathan. 'We were all really sad when you stopped doing plays.'

'Well, you were a brilliant bunch. I was sad to give it up. But, there's no time. You'll see, when you get to my age.'

Nathan said that Matthew didn't look so old, and Jeremy felt a chill. They all sipped and smiled. Mrs P looked down at her shoes.

Matthew cleared his throat. 'Are you still in touch with any of the others, Nathan? Are they here?'

Nathan said they'd all gone in different directions after school. A couple of them had had children, not him though.

'And what are you doing these days?' said Jeremy. 'Are you still acting?'

'No time,' said Nathan. 'I'm a nurse.'

'What kind?' said Jeremy.

'I'm a theatre nurse.'

'So you've not left completely left the theatre,' said Matthew, and Jeremy laughed because there was something in their wedding vows about indulging your husband's terrible jokes, at least in public. He imagined Nathan's seemingly gentle spirit in a brightly lit room with some egomaniac surgeon who was breaking into an anaesthetised body, bone by bone. He wondered how Nathan liked such work, and if they made Nathan take out his eyebrow piercing in the operating theatre or if they didn't mind that sort of thing as long as nobody was awake to see it.

'And you're still living in Manchester?' Matthew said.

Nathan nodded. 'Where do young, cool people live, these days?' Jeremy asked.

'Town. One of those new ones.'

'Which one?' said Matthew.

Nathan named the building. For a fraction of a second, only long enough for Jeremy and Matthew to notice, and for each of them to notice that the other one had noticed, nobody said a word.

'That's a great building,' said Matthew, finally.

'Yeah. It's expensive.' He dropped his voice. 'It's kind of a sublet situation. One of the doctors at the hospital is letting us stay in her flat, me and a couple of friends.'

'Sounds quite crowded?' said Jeremy.

'She's in Australia,' said Nathan, laughing. 'Just for a year. But she's thinking about moving there.'

'And she's charging you rent?' said Jeremy.

'Jeremy!' said Matthew.

'It's fine,' said Jeremy. Mrs P inclined her head ever so slightly to the left.

'Just enough to cover what she's paying,' said Nathan.

'Do you like living there?' said Matthew. 'We used to live in the city centre. About a hundred years ago.'

'It's fine. It's in the centre of town, so I can walk to work and things, which is good. The shower's broken but my mate says she's afraid to tell the landlord in case he raises the rent.'

'I'm sure that wouldn't happen?' said Jeremy, quietly.

Nathan shrugged. 'Yeah, probably. The rent's so high as it is! My mate can only afford it because her family's loaded. I'm sharing with one of the other nurses or it'd still be too dear.'

Nathan laughed again, but it was like he was laughing into an empty space. Mrs P's eyes were on them all, flicking from husband to husband, and to the young man. And Jeremy knew she'd seen what he'd seen, that Matthew had changed hands so quickly that Jeremy hadn't even had time to reach out. He slid his arm out of Matthew's and his eyes wandered to the plate of sausage rolls. They were on the coffee table, still a few left. Maybe if he was quick—

Nathan said, 'So, Mr Brown—'

'Matthew, please,' said Matthew, cheerfully.

'Matthew,' nodded Nathan. 'You're still so young. What will you do, now you're retired?'

CATRIN KEAN

DŴR

A GROUP OF people huddled under dripping yew trees, bow-headed under bright umbrellas. A shrouded mountain rose above them, and somewhere the sound of a river rushed, fat and silver with rain. I'd missed the service – a work phone call and a hold-up on the motorway meant I was late – and now I couldn't find the courage to join them. So I watched from behind the high iron gate, and then slipped away down the hill, a little unsteady, slip-sliding in my city shoes.

My father's house was in the crook of the valley, in a terrace hunched under the mountains that rose up on three sides, curtains of rain sweeping across them. In my pocket I had the key he'd sent me and I hesitated a moment, feeling a visceral urge to turn and walk away, to drive back home to London. But I put it in the lock and went inside, a brass bell above my head tinkling my arrival.

I smelled damp.

It took me a moment to adjust to the light, which had a green tint to it, as though the house was underwater. I found a light switch and a dusty central light with a '50s lampshade came on. I was in a sitting room with not much in it except a '50s armchair and a glass-topped Queen Anne coffee table. Thread-bare rugs partially covered the wooden floorboards. On the mantelpiece was a framed photo of a small child on a swing, laughing, hair flying like a flag. So disconcerting, to see a photograph of yourself in a stranger's house. I couldn't remember it being taken, or anything about it.

I went through to the kitchen which was equally sparse – an old leather sofa against one wall, a formica table with an old portable radio against another, rugs on the floor that looked as though they had patches of damp on them. At the far end there was a range which looked like it might be cosy, but I had no idea how to light it. To the side was a conservatory with a corrugated plastic roof, rain thrumming.

I went upstairs. I wasn't sure what I was looking for – something to tell me who he was maybe, but there was nothing personal – no pictures or ornaments. But in the bathroom, his toothbrush in a jar and a throwaway razor made me catch my breath, and then when I looked into the bedroom I saw a pair of striped pyjamas folded neatly on the pillow and I suddenly wanted to cry. It wasn't grief – how can you feel grief for someone you barely knew? I didn't know what it was.

Rain clattered on the roof.

I wished I hadn't come: there was nothing for me here. I stared out of the window at the navy, blurred night and the lights in the houses that rose higgledy-piggledy up the hill. It was too late to leave now – I'd go first thing in the morning, call an estate agent, forget all about this place. I went out into the drenched night, fetched a blanket from my car, huddled up on the sofa in the kitchen and tried to sleep.

But there was a sound, above the squall of the rain. Water, rushing and turbulent, and close. I realised I'd heard it earlier, but had just pushed it away. I opened the back door and shone my torch out onto an overgrown garden, afraid that the house was in the path of a runaway torrent, but there was nothing but the drip and spit of an ordinary wet night. Maybe the river that I'd seen on the map was closer than I'd thought. I wrapped my blanket around myself and tried to sleep, listening to the sound of the water, its rise and fall like a song.

Like voices.

I hadn't seen my father in years. I was the result of a brief and I guess passionate affair, but he and my mother were from different worlds, and he didn't stay in hers for long. He sent Christmas and birthday cards, and sometimes I replied. He'd worked abroad for a while and then came back here, to the valley where he'd grown up and where his father had worked in the mine that was now long gone. I thought I had a memory of him telling me about his father sitting in a tin bath in front of the fire scrubbing coal dust from his skin. But now I wasn't sure whether that was a memory, or something I'd imagined.

Somehow, I slept, and I woke, stiff with cold, to a barely-light wet morning and a knocking on the front door. I could see, through the frosted glass, the shape of a man. I opened it and the little bell tinkled above my head. The man was old, and wore a coat with a hood. He had a dog with him.

'I'm sorry about your dad,' he said. 'He was a good friend of mine. I've been looking after Bobby till you got here.'

I stared at him, confused. Behind him, gusts of rain span and spat across the street and tinkled in the drains. Then, the man handed the lead to me and I realised he meant the dog. I took it without thinking and then tried to formulate something to say. I was going home today; what on earth was I going to do with a dog? But before I could speak he said, 'I won't intrude but I'm at number twenty-four up by there if you need anything.'

And he was gone. The dog, a skinny-legged scruffy little thing, shook water from its coat.

I had five missed work calls on my phone but I didn't call them back, as even though I hadn't asked for this dog, I supposed it needed to be fed. I found some tins in the cupboard and while it ate I googled local dog rescues. I called one, was told they were full but I could join a waiting list. The dog stood by the back door and looked at me so I let it out, and then tried another rescue centre, which was engaged.

Maybe I should just drop the dog back to the man at number twenty-four.

I peered out of the back door, but couldn't see the dog. There was a brown fleece-lined hooded coat hanging by the door, that smelled of earth, and a pair of old slip-on boots. I put them both on. The coat was too big for me, and warm, and my feet skidded around in the boots. I felt strange, as though I'd climbed inside someone else's skin. I went outside.

The garden was stone-walled and mossy. In a bed running along one side, long-forgotten bamboo sticks rose from beds of nettle and dock and dandelion. The dog was waiting at the far end of the garden. A steep wood bordered it and as I got to him he slipped through the gate and up through the dripping trees. I followed.

At the top end of the wood was a raised grassy area, clearly man-made from the days of the mine. The dog wandered ahead, sniffing, and then slipped under a stile where the mountain started to rise. This must be the dog and my father's regular walk. I followed, listening to the sound of the dog's breath as he brushed through scrubby undergrowth, along the bank of a stream that scrambled over rock, singing over stone. The air was cool and fresh-scented and fistfuls of rain slammed sideways and I had icy drops in my eyelashes. The mountain curved above us, tumbles of white water dropping down through its crevasses. Higher up, stone walls criss-crossed and clouds hung like waterfalls.

And then, through a clump of wind-sculpted mossy trees, a real waterfall, a dance of white and black water, drunk with rain, and then, almost as though it was spoken by a real person, I heard a word in my head: dŵr. The Welsh word for water that my father had taught me. I hadn't thought of it in years.

Dŵr.

As the dog sniffed around the bank, I sat on a tree trunk listening to the waterfall and the wind, feeling it all move through me. And then, at my feet, I saw rusted metal ropes, twisted and pushing through the earth like tree roots, and I wondered what they were the ghosts of. I remembered, aged about five, coming to this valley or somewhere near with my father to visit my grandfather, who was sick and wore an oxygen mask. And as we drove my father mapped the area out for me, though not the one we could see, but a subterranean one: mine shafts that linked to other mine shafts and on and on under the mountains, like a vast underground city where people worked and laughed and cried and sometimes died. I wanted to ask him now: what are these metal ropes? What's beneath us?

But it was too late.

I turned back. The dog and I followed the stream as it twisted down back down the mountain, towards the village that was tucked into the valley.

And then, just before we reached the old slag heap, the stream suddenly disappeared, went underground. I got onto my hands and knees, pulling the grass aside, earth under my finger-nails, and peered into the blackness of a man-made culvert; something else that was beneath us and hidden.

My father's house was directly below us.

The sound of the stream followed us across the old slag heap, down through the little wood, and through the garden. It followed us into the house.

In the kitchen I removed rugs until I found the trap door. I pulled it open and the sound of running water rose up from the darkness. There was a steep stone staircase leading down into the gloom. A torch hung beside the door. I carefully followed its beam down the stairs. A scent of moss rising. At the bottom I swung the torch around.

I was in a cavernous, dripping space with sodden stone walls. And through the centre rushed the stream, twisting and tumbling, its voice filling the void. Beside the stream was a table and two chairs: on the table was a bottle of single malt whisky and two glasses. I'd seen this particular malt on the shelves of chic whisky bars: my father may have been frugal in many things but clearly not in this. The dog tapped his way down the stairs and settled under one of the chairs.

In the last year my father had been a little more communicative. He didn't do phones, but he'd sent more notes and cards than usual. With one note he had sent a key. 'I'd love you to visit,' he said. 'Here's a key in case I'm out when you arrive.'

'I'd love to,' I replied, which wasn't true. 'But I'm very busy with work at the moment.'

'You work too much,' he replied.

I sat wrapped in his warm old coat and I thought of his toothbrush and his folded pyjamas and his dog who lay at my feet, and the pain was like a punch; it made me gasp. He liked to sit here in this strange underground place, listening to the water, and he'd wanted to share it with me.

But it was too late.

I poured myself a glass of whisky. Then on a whim I filled the other glass too, and I clinked it. 'Cheers, Dad.'

I drank, and the heat filled my throat. My face was wet. The torch-light picked up the shadows in the eddying water. The sound of it felt as though it was rushing right through me. Calming me.

Dŵr.

And then I heard, just behind me, a sigh. A breath. And I knew he was here, and he knew I had come.

ELIZABETH STOTT

A FICTIONAL DETECTIVE

A FICTIONAL DETECTIVE sits in his comfortable wingchair, his window curtained for the night. He reads a book written by a retired coroner. *Death by Misadventure? – The tell-tale signs of murder.*

Sometimes he thinks he hears music from an adjacent apartment. There will be a telephone call. Or a telegram. Or a note slipped beneath his door.

A fictional detective sits in his comfortable armchair, his window curtained for the night. He reads a book written by a retired coroner, concerning the hallmarks of the poisoner. He can hear the trains in the distance, rushing. Maybe it is music. A violin, a clarinet, a horn . . .

Someone slips a note beneath his apartment door. There is no sign of anyone in the corridor.

This is how it is for the detective. Day after day. Night after night. He cannot seem to leave this life behind. His youth seems like a story. It seems he is created only to solve the endless crimes of fiction. Murder follows him like a curse.

The detective travels frequently about his business. Often by train. Whenever he goes to the station, he worries that someone will fall, or perhaps be pushed, on to the tracks.

Steam shrouds the platform. A whistle blows like a scream.

He travels frequently about his business. He hopes that nothing bad will happen to spoil his journey.

He travels often by train. He goes first class in a comfortable compartment where he can think. Where the blinds can be closed at his convenience to block out the light. Or opened to watch the world rushing by.

The detective imagines a time when he is able to go about his day without a murder close at hand. A body hidden in a wardrobe. A woman unwittingly drinking poison in her tea.

The fictional detective stays at a country hotel where he intends a quiet weekend. He is not a well man. He booked as someone looking for restorative rest. Doctor's orders. He asks for hot water and tea things to be brought to the bedroom.

His window overlooks the grounds. A garden, tennis courts, trees. He sits in a comfortable club chair. A little soft, maybe. He sips his tea.

Tomorrow, perhaps, he will sit out in the sun and take his tea in the garden. Relax. Meet the other guests. Tonight, he just wants rest. A night undisturbed by the worries of others. No note slipped under the door warning him of ill-intent. No unexplained noise. No trains screaming by.

The fictional detective lies in his bed. His window is curtained for the night. The floral curtains, at odds with his sense of decor, now hidden in the darkness.

His thoughts turn to slumber, but his ears tell him that all is not as it should be. A door closing when all is quiet. A footstep, furtive, overhead. Music playing softly. Or the sound of a woman sobbing.

He does not sleep well.

In the morning, he comes down to break his fast. He has asked for something not too heavy. Nothing that will trouble his heart.

Nothing abrupt, like a dropped knife. Or a sharp word. No heavy atmosphere from a couple with the cloud of an argument hanging over them from the night before.

All seems well, but a newspaper will be placed upon his table. If he turns it over, he may well see the front-page announcement of a death. Possibly of a well-known detective.

He travels frequently by train. He travels first class.

A comfortable compartment where he can think. Where the blinds can be opened wide to see the world rushing by. Or closed at his convenience, to block out the light.

His apartment window is curtained for the night. They are heavy curtains. Made to match the upholstery of his chair and other soft furnishings. Soft things have little place in his life. His choice of fabric is a smart check with a feature fleur-de-lis motif in the centre of each square.

He can hear the trains in the distance, rushing. Maybe it is music. A violin, a clarinet, a horn . . .

The detective imagines a time when he is able to take a holiday without a murder close at hand. At his hotel, say. Or on his ship or train. Or some bad omen like a newspaper announcing a death.

Or the story of a young woman who dies tragically after an accident.

He can hear the main-line trains tearing through the night. Tearing through the heavy curtains of his apartment into his dreams.

He travels frequently by train.
    They scream at him at night.
    He travels first class. A comfortable compartment
where he can think.

Where the blinds
can be closed for his convenience
to block out the light.
Or opened to watch
the world rushing by.

The years go on like this.

He imagines a time when, as an old man, sitting at a dining table in a country house breakfast room where he is sipping surprisingly agreeable coffee, there is not a disturbance of some kind. A dropped knife, a breakage of china, a peremptory comment to a young waiter who started just that day.

Or the arrival of a couple with the cloud of an argument hanging over them that will spoil his morning repast with a heavy atmosphere.

Maybe he could relax, then. Live in the moment. Enjoy a companionable game of bridge, or chess.

Enjoy a sunny afternoon when the young things are playing tennis.

Not the detective, of course. He is too old for these games. He will be watching from a comfortable deckchair, wearing his Panama or boater, reading a book of non-fiction.

Not a book written by a retired coroner. But something lighter, a field guide to butterflies, perhaps, or a modest tome on architecture.

He will watch the young things play doubles. Listening as they shout encouragement, the umpire cry, 'Love all'. He will observe a young man hit the ground with his racket in temper, his pretty partner throw up her arms in frustration. *Not again!*

He watches her remove her jacket, her hair tumble from its clasp on to the shoulder of her white tennis dress that catches the sun, showing a silhouette of her body beneath.

A beetle-browed man, from the other side of the court, scowls.

He (the beetle-browed man) watches the young woman as she serves, her soft, bare arms pale.

'Net,' says the umpire.

The beetle-brow scowls even more as she serves again. An ace this time.

The detective admires the young woman's tenacity, her determination to win.

The beetle-brow almost smiles.

'One love,' says the umpire.

Some ladies take tea. Then an attractive older woman makes eye contact with him. Perhaps an eyebrow is lifted. She smiles in his direction. He doffs his hat.

Is it attraction?

That sort of thing was a long time ago. More likely now it is sympathy. Pity for an ageing man in a deckchair sitting alone.

A young woman approaches the elder. There is a resemblance to someone he knew a long time ago. The young woman brings a chair alongside the older lady.

They settle. Things are pleasant enough.

Perhaps this time it will be different; the people agreeable, there will be no knives dropped, nor arguments at table.

No shriek from the library whilst pre-dinner sherry is served. No body discovered by some poor maid.

Perhaps he will get to sleep the night through without an urgent knocking at his bedroom door.

And no one will need to see him in his pyjamas and dressing gown, his feet in velour slippers lightly worn at the toes, his hair in disarray.

Or see that the cord on his dressing gown is frayed.

That his eyes are bleary with fatigue for a life spent watching others commit crime.

Those who kill
those they should love.

Perhaps the couple will make it up, get married and live happily ever after.
    Maybe the beetle-browed man will win out in a different story.
    It's a conundrum.

The train arrives at the station. The whistle blows like a sigh.
    He (the man who was the detective) is already aboard, the blinds of his carriage pulled down.

CHRISTOPHER BURNS

JUNCTION

I RECOGNISED HIM soon as I saw him. The haircut, the clothes, even the walk were what I had expected. From the way he approached my park bench, however, it was clear that he was unconvinced about our meeting. Perhaps he was still wondering exactly who I was, what I wanted, and even why he had agreed to see me.

'I think you must be . . .' he began, and deliberately let the sentence tail off as though challenging me to finish it. I thought that its completion was unnecessary. Not to show surprise should have been recognition enough.

'Maybe we should shake hands,' I suggested.

'I don't think I want to touch you.'

A refusal was not unexpected as I'd had my own doubts, but his brusqueness was unsettling.

I had chosen to sit at one end of the bench so I raised a hand to indicate the unoccupied area to my left. For a few seconds I wondered if he was going to remain standing. Possibly he would even turn and walk away, and I decided that I could not blame him if he did. So I attempted reassurance.

'I'm not going to do anything stupid. I already know that you don't.'

But he was unable to hold my gaze and instead stared out across the park. His face looked eerily young. I spoke again.

'In the time I've been allowed here I've usually sat on this bench and thought about things.'

'Things in the past, you mean?'

'Not always.'

For a moment I believed I was speaking the truth, but then I realised that almost all my conscious time was taken up trying to recall a life whose details sometimes eluded my grasp. But despite my imperfect recollections I had no doubt about the shaping, defining power of the past. Clearly it had not been either intellectual or ethical determinants that had made me who I was, but actual events. How I had acted must always have been more important than what I had believed.

After a few more seconds my visitor reluctantly sat down at the far end of the bench. As though ready to stand up again at any moment he leaned slightly forward and looked across the springtime trees, daffodils, new grass and the shining pond with its chattering ducks. I wanted to reach out and touch his hair, but knew that I should not.

'This is the first time I've visited this park,' he said.

'I've sat here for days,' I told him, although I was not sure if that was true.

The bench was fixed on top of a slight rise overlooking the arterial pathways. Despite the sunlight the air was slightly chill. Passing below us, and only occasionally glancing upwards, were dog walkers, office workers taking short cuts, and friends meeting by arrangement. There was enough space on the bench for two more people, and I wondered what would happen if one of those strangers should unexpectedly walk up the rise and chance sitting between us. Perhaps I would be recognised. Silent and with my eyes down I had sometimes walked among these people and listened to their conversations.

Although I was unable to look away from him, my visitor still did not want to look back at me. Perhaps he believed my intention was to exploit him. The thought unsettled me, as though I should question my own motives.

I cleared my throat, aware that it was a sign of nervousness, and spoke again.

'You're a little late. Not that clock time matters. Not now.'

'I'd have been here as agreed if it wasn't for all the traffic.'

I believed him. Before he arrived I had walked to the park gates and seen that the road was busy.

'Of course you were always punctual,' I told him.

'I try to keep my promises. And if you're telling the truth then you must have known that I wouldn't let you down.'

A passer-by threw some grain to the ducks and for several seconds their demanding, slightly absurd quacks carried sharply across the park.

'I tried to ring you back but my phone hadn't registered your number,' he continued. 'Because of that I thought your call might not have actually happened. It seemed possible that I'd dreamed our conversation. For a while I wasn't convinced it had actually taken place.'

'Your number was easily remembered,' I said, although I could not quite recollect how I had rung him. I just knew we had agreed to meet.

'Maybe I'll look back on this as happening at a different time and in a different place, maybe even in another country,' he said. 'You must know that memory can never be trusted. It betrays us too often. It could be betraying me now.'

'I can assure to you that it's not.'

And then he turned and looked me straight in the face.

'You're a lot older than I expected. And you don't look well. Are you ill?'

'My health has been better,' I admitted. 'Maybe I was given this chance because I haven't got long left. But I can't know that.'

'Are you looking for sympathy?'

'At my age sympathy is of little value.'

'And I didn't expect you to be wearing glasses. How long ago did that happen?'

'I've worn them for several years. I need them now, just like I need this hat to keep my head warm.'

'You've lost your hair?'

'That was a long time ago, too. You hope these things aren't going to happen but they do.'

He shrugged. Old age meant little to him.

'I wasn't surprised when I saw you,' I told him. 'You're exactly what I expected.'

'I'm sorry I couldn't be more of a surprise.'

'I haven't forgotten anything important about you – how could I? And if sometimes my recollections aren't as sharp as they could be then I can look at the photographs.'

'You've kept them?'

'What else would I do with photographs?'

'Even the ones that were taken later than this?'

'All of them.'

'I don't know if I want to see those. I don't think I should.'

'Even if I had them with me I'd refuse to show them. There are some things you shouldn't know.'

'Are you expecting me to ask?'

'I think you're too clever for that.'

'And I think that's the kind of assumption that you shouldn't make.'

Two joggers ran along the path below us, their breath laboured, their shoes slapping on the asphalt.

'I don't even know what to call you,' he admitted. 'I think I'd feel better if I didn't call you by name.'

'If that's what you've decided then I have to accept it. But I'll always think of you as Kenny.'

'If that's what you want. But I can't think of you as anything.'

For a few seconds I felt unreal. I knew that if he spoke my name it would somehow anchor my existence.

'This can't happen, can it?' he asked. 'Common sense is against it. The laws are against it.'

'But it *is* happening.'

'Is it?'

'Kenny, we both know that it is. Whatever the laws are, they haven't prevented our meeting. They've enabled it.'

Repeating his name was like an intake of oxygen; it re-established my sense of control.

'What you're arguing is that we can trust what's going on,' he said. 'But I can't stop wondering if everything around us actually exists. Maybe I'm hallucinating. It's as if somehow I've been able to walk into a mirage, and all this is a fantasy, a deception.'

I wanted to grasp him by the shoulder but resisted. It would have been good to touch him.

'Listen to me,' I insisted. 'We're talking to each other on a bench in a park. We can feel how solid it is beneath our weight. This whole area has spatial coordinates; you can check what they are. Living, breathing people are walking along the paths and there are ducks on the pond that we can hear as well as see. It's chilly even though the sun is shining. The daffodils are out. It's spring. All of these things are real. They're not false.'

'How can you be so certain?'

'Kenny, I've had more time to adjust than you have. I've thought everything through. Over the last few days I've been able to come to terms with the opportunity and be grateful for it.'

'If that's the case then you must know what you want out of this—' He considered a moment before completing his sentence. 'Trick world,' he said.

'I didn't want anything other than to meet you. I was given that chance. That's all. No one would refuse an offer like that.'

'You're content just to be here?'

It was true, and I nodded.

'But I don't know what you expect of me,' Kenny said. 'You don't appear to be anything distinctive; you just seem to be an old man who needs to be reminded of his own youth. Is that why I'm here? I hope that watching me makes you happy, because I don't like looking at you. It disturbs me too much. All I'm getting out of this encounter is uncertainty and a kind of fear. Nothing in my world is stable any more.'

'Give our meeting a chance and you'll soon see its value.'

'You act as if you know everything, but I can't be certain that you do. Maybe you actually know nothing. Maybe all this is just a ruse. We both know that there's a way of proving that it's real but it seems that you don't want me to ask. Exactly how much can you tell me about what happens after this?'

I could understand why he challenged me, but I still found it annoying. The irritation came through in my answer.

'Not only can I *not* tell you such things, I know that I *don't* tell you them.'

'That sounds as if you actually have no idea what's going to happen.'

I shook my head and he leaned forward a little. It was the closest we had been to each other.

'Why don't you make something up?' he suggested. 'That could be the way to convince me. After all, what would it matter? If you invented an untruth it would become as insubstantial as a dream. When its time came I would go on living my life completely unaffected.'

And I began to wonder what I could say to Kenny that would convince him and yet have no consequences on his life and therefore on mine.

'We both know you don't want to be told a lie,' I reasoned. 'You need me to tell you something that will actually happen. You must see it as a matter of trust.'

'I'd like to see it as a prophecy.'

'I already know I don't tell you anything important. You must realise why.'

He thought for a few seconds and then continued.

'It would depress me to think that I never got out of this town.'

I said nothing. He appeared to be considering possibilities.

'Travel will be a safe subject. It has no dangers. Just like thousands of others, I must go abroad, even if only for holidays. Tell me about some of the countries that I visit.'

Immediately a series of vivid but unconnected images flickered in either my memory or my imagination; I was not sure which. They were motionless but colourful, like photographs of landscapes and buildings glimpsed in a guidebook held in the hand but skimmed through with neither engagement nor interest. And yet I was convinced that my travels had been both varied and rich, and that afterwards I had often entertained my friends with anecdotes about them - although for the moment the names of those friends escaped me.

'Yes,' I said, 'I'm sure you'll travel. Given the chance, most people do.'

It was an evasion and he recognised it as such.

'If you won't even tell me which countries I visit,' he said, 'then there's no chance you'll tell me about my love affairs, is there? Tell me if there is.'

'I remember that I refuse to answer that question.'

'It wouldn't bother me if your answers were so generalised and unspecific that they turned out to be worthless. I just want to know that I can look forward to some excitement. God knows I haven't had much so far.'

Yes, I thought: I've had good times; intense times. And even though I could tell him nothing I began to revisit my relationships and assignations. The memories were layered and vivid, but as I tried to recover the specifics they became shallow and inauthentic. Unexpectedly my passions had become carnivalesque, like the products of a dreaming mind. Even the settings, the décor and the beautiful compliant women belonged not to reality but to elaborately staged masques. I was not even sure of my own identity within them.

I shook my head. The memories were unreal, perhaps even implanted. A chill like the touch of a knife ran through me as I understood at last that amnesia was eating ever more rapidly and deeply into my past.

Kenny became aggressive.

'You look puzzled,' he said. 'Can't you remember what happened? I'm sure I wouldn't have forgotten about love affairs.'

'That kind of knowledge would wreck your future and my past. We couldn't even be certain that I'd still be living.'

He considered for a moment.

'In that case I'll ask you a very simple everyday question.'

'Kenny, you have to stop this. Think of all the paradoxes it could throw up.'

'The answer will be either yes or a no; all right?'

'I don't know. Maybe.'

'The question is this – do I marry? I don't need any other details. I don't even want names. I just want to know if I ever get married; yes or no.'

And I thought that perhaps I could, without harm, give him an answer that wouldn't really matter. I need not disclose any identities, professions, families or geography. I could be discreet to the point of secrecy.

Then, shockingly, I realised that I no longer knew what the answer was.

Only a few seconds ago I had known – or could have sworn that I had known – and yet suddenly lives other than my own were no longer reachable. I did not know if I had ever had a wife or wives. Whoever she had been, or whoever they were, had withdrawn into a darkened corner of my mind where even their outlines were no longer legible.

A sense of panic swept through me as I became momentarily incapable of rational thinking. Perhaps all such details were being scoured from my consciousness. Perhaps soon I would be helpless, stranded, and bereft of personality. Only after a few seconds did I realise that at least some of the essential elements of the self were still functioning, because I knew who I was and why I was there.

'I can't tell you that,' I said.

Kenny was staring hard at me. 'You mean you refuse to tell me.'

'I don't know the answer,' I confessed. 'I can't remember what happened. The memories are gone. Kenny, I'm not lying.'

And it seemed to me that I stood in the shallows of a vast fathomless lake of forgetfulness, and that in a few more steps the blackness would close over my head completely and for ever.

Kenny became scornful. 'This meeting has been a fiasco. I should never have agreed to it. Whoever you are, you're a fraud and a liar. You have nothing to do with me. I was a fool to think you might have.'

Even though I could no longer remember any of the women I had loved, his rejection seemed more wounding than that of any lover. As he stood up I held out my hand in an appeal, but he was too quick and within a few paces was standing out of reach.

'I'm going,' he said. 'Don't call me back.'

I did not know how to prevent him. I hadn't remembered him leaving so quickly. Or maybe I had forgotten that, too.

'Please don't go,' I pleaded. 'Seeing my youth again means everything to me.'

Kenny took three steps farther away but he was still looking at me.

'There's something wrong with you,' he said. 'You need treatment. Have you been stalking me? If you have, you've got to stop it now.'

A sense of despair grew within me. The failure hadn't been entirely my fault. Kenny had simply refused to accept the limitations on what I was able to say.

'Why would I lie to you?' I asked. 'We're the same person. In a few more decades you'll look in the mirror and find my face looking back at you. I can already see it in your expression now.'

But he turned and began to walk away. For a moment I considered pursuit, but I knew that could only exacerbate our problems, so I called after him.

'Think it over. We should talk some more.'

And then, when he neither turned nor broke step, I shouted again.

'I'll be here tomorrow, Kenny. Meet me tomorrow.'

It was too loud. I glanced at other visitors walking through the park, but no one turned their head and neither did Kenny. In a few more paces he reached the gate and then disappeared beyond it into the ordinary world of streets and traffic and our youth.

When I looked down I saw that my hands were spread out, almost as if they could grasp all our hopes and all our paradoxes and hold them close until Kenny and I could meet again.

It was the last time I saw him.

Because there are no other choices I still wait at the bench during the hours of daylight. It is unclear where I go to at night. Meanwhile the life of the park continues uninterrupted on the paths and lawns and along the edge of the pond. For those visitors everything is normal, but to me my presence has become hopeless, as if I were an old forgotten soldier guarding an abandoned post. I also know that I am changing in frightening ways over which I have no control. Recently my hand has become almost translucent, and if I hold it up to the light it seems to be made not of flesh and bone but of something resembling melting ice. Even my clothes are losing their colours and degrading into an undifferentiated grey.

A few days ago a young couple came to sit on my bench. They were so absorbed in each other that I decided they had not noticed me and were about to rest on my part of the seat. I stood up, moved to one side, and tried to say that they should look where they were going. Momentarily puzzled, the woman glanced round, did not notice me, and then looked back at her companion. Suddenly I realised that I could not be seen and that if I was heard it had only been very faintly.

Later I began to understand that I have become invisible to everyone in the park, and that whenever I speak my words will be distant and indistinguishable, as if hailed from the limit of audibility. Perhaps I should have expected this. I had believed myself to be a messenger from the future, but now I have to think of myself as a consequence of the past. I am not truly real, and my presence clings to the outermost edge of existence.

Of course such beliefs are persuasive indicators of madness. It may be that it I am the one who inhabits a trick world, and no one else. Perhaps nothing I have described so far has been empirically true. What I subsequently learned about Kenny would necessarily be part of that illusion, and yet I cannot accept such a conjecture.

For the sake of my own sanity I am convinced that several days ago I sat on this park bench and talked to my younger self. I must have no doubts about this.

I cannot tell, however, how long I will be able to continue waiting here. There is little point to my vigil because it is impossible that the two of us will ever meet again. Whatever our time together was, it ended as brutally as if it had been cut by a knife.

A little later than our meeting, or possibly just before, Kenny was killed at a road junction just outside the gates. For the rest of that day and part of the next, the park visitors exchanged the news excitedly, as though they had personally witnessed the accident.

His death has consequences. The most obvious one is that in any normal sense I cannot be alive. When Kenny was killed his future must necessarily have died too. My past was obliterated at the same time as his life, so it is impossible that he grew into the older man I believe myself to be. And if I am not a Kenny grown older and wiser, then I must be something else.

After brooding hard on the paradox I have now reached a rational conclusion.

I must have been created as a kind of hypothesis. As Kenny lived out his everyday youth he conjured a counterlife from speculation and invention: I am that other life, somehow given duration and presence. But his dreamed futures cannot have been imagined either rigorously or systematically, as I have been equipped with both memories and fantasies that are facile and without texture. Sometimes they are little more than categories. My inability to remember was not my own failure, but that of my younger self. Kenny must have been like a writer scribbling chapter headings for a memoir he would never complete.

I am not a person; I am not even a simulacrum. I am a wraith, an invention, an immaterial and unobservable intrusion in a world of measurable substance.

And I must also acknowledge that there is another interpretation. It is even worse than insanity but I am unable to ignore it. One can recover from madness, but not from the possibility that Kenny released me into the world only in the final moments before he died. Perhaps, at this very instant, I have actually been aware for only a few moments, and that what I now experience as slowly passing days are but fractions of a second.

It could be that I never met Kenny at all. Perhaps I merely imagined him as he failed to reconcile himself, not with a future he had lost, but with a future that had never belonged to him. Maybe the park, its people, my presence, and even my thoughts exist within a constricted moment of time, scarcely longer than the drawing of a final breath. I am distinctive, unique, a singularity who cannot judge if a few seconds have passed or an entire year, and who assures himself that he is alive but secretly knows that he cannot be.

At first I was scared but I have learned to accept whatever my fate will be. And if I sense that time is passing, I have to believe that it actually passes at the speed at which I witness it. I am unseen, unheard, and alone, but whatever my physical state there is a core to me that remains human. I will continue to honour that even as I accept that I do not know what my future has to be.

There is little left of me. Perhaps I will merely fade away, like a lamp that imperceptibly wanes until it holds the merest hint of illumination. What will be left of me then - a disturbance in the vision of passers-by, as if the atmosphere had somehow momentarily warped? Or will I be a scarcely audible whisper that only some are able to hear but not understand, and the reason that they will turn to their bewildered companions to ask if they heard a noise like someone breathing?

I stand guard by the bench as a cloud darkens the grass in the park. A breeze troubles the surface of the pond. My body and even my clothes seem no longer to be material, but composed of fog. When I put my hand on my chest the skin offers no resistance. I feel that my fingers could flow into my ribs like a stream of mist.

The air temperature dips and it begins to drizzle. I cannot feel the raindrops as they pass through my body and fall on the ground beneath me.

IMOGEN REID

FABRICATION

more often than not you see the room in Long-Shot with the darkness pressing in all around you, your right shoulder wedged firmly into the wooden jamb framing the cheap plywood door you lean on, a tense posture triggering a dull ache that extends the length of your arm culminating at the tips of your fingers with the tingling sensation that animates them, driving them into the chipped paint so that the tiny shards lodge themselves beneath your nails, Brilliant White, Non-Drip, Quick Dry, Durable and Long Lasting, Available in Variety of Colours

it's the pain that focuses your attention on the scene you see in front of you, the same scene you've seen day after day, a scene so familiar you are convinced you could recount the position of each object with your eyes closed, as if an optogram had been imprinted on your retina; a scene so familiar that you no longer see it, or rather you see what you expect to see, you oversee layers of the past unhinged in the present, amplified and embellished in the darkness

at the far end of the room in an alcove, to the right of a four-pane window, an eerie glow emanates from a partially obscured computer screen ensconced on the desk beneath it, and your eyes strain to make out the indeterminate shape shifting back and forth in front of you
a small patch of creased white fabric swings slowly forward towards

you, followed by an elbow, a shoulder, a shirt collar, a loose tie with a knot that hangs like a noose at the neck, black or possibly blue in colour, the kind of blue that dissolves in the ink-stained darkness that effaces the part-formed silhouette of the man shifting slowly back and forth in front of the desk

a shabby office chair pivots silently on its adjustable axis, steered by the push and thrust of his haunches, into and away from the eerie light radiating from the computer screen, intermittently illuminating this or that feature, which undeniably belong to the unidentified man whose body, drained of vigour, sinks into the standard grey upholstery as the chair swivels into and out of the light, or the darkness, like a pendulum slowly gathering speed until it reaches the familiar time of 24 frames a second. In the background the image remains crisp, in the foreground the details are unfocused

on the table, to the left of the computer, a lit cigarette nestles in the curved rim of a glass ashtray, and you watch as the smouldering embers accumulate

above the desk, tacked to the wall, a yellowed newspaper cutting hangs at a slightly skewed angle, it's barely held in place by the steel pin piercing the rough-hewn frame that surrounds the black and white image at its centre, leaving the loose corners of the fragile paper free to catch the gentle breeze stealing through the tiny fracture in the windowpane; the torn edges tremble like a shackled butterfly, its foxed wings straining against the impossibility of flight. Beneath the image a faded caption reads 'Suspect Found' or possibly 'Drowned'

you have no recollection of being there, or of where or when the photograph was taken, but the matt black ink is insistent, despite, or perhaps because of, the faded tones, an official document tarnished by

time
lends authenticity to the image, drawing a line under the fact, it is you, you are sure of it? the same leather boots scuffed at the tips and worn at the
heels
fitted with Blakey's Segs Protecting, Prolonging The Life of Your Shoes, the same ill-fitting jacket, its patch pockets flaunting a visible mend skilfully darned with a coarse red yarn that clashes with the original weave, a decorative trim devised to detract from a hole in the lining, which fell all the way down to the hem where a small pebble, or perhaps better a stone, nestled amidst a collection of unidentified debris and lint. The same brown slacks, which retain the shape of your body like a cast of your legs, backside, and knees, the same white shirt with the dark blue tie hung loose at the neck, so dark it dissolves into the matt black ink concealing the colours of these long-lost garments, the details of which sharpen or fade each time you recollect a new memory. But the face could be any face effaced by the network of ben-day dots that compose it, the face is more gap than it is substance, its identity remains undecided. Beneath your feet the repeated pattern dissolves into the threadbare carpet like capillary waves lapping around your feet

you can't recall being there, but you can feel the frayed edges of an unwritten narrative slowly crystallise around the grainy image tacked to the wall, barely held in place by a steel pin, its fragile edges fluttering in the breeze like shackled butterfly wings. Beneath it, in front of the desk, partially illuminated by the eerie glow emanating from the computer screen, the chair turns and re-turns silently swivelling on its well-oiled axis, the monotonous rhythm neither surging nor subsiding,
now
and then again
the angle of viewing ceaselessly changing

you are running down an empty street, the cold air burning your lungs as the darkness spreads out in every direction around
you
the piercing sound of iron striking concrete reverberates in your head, Blakey's Segs Protecting, Prolonging The Life of Your
shoes
pound the pavement, your right hand grips a battered torch, your tensed fingers wrapped around it, nails digging into the chipped enamel so that tiny shards of white paint lodge themselves beneath them, Brilliant White, Quick Dry, Durable and Long Lasting, and you barely notice the thunderous sound of footfall cut to a muffled thud as the cracked concrete gives way to loose
soil
sticks to the soles of your
boots
fit perfectly into the trail of muddy depressions that define the well-trodden route mapped out ahead in advance of
you
the torch light skirts the undergrowth loitering on litter and detritus, a silicone-coated commuter mug with a broken spill-proof lid, its non-slip grip scorched and blistered, the tiny lacerations revealing the corroded stainless-steel liner beneath it, a crushed plastic water bottle snapped at the neck, the screw-cap still attached, a glut of bloated cigarette butts saturated with rain, an upturned swivel chair, an assortment of discarded packaging, their trademark logos bleached by the sun, blanched remnants that give nothing more than a taciturn hint of the contents they once contained, the abandoned, the lost, and the wilfully hidden, concealed beneath the decomposing foliage banked at the sides of the muddy
path
is strewn with unremarkable pebbles, or small

stones

that get caught in the tread of your rubber soles bear a striking resemblance to the pebble, or stone, that slipped through the hole in your left pocket before falling all the way down to the hem of your ill-fitting jacket, the same pebble or stone that beats against your hip like a metronome setting the pace of your stride, its monotonous rhythm neither surging nor subsiding, and you are convinced that the weight of this tiny object is incrementally increasing, dragging you down like ballast as you struggle to come up for air. And you feel the coldness bite at your ankles before you hear the flashbulb pop, the hiss and whine of gas, or smell the heady stench of smoke, and you can't exactly see the blast of light as the electric current passes through it

burns

your eyes printing an optogram on your retina, and the capillary waves continue to gravitate around your waterlogged

boots

dissolve into the concentric circles that decorate the threadbare carpet disintegrating beneath your feet, the pungent sent of tobacco hits the back of your throat, and the bittersweet taste makes you gag. In the background the image is blurred, in the foreground, slowly swinging towards you, a small patch of creased white fabric followed by the part-formed silhouette of a man seated on a shabby swivel chair, his dead weight sinking into the standard grey upholstery as he steers the well-oiled axis into and away from the eerie light emanating from the computer screen ensconced on the desk before him, coming and going, toing and froing, so on and on and so forth

behind the chair, but in front of you, a small spider embarks on a rapid descent from the ceiling, abseiling towards the floor on a dragline drawn from its spinneret, pausing, briefly, a few centimetres above its target when the breeze stealing through the hairline fracture in the windowpane catches the silk thread causing it

to oscillate, momentarily suspended, hinged legs flaying, the tiny creature drops deftly onto the carpet and makes its way towards the well-worn
jacket
retains the shape of its former occupant, the shoulders, elbows, and trunk, like the cast of a missing body slung across the back of the chair so that it hangs at a slightly skewed angle, its patched pocket darned with coarse red thread, a single strand dangling down towards the patterned carpet drawing your eye to a pebble, or perhaps it's a small stone, which must have slipped through a hole in the lining, there's nothing particularly remarkable about
it
concentric circles gravitate in decorative motifs, like capillary waves. To the right side of the jacket, stacked randomly against the back wall, there's an assortment of plastic bags and storage boxes stamped with trademark logos that say nothing of the contents within, and you watch the tiny spider disappear into the gap between the skirting board and the threadbare carpet, above which the computer sits on a laminated desk, its screen casting a white light that intermittently reveals the slumped silhouette of a man swinging back and forth on a shabby office chair. To the left of the computer, strewn across the table, a silicone-coated commuter mug, a half-filled bottle of water, the screw-top lid placed by its side, and an ashtray containing a glut of crumpled cigarette butts. Above the screen, fastened to the wall by a steel pin, a yellowed newspaper cutting flutters in the breeze like a shackled butterfly, its foxed wings so brittle it looks like the image printed on it is about to disintegrate, and the face could be any face dissolved by flashlight and ravaged time, you are certain you do not recognise it, and the caption beneath it reads something like 'MISSING: Presumed Drowned', or possibly, 'Body Unfound'
now
and then again

the chair turns and re-turns silently swivelling on its well-oiled axis, its monotonous rhythm neither surging nor subsiding, like a pendulum folding past into present into future, the toing and froing, the coming and
going
nowhere exactly, unrooted while fixed to the
spot
beneath you, the decorative motif melts into the threadbare carpet and the concentric circles seem to gravitate around your feet like capillary waves, and the dull ache that extends the length of your arm focuses your attention on the same scene you've seen day after day, a scene so familiar you are convinced you could recount the position of each object with your eyes closed, as if an optogram had been imprinted on your retina; a scene so familiar that you no longer see it, or rather you see what you expect to see, you oversee layers of the past unhinged in front of
you
start again

NAOMI WOOD

FLATTEN THE CURVE

ANXIETY WAS DEBORAH'S thing. In fact, it was her friend. Back in January, she'd been anxious about the pandemic before anyone else: she'd stockpiled the baby's formula, and amber soaps that smelt strongly of Dettol. And when the pandemic had finally shown up, Deborah had felt a strangely pleasing sense of confirmation:

Hello. Here you are.

I've been waiting for you.

Maybe my whole life.

It turned out the virus was – and had been, as suspected – everywhere: on the baby swing, the button at the traffic lights, on the dog come to slobber moronically over her daughter's pristine hands.

But when the disease arrived her anxiety oddly lessened. She'd read how neurotics actually became less neurotic during the Blitz because the bombing raids only confirmed what they had suspected all along: the world is frightening; the world is bad.

And: I knew I was right about this, all along.

Never before had Deborah felt as if her vision of the world was in alignment with reality. Now she was just like everyone else. Or – ha ha! – everyone else had the bad luck to be just like her.

That March Deborah decided to make their house impenetrable. They only left to go into the garden, or, when the kids were really going cuckoo, Cal took them to a nearby school field. They bathed their groceries. Sprayed the post. All their friends were doing this, too. Cal had had pneumonia three years ago. Men like him – late forties, fit enough – were dying in the ICUs.

Despite the newness, this withdrawal also felt deeply familiar. Deborah was already an expert in declining pleasures. She could diet for months and instead of re-integrating foods she would take more out: no sugar, then no fruit; no carbs, then no alcohol. More than other people, she could deny herself nice things for longer. She found she just never wanted things as much as other people wanted things.

One morning Deborah took the children into the garden. She watched the baby as he poured the flowerpots onto the patio. Two lines marked where he'd wet through his nappy. The baby was loutish and oversized; nothing fit. On her phone she googled 'How big is a one-year-old?' and clicked on portable children with slim waistlines. She wondered if she was bored. At first she'd been devoted to their internment, but it was weeks since she'd even put her foot outside the front door.

She heard her neighbour open his gate and soon squares of Andrei's chestnut curls were visible through the trellised fence. He and his wife were Brazilian. He was on a work call; Andrei was something in marketing. Before lockdown Deborah had seen Andrei almost dance to avoid a dogshit on their road. He'd looked beautiful, agile.

Deborah carried his body in her mind like a souvenir. Really, she couldn't even remember if she had genuinely found him attractive: maybe she'd made it up, now that her old life had the helpless sexy voodoo of a forgotten dream. Anyway Deborah only ever talked to Andrei from ten foot behind the shared fence, so that his breath could be ventilated away in the breeze.

She wondered if Julia and Andrei ever heard them having sex. Deborah never heard them having sex. Come to think of it, she never heard the neighbours on the other side having sex either. Deborah suspected they had a second home and were swapping between them. She thought lesbians would be more right-on but maybe that was another heteronormative way of thinking. They had hand-drawn pictures of NHS rainbows in the windows, despite the fact they had no children.

'How's things?' Andrei said, after hanging up.

'Oh, you know,' Deborah said. 'On it goes.'

The baby gave her a gummy smile, and Deborah stroked his back. 'How's Joey?'

'He's fine. Now he doesn't even ask to go out!'

'Same with Zara.'

It had been hard work, at first, separating Joey and Zara. It was like the Montagues and the Capulets! But now the kids just gazed at each other through the windows.

'We could play badminton,' Andrei said. 'One day, over the fence.'

'Yeah,' Deborah said, as she traced the arc of the pathogenic shuttlecock. 'That'd be nice.'

Zara wandered into the garden with her magnifying glass. Lately she'd been pretending to be a spy. She was wearing a swimsuit, which was dangerous, since the material's ultra-silkiness seemed to make her giddy. She was an embarrassingly sensual child, prone to erotic dancing in her bedroom window, which Joey would sometimes watch from his trampoline. Deborah wanted to tell her six-year-old to stop but didn't know if this would make it worse. 'Hi, baby,' she said, cupping Zara's chin, resisting the urge to kiss her, since maybe all the kissing was the problem.

Zara held up the magnifying glass. 'I can see you,' she said. 'I can see everything.'

Next door the netted walls of the trampoline began to tremble. 'Oh,' said Zara. 'I didn't know Joey was there.'

'Zara!' Joey said, his hair mushrooming at the apex of his jump. 'ZARA!'

'Do you want a dozen eggs?' Andrei said. 'I have several pallets of eggs.'

'I'm here! I'm here!' shouted Joey.

'No,' Deborah said to Andrei. 'Thanks.'

'Don't go, Zara! Don't go!'

But Zara giggled and wandered off inside, and the baby pulled a plant from the soil, and Deborah thought of expensive hotels, clean and sexy, without history.

The weather that April took on a peculiar, LA clarity: nothing but blue enamelled skies, endless brightness, hot rooms with little mystery. She sensed Cal was bored too, though he was enduring house arrest better: he'd found an exercise regime, the garden bloomed, he spent more time with the kids. The more he flourished – tonally, physically, spiritually – the more it nettled her.

Deborah worked in contract HR. At the start of lockdown her company had been accommodating of her flexible working request, but recently they had tired of it and had asked her to come back full-time. Now, she and Cal swapped work and childcare in a terrible cascade of two-hour shifts. Someone was almost constantly trying to put the baby down for a nap.

She thought she would be able to endure this for months, but already she was beginning to fray. Honestly, she'd had her fill of joy and togetherness, and was done with all that. The problem was the autocycle of cleaning, cooking and caring. The problem was the lack of change: the next calenderless day, there was still nothing to do, even while the sky burnt, a blue tub.

Without a haircut, there was a new density to Cal's beard; he'd started to oil it with clove. He had long hair and dark shamanic eyes. Often people thought he was Arabic. In the sunshine he'd tanned deeply, and his hands had grown rough from gardening. He looked better than ever, but Deborah felt her attraction to him lessen. A friend said she loved lockdown because she and her husband could fuck over their lunch-break. Cal and Deborah weren't doing much fucking. But neither were Julia and Andrei, or the lesbians, who'd mysteriously come back.

'Nine hundred and thirty one people died yesterday,' Deborah said, over dinner one night. Every evening she told Cal the daily body count.

Deborah always watched the news, because it gunned her towards the fact that they were doing all this for a moral purpose. When she watched the broadcast bar charts she willed herself to grieve for the dead, but it was hard to hold twenty, thirty, forty thousand people in her mind at once. She imagined the dead in buses, in concert halls, in stadia. She felt bad about this too: she wanted to be more horrified, but the more she tried to conceptualise the dead the bigger the metaphor she had to reach for, and the more impossible they were to imagine.

Deborah looked at her dinner: roast leeks, cauliflower, rice. She knew, then, that the vegetables just could not rise to what was needed of them.

Cal was vegan. There was little that could be done about that, either.

A sound came from the sky. They hadn't heard a plane in a while. They lived in the city, but the city was stricken, subdued. 'Do you think the best thing to do is just lie down and take it?'

'Take what?' said Cal.

'Like, stop militating? Be more Buddhist, accept surrender: that wanting things only leads to grief. Etcetera?'

Cal looked at her bleakly. 'What is it that you want?'

'I don't know,' she admitted, though she thought: not this.

They didn't speak for a while as Cal checked his WhatsApp. She herself didn't look at her phone at the table. And anyway, she hated WhatsApp. The constant messages made her feel under siege.

'I spoke to Satomi yesterday,' Deborah said. 'She told her

husband: "Give me the virus! Put it in my veins! I cannot spend another minute with my children!"'

'Isn't Satomi Buddhist?'

'I don't know. She might be.'

They carried on eating. They'd used food against the tedium, and now she felt softer, inflated. Deborah looked around the dining room. They'd only just bought their house, and she wondered if it would be renewable, or if it would always remind them of this year's terror and lassitude. She knew they were the lucky ones: a bedroom for each child, a garden, but reminding herself of her luck didn't help raise the shelf of her mood. 'All of this. Why doesn't it seem relative? All that shit, I mean' – her voice gathered reverb – 'the makeshift morgues, the tiny funerals, why doesn't all *that*' – she gestured to the window – 'not make *this* more bearable?'

'This is hard.'

'I always thought I was the queen of this. Endurance.' She thought it would be the same as quitting cigarettes, sugar, booze. 'Turns out, I don't think I am. I'm actually intensely fragile. Weak.'

Cal pulled her onto his lap. She touched his beard and its Death-Star blackness. He was so handsome. She loved him, and yet wanted more of him. It seemed like he was going to say more, but the baby cried out, and instead Deborah went to him.

Upstairs she soothed him easily. He didn't fight her, and so nothing of the moment had its usual ambivalence. She kissed him while he slept, kissed him so many times she risked waking him, until she persuaded herself to put him back in the cot.

She peeked around the curtain. The window was open, and she saw Andrei, on a call again, speaking Portuguese. She wondered about the type of woman with whom he would have an affair. He looked up at her and smiled.

She put her finger to her lips.

Andrei made a 'mea culpa' gesture, sneaking off to the shed, though she hadn't meant to tell him off.

Downstairs she heard Cal doing the dishes while watching skate videos on his phone; she could hear the flame-like crackle of the opening credits, and then the grind of wheels. Sometimes, in the evenings, all they could do was commune with their phones. They wasted the evenings because they had no energy for them. In the evenings they were done for.

The breeze sucked the blind in and shot the room with light; that must have been what roused the baby. Deborah thought of the time she'd flown fourteen hours, Tokyo to London, and the light from the cabin window had been an endless afternoon. Yes; this drift, this waiting, this negligent eating.

Despite Deborah's crisis in resolve there was still twice the amount of work to do in about half the time. Other companies contracted out their legal policies to Deborah's, and her company advised, in terms of HR, what was legal and what was not: most of it was. She spent her time showing clients how to furlough, how to recoup government money, how to report losses to get Covid grants. Sometimes, it felt rotten. Cal worked as a manager of a water-aid charity. Sometimes that made her feel bad too.

During her Zoom today Deborah talked casually to her colleagues about parenthood in a way she knew the other women found offensive: how the baby played with hair straighteners, the oven, the plugs, but when she heaped on the sourness, the men laughed even more, and she felt like one of them. She didn't know why she did it: why she couldn't report that life with the kids, now that they all operated in a constant perceptual indoors, could also be benign, even delightful.

Downstairs, children roared. Birdcalls zapped from tree to tree.

Her little desk was shoved against the window; their bed was in the background. She feared the children coming in, yet longed for them to interrupt her, so that she might say to her colleagues:

Look! Look!

This is what I'm dealing with!

Her boss arrived and the call moved on. Most of their discussion was about a retail brand: an Asia-Pacific multinational which had been investigated for taking a governmental Covid loan and spending the money on an ad campaign. And if their fraud wasn't yet in poor taste, Deborah thought its slogan, 'Click for Calm', which encouraged shoppers to surf out the national crisis via online retail, was almost as bad. Was the alliteration meant to echo 'Clap for Carers'? But she kept her opinion to herself. The CEO said it would soon blow over.

Zara wandered into view behind her.

'Oh, hello!' nearly everyone said, apart from the CEO.

'Say hi, Zara.'

Zara said nothing and flopped onto the unmade bed, the look in her eyes positively bridal. 'I have to go,' said Deborah, conscious of Zara's ritzy swimsuit. 'Time for home-school.'

'Have fun, Deborah!' someone typed privately in the chat, with a winky face. 'I've been learning patisserie!' Then an emoji of a baguette, which was not, she thought, patisserie, but just a baton of bread.

Zara was in fact getting close to no home-schooling.

'Where's your magnifying glass?' Deborah said, closing the laptop. 'Aren't you still a spy?'

'Lost it.'

'Close your legs, babes.' Really, it was rampant; when had this happened? 'Are you missing your friends? And school?'

'No.'

'Where's Daddy?'

'Doing yoga with the baby. Can we play aliens?' said Zara. 'Or mermaids? Or babies?'

Babies was hands-down the worst.

'*Flam flark manoosh*,' Deborah said, as Zara pulled her into her bedroom. 'I'm from planet Zog.'

They played for half an hour, quite pleasantly, and Zara's face grew joyful as Deborah really committed to her role. Finally, when Zara had grown bored, she climbed onto the window sill to watch Joey on the trampoline, and banged her palm against the glass: 'Joey!'

'Zara!' he said at the height of his bounce, then 'ZARA!', again at the top, then 'I LOVE YOU!', which made Zara dissolve into hysterics.

Julia was also in the garden, in her terry-cloth dressing-gown. Deborah cranked the window to hear if the call was interesting, but knew from Julia's tone that it was her mother, who frequently called from São Paulo.

Deborah looked for Andrei. She sensed he was a little more decisive than Cal, a little more straightforwardly *masculine* – no yoga, no charity work; just selling people shit, and occasionally doing weights in the garden. She wondered if he was a reflective man. She wondered if he and Julia kept secrets from each other. She was thinking about him more – on a Zoom call his face often rose unbidden in her mind. She noticed that when she thought about him, she felt a tug of something like desire. She thought about him especially at night-time, when Cal was on his phone, and she was already in bed, and when she did her brain went dark, as if it were filling with water.

A cloud of apple blossom filled the air around Joey, kept aloft by the trampoline's electrostatic. It was so beautiful that for a moment Deborah forgot herself. The suspended snow hovered about him, then, like a magic trick, it showered down, and the image was over.

Deborah started waiting for Andrei in the garden. She couldn't work out if it was Andrei specifically that she desired or whether it was any stranger that might induce in her again the feeling that she lived inside a body.

Andrei had begun to sunbathe topless, or to work outside

topless. He seemed to do very little parenting. Sometimes she heard him and Julia arguing, which reassured her, since she and Cal were arguing too, over the smallest things – things that would have never upset them before, but then neither of them had agreed to be holed up day and night in all this starchy proximity.

More time happened. There was a meteor shower, which she somehow missed, and the sky at night was so clear that the stars shone with cold intensity. Satomi had posted her a book on Buddhism that she said was helping her endure lockdown. Deborah tried to bear in mind impermanence, as the book suggested, especially in relation to her own suffering, but it didn't help. She'd thought she was a master of not wanting things, but now all she did was want things she could not have: she wanted to see her friends, she wanted to dance in a club of sweaty bodies with a raging EDM track; and, most of all, she wanted Andrei, who did something weird to her saliva glands.

At work she'd buried the 'Click for Calm' campaign by hyping the company's new diversity stats, and the CEO thanked her for it.

The birdsong grew increasingly insane, like a tropical aviary outside her window at 4 a.m. She began to eat the children's vitamins.

The lesbians had gone again.

Meanwhile the numbers of dead were so big it was impossible to visualise, even with metaphors. At 8 o'clock on Thursdays she and Cal stood on their doorstep and clapped for carers, though she didn't put in much effort. Her aunt had told her that in China there was a tradition that a citizen should *eat bitterness* – that one just had to endure things, without speaking, without complaining, and above all, without applauding.

Eating bitterness seemed better than clapping. The clapping felt no good. She thought some of these people clapping were probably also willing vectors: people who went out, and socialised, and didn't care about killing others. She thought of all the brown and

Black doctors and nurses and porters dying in the NHS, and only reluctantly smashed her hands together, thinking it was altogether too cheap, too minor, for this tragedy.

She continued to watch Andrei obsessively in the garden. 'Olà, Deborah,' he'd say to her, as she watched him from the baby's bedroom. When he spoke in Portuguese it turned her on. 'Olà, Andrei,' she'd reply girlishly. She tried seeing into their bathroom. After a nap one day she found herself masturbating, imagining him banging her against the fence that separated their houses, and it was so hot that she came in just a minute or two.

One evening Deborah cooked a beef bourguignon. She knew it would upset Cal but still did it anyway.

'What are you doing?' he said.

The kitchen smelled of animal fat and boiled red wine.

'The baby only eats mush, you won't eat meat, Zara won't eat flavour, am I the only one who consumes *normal* food?'

He told her she was being crazy, but she could tell he was wounded. He went back to the year's best Vines, and they sat watching the folkloric internet try to wash away their unhappiness.

'What's wrong with you?' he finally said, sprawled on the stained sofa, because they weren't allowed nice things until the baby was older. 'Why would you want our kids to eat that? An *animal*? We agreed they'd be vegetarian.'

'I'm sorry,' she said, wondering what, in fact, was so wrong with her that she'd made their children a meal from the constituent parts of a cow.

'Do you even *care* about climate change?'

'Yes,' she said, wildly ashamed. 'I care! Of course I care.' On the screen, a man fell off a roof and into a pool. 'Maybe I could make you dessert? Out of jackfruit, or something?'

'No. You can't just . . .' Cal looked around the room. 'De-leverage.'

'I don't know what that means.'

Cal looked at her, and she thought he was going to say something long and filmic, but he didn't. 'What's wrong, Deborah?'

'I don't know.'

'I don't know, I don't know! That's all you ever say. Well, figure it out. I can't live with you like this.'

Cal went to bed, and she wondered if she should join him. Maybe if they had sex it would make things better, but she'd probably kyboshed that with the brisket.

As soon as he was upstairs, Deborah drank the rest of the cooking wine, then opened a new bottle. She drank another glass and scrolled a gossip website. For an hour she looked at pictures of the Kardashians, then George and Amal. She wondered if lockdown was an escape for them, since they hated their celebrity, though that, too, could just be a ruse. She scrolled through Adele's furious weight-loss; then to a story about Grimes and Elon Musk who'd just named their baby 'X Æ A-12'. She wondered what those figures signified. Maybe it was a Buddhist chant? Deborah said 'X Æ A-12' a few times, wondering if it might help quell her desire for Andrei, which also felt like a sum with no definitive answer.

She put on a coat and went outside in the hope of finding Andrei in his garden. Maybe, with his wife in the house and Cal asleep, they could get into something deep; something lovely, and rare. She could smell weed from their side, but when she stood on the picnic table she saw it was Julia, smoking a joint.

'Hi, Deborah. Wish I could offer you some of this.'

'Oh, don't worry. Probably shouldn't.'

Julia took a toke. 'When was the last time you went out?'

'Like out, out?' said Deborah. 'Not sure. Forty, fifty days?'

'That's incredible. We at least go to the supermarket. Or the park.'

'Cal had pneumonia. We're just being careful.'

'But aren't you going out of your mind?'

'It's like a movie about the Jews in Germany,' Deborah found herself saying, and though she herself was Jewish, she felt on shaky ground. 'You keep thinking, "It's 1938! How can you not see the danger? Get out of Berlin! Just get out of there!" And I see old people on our street and I think – "It's 2020! Just stay at home! Just an extra day!" Instead they're out there, in Virusland, hugging their friends like they *want* to die.'

Deborah felt ashamed of her holocaust analogy and sought to row back. She was drunker than she'd realised. 'At least, that's what I tell myself,' she said. 'You know. To keep us going.'

'I mean, boredom does weird things to people,' said Julia.

Deborah shrugged. 'Can't be bored, dead.'

Andrei came out of their back door. She realised he had, at some point, turned almost triangular. Such a neat little waist. She wondered if it was a stereotype to think that when he walked he almost Samba'd. '*Ciao, amore,*' Andrei said. For a racing moment Deborah thought that was for her. But also: wasn't that Italian, rather than Portuguese? 'Hello, Deborah,' he said.

'Are you going out?' she said.

'Just the supermarket,' he said with a wink.

Julia rolled her eyes. Andrei unlocked the padlocked gate and disappeared down the shared alleyway. '*Adios!*'

Now Spanish?

'He has a poker night at a friend's house,' Julia said. 'They play cards. Drink whiskey.'

'Inside?'

Julia shrugged. 'Everyone bends the rules a little.' She finished the spliff. 'Night, Deborah,' she said, and went back inside.

Deborah felt suddenly disgusted. It was as if Andrei had deceived her directly. He was one of *them*: a person willing to kill someone because he couldn't be bothered to stick to the rules. Andrei was killing people. Potentially, anyhow. She thought of her moral internment, her suffering – one of the four noble pillars in

Satomi's book – and of all the times she'd ever fantasised about him. She rested her forehead against the gate. Here is your pillar, she said, and she began to hit her head against the fence. *Bang, bang, bang.*

'Wake up, Mama!'

Deborah felt one of her eyelids being opened by her daughter's magnifying glass.

'I'm here,' Zara said, 'to arrest you.'

Deborah sat up, her hangover instant. 'Oh, fuck.'

'Mummy, don't say that word. The baby's crying.'

The bands of Zara's swimsuit sparkled in the dim light.

'Why are you wearing that?'

She looked at her swimsuit. 'I wear this every day.'

'You do? Why don't you put something else on, sweetie?' Then she changed her mind. 'Actually, do what you want.'

Deborah went to get the baby. The cot-sheets were wet with leaked pee, and he was still wearing the dungarees from yesterday, without a T-shirt, so that he looked like a miniature mechanic. Ultimately, the baby would be bad for her hangover, but right now his solidity prevented her squid-like anxiety from returning completely. It was the booze. The booze always made her way more anxious.

'I'm here,' she said, cuddling him, 'I'm here,' while genuinely feeling as if the sense of who was here might disintegrate at any moment. *Thump, thump* went her head, and she remembered how she had banged it against the post, and then the shock of Andrei's illegal outing; and how much she had drunk, afterward, because her idea of him had been so wrong, and the pain of her disappointment had been so surprising.

Downstairs she put the two empty bottles in the recycling, then retrieved one and put it on the side so Cal would pity her. She made the children pancakes and gave Cal a lie-in so that later she'd have something to trade. She made Zara a heart-shaped pancake, and the baby threw his to the floor.

'Look, Mummy!' Zara said, cutting off its top lobe. 'My heart is BROKEN!!!! Do you get it? Huh? Huh?'

'I get it, baby.'

When Cal woke she told him she was hungover. He kissed her and said he'd take the kids out for a long shift. He was so kind; she was so awful.

'Have you forgiven me for the beef?' she said. 'I'm sorry. I think I'm going mad inside.'

'It's fine. This is weird,' he said. 'This is all very weird.'

When they were gone she went on a bad internet dive. She read how global warming was melting the Arctic permafrost, and when that ice went millions of microbes, which had no intimacy with the human immune system, would be released in vaporous plumes: anthrax, smallpox from the Kolyma river, raging botulisms; who knew what else the ice hid? Then the fish would eat the microbes, and a local hunter would eat the fish, and then the hunter would sleep with his wife, who would serve coffee to the Canadian oil-seeker, who would journey home to Toronto, closing his eyes on the suburban train towards home; his breath, real as cloth, billowing like iridescent laundry into the extinct future.

Eventually, Cal and the kids came home, and again their bodies, their delightful realness, consoled her. She thought how she had three people to love, and how she would die if anything ever happened to them.

Later, while the baby was napping, and Cal was in the shed, she watched *Frozen* with Zara. She liked this movie. She wondered if she too could harness her anxiety as her superpower, just as Elsa could eject icy shafts of power from her hands. She wasn't sure, though, that her anxiety was anything but a darkness, and one that she could much better live without. Elsa was discovering this for herself, but Deborah was sleepy, and there were long stretches where Princess Anna was kind of annoying. Just as she was dropping off to sleep, Deborah heard the back door slam.

She roused herself, ready to find Cal in the doorway. He would soothe her completely, tell her that he loved her, and that everything would be over soon.

Instead it was Joey. He was smiling at her as if this was all completely normal. She stared at him. The garden gate. Had Andrei forgotten to lock it after the illicit game?

What was Joey doing inside her house?

'Please,' she said, her mind feeling sharp, and not at all hungover. All of their work suddenly ruined, by someone as stupid as Andrei. 'Please don't move.'

'Hello,' Zara said happily. 'How did you get in here?'

Without warning Joey leapt towards her and they fell together onto the cushions. 'You look nice,' he said, hugging her tightly.

'Joey! Joey!' came a voice from down the hall. The sound of Andrei's footsteps followed; then, he, too, emerged in the doorway. The funny thing was that up close, Andrei didn't look like how she had imagined him; not at all. 'Joey!' Andrei looked astonished. 'Oh, I'm so sorry, Deborah! Joseph, no!'

'Andrei,' Deborah said, though she was thinking only of Cal. 'Andrei, please get out of here.'

Just then sunlight spilled into the room, illuminating Zara and Joey, who were on the floor like Romeo and Juliet entombed – and Deborah saw the dust of the pumped cushions, circulating the room like dander.

ROGER LUCKHURST

YOU

YOUR BACK STORY is nothing special. You have no hidden trauma. And even if you did, it wouldn't matter. Not to us. All we care about is that your vessel was cracked in the firing, the glazing crazed, and we can find a way up through the chinks and out into the open air.

It's rare. You don't know how rare. We have to wait, hope the cracks widen, enough not to break the pot. It's a delicate balance. Impossible, really. We lose nearly every one of you.

Your mother looked hard at you, sometimes, there in the crib. Not that you would remember this, but she had wild thoughts about changelings, the old switcheroo. There was something unnerving in you, an old soul. Ancient. Pitiless. The way you looked at her. Sheesh. It was the Irish in her. Superstitious. She asked the doctor once, voiced those barely thinkable thoughts, but she was the one who walked out of the clinic with a prescription, not you.

Your father was less concerned. He judged you a day-dreamer, being an unimaginative man himself. He was right, though, that you wouldn't amount to much at school. Lessons were futile. We had so much to tell you. We've got a pool of knowing, here, bottomless. You didn't need lessons.

Still, you found out something important at nursery school. Something clicked. You thought everyone heard this chorus, felt the patches of warm and cold, spaces bathed in clamour, others emptied, blasted as tundra. You said something in Miss Sandra's class, something off, alarming, and you saw the way her eyes narrowed, her attention sharpened on you. *Where did that come from, the little devil?* We felt the danger at once, all of us, and tamped it down. Like we curled up, folded our little antennae in. We've all been here before, we yammer on, get all excited, and before you know it you've been carted off, tested and poked, throttled with Librium or barbiturates, burnt out with electricity, and soon enough the pot is broken.

You learnt that day: *don't* show; *don't* tell. We learnt something too. Remembered how precarious this was.

It's a trade-off, right? We were co-operative, most of us, we'd keep it in check if we could be sure there'd be times when we were allowed out, when the sluice gates could swing open and we'd have free run. But it's hard being a teenager, isn't it? You tested your boundaries all the time, experimenting cutting us off with imprecise mixtures of alcohol and drugs cadged off older kids. Your friends, such as they were, sought disinhibition, opening up the channels. You were in search of the opposite: blockage, amping the noise to drown the signal. You edged towards obliteration all the time. We had words. Things were thrown. Addiction comes with this territory, it's part and parcel. We didn't want that. Your mother was scared; your father hit you once, enraged at his own fear, the room and all your old toys dancing around him, unmoored from the real as we lit you up like a merry-go-round. He didn't do that again.

You were smart, could have been smarter than all of them if only you had just listened. Yet you left school without much to show for the years of bullying, the kicks, the hair-pulling. You got better at what might suppress our clamourings, and spent years in a blur of night-clubs, loud beats, dancing, dropping the little pills hard-eyed twinkers pressed in your palms. You longed for spaces where the walls were not verbose. You met a girl, sometimes a boy, and went back to their pad, hoping they lived in somewhere new, anonymous.

You fucked their brains out, hoping that they would do the same to you. You had to leave before morning, needing to be out of the rooms before all the histories unfurled out of the shadows of the long corridor to the bathroom or from the ceiling voids above. There were times, just before dawn, when it felt that the cracks were at their widest, and you had to be alone for that. You couldn't fall to pieces in front of anyone. It was your greatest fear.

On the way home, Sunday morning, you might find yourself hovering at church doorways, wondering whether to wait for the early service, seek consolation, hands of benediction, the shadow of a priest's worried face through the grille. We'd be quiet, wait out the impulse. You always chickened out.

You needed money to move out. Your mother half-knew by then, she'd pieced it together the way mothers do, and she was often sitting tensed in her armchair in front of the telly, anxious when you were gone but stiffening in fear if you came close. Your father propped up the bar at the local every night, drinking towards a permanent blur. He avoided you, flinched when he passed you on the landing. Bad juju to your own kin.

So you took a job. Then another. Then another. Moved out, a bedsit attic where the walls were quiet. The room was okay, but the carpet on the stairs was a river of old miseries you sloshed through every night, swamp hands reaching up through the leaf swirls to will you to tarry and suffer every turn of each bleak tale. You took those stairs at a run, three steps at a time. And then you began the long road of short lets and rapid exits, the knight's move across the squares of the A–Z.

Remember that time you hadn't done your homework properly, and took a let on that flat you'd only seen on winter evenings, in the dark? And you unloaded the van through the shabby hall and into the back double bedroom. You twitched the net curtains over your first brew of tea and only then saw through the thicket of trees at the back of the garden the headstones of an old cemetery, long closed and sealed up. Well, that was a long month. You did your homework after that.

You discovered as you got older that it wasn't always predictable. Old houses might be entirely benign, the merest echoes, a choir of gentle melancholy, while the modern blocks, those big post-war builds, could be awful, littered with clumps of terror in the communal hallways or the scrubby forecourts where the cars were up on bricks or dumped local papers mulched in bundled bales. Yammerings of garrulous widows in lift C; the depression of war veterans leeching through the walls on the fourth floor. On nights the tuning was good, however these atmospherics worked, you would see what they had seen. Chest wounds sucking air through ragged holes, the bodies piled up, the stench of the dead in fox holes, a flung child, the back of the skull torn out by large calibre automatic rounds. As you passed level 12, that black hole of a back room where the priest hadn't made it in time, calling to you, begging you, demanding you press the button, stop, slump awhile against the mouldering hallway walls and take on the burden.

You learnt, for work, to take desk jobs at offices in shiny new buildings. Less clamour in those. Factory refits were a nightmare. The agonies of them. You learnt you needed to be drowned in paper, work through bureaucratic processes that demanded many steps to be done with absolute attention, a strict sequencing, repetitive protocols, form letters. Rent arrears notices in understaffed local councils. Insurance claims, looking for niggles to avoid pay outs. Product returns in complaint departments. The larger the open plan, the more the voices of the living gained the upper hand, and everything else, all the background noise, merged into a soothing murmur, a chittering of insects.

We weren't opposed to the girl, you know. Not if it kept you happy. You liked the way she respected your boundaries, asked only the questions you invited. It took her months to even get you into the pub after work. She saw the woundedness in you, didn't she, caught glimpses of something maybe worthwhile behind your hooded ways, your caution. Your adherence to strict routines seemed to make you safe. She'd had some bad experiences before, it was obvious. Months later, she traced her finger over that wound in your arm like it was a record groove that would speak its secrets if her fingernail found the right pressure. Of course, you couldn't tell her what the scar was, could you, the agony at its worst, that awful pair of shriekers you picked up from the house by the canal, the screams no one could dampen, not even us, and you took the curled slither of the smashed glass and started to carve, so desperate were you for some other pain.

You thought she might be the one, you really did. She didn't seem to carry any baggage. Nothing clung to her, demanding your witness. After a year, you gave in, took the train north to see her parents, that new-build bungalow on the hill, the old mills in the valley below. Her mother and father, older than you expected, standing at the door of the porch framed by white PVC windows, close together, a loving picture, his arm resting on her shoulder, and her waving, waiting for you with a big welcome at the end of the long path through sculpted hydrangeas under a lowering sky.

You thought this visit would work out just fine, didn't you, your anxious clench slipped a notch or two, just for a moment, but when you got within range, my God, the vortex of poison that twisted around that old man's face, that poured from his eyes, his mouth. A wall of rage and bile, all his vile abuses tumbling out of him, poisonous yellows and greens, galloping at you like unleashed wolves. You looked at the girl, and saw something else in her face that you had never seen before, and you panicked. You ran.

At 28, alone now, for the best, you had those incidents of fainting dead away in the street, on buses, in the café. A light-headedness, a flash of a migraine arc uncurling in your retinal nerve, a rising chorus of voices come to meet you. You thought the curtain was going to be pulled back, didn't you, and it was as if your brain had to shut down the possibility. The third time, an ambulance called, the callous stare of schoolkids in a circle around you on the high street, terribly embarrassing, and the A&E doctor insisted on an MRI, those machines clattering with bad memories. They wondered about the migraines, considered late onset epilepsy. Oddly, you clung on to this possibility like it was jetsam in a violent sea that might carry you to a far shore and safe ground. To have all this pinned down to a bundle of misfiring neurons – imagine! It would be the final reveal that would make sense of it all. But the results came back negative, the neurologist shrugged, and they pushed you out onto the street with some codeine and a suggestion of bed-rest.

It was just a few weeks after that you went to that little Spiritualist church – do you remember? What possessed you? Desperation. Maybe aggression. Okay, we could go with the flow. A cold week night, a handful of visitors, you'll remember that mother, wracked with grief, the husband stolid, numbed, exasperated, not at all on board with this but prepared to try anything. That fucking charlatan of a man, his hokey patter, the melodrama of his slip into trance. Give us strength. He fished haplessly for the dead child's name, a terrible cold reader, but the mother was more than willing to meet him halfway. But when he turned to you, we decided to give him it both barrels, and we opened the cracks, as wide as we dared, wider than we'd ever done, and blasted him with it. He packed it all in soon after that.

In the end, we found an accommodation, didn't we? It was about volume control, keeping it steady, the knob at 2 or 3 like an old crystal radio set, burbling in the background. Like *Sing Something Simple*. Like *Lake Wobegone Days*. You could get through a morning meeting, then a working day, then a whole week, the tasks in front of you absorbing your attention. You found a place that had only three or so voices in the walls, nothing too rococo. They let you sleep, didn't jolt you awake. True, there was a pocket of bad vibes at the end of the street, the corner where you crossed to avoid the residue, the visceral pain of those last minutes the young girl spent under the wheels of that truck. But if you went a zigzag path, you dodged all that.

You couldn't travel, not really. You circumscribed things. You took off, sometimes, to remotenesses in Wales or the Western Isles, but learnt to avoid any truly ancient places. Barrows, stone circles, menhirs: they all were peculiarly awful, less a set of voices than a wash of dark colours, a noise of howling wind, a smell of blood and a weird tonality of ecstasy and terror that seemed to ride the contours of the land.

It's a limited life, we know. But we don't make the rules. We don't understand them any more than you do. Your back story is nothing special. You have no hidden trauma. This is how it will be until you join us, and we begin again the search for another vessel.

PIPPA GOLDSCHMIDT

LORD OF THE FRUIT FLIES

HERMAN MULLER ARRIVES at Kings Cross rather earlier than necessary, but he's exhausted and the station waiting room seems as good a place as any to sit quietly. There have been many such journeys across Europe in the past few weeks; on proletariat-friendly Soviet trains with wooden seats and battle-scarred Spanish trains with smashed windows and lavender-scented French trains with plump cushions. Herman hopes this journey north to Edinburgh will be the last for the time being.

He settles the suitcase onto the padded bench next to him before opening it. Inside, shining in the weak London sun, are rows of small glass vials holding his travelling companions; each vial containing a different strain of genetically altered flies created by him. In his lighter moments he thinks of himself as a travelling fly circus. There have not been many such moments lately.

The vials all need to be properly sealed and he goes through the ritual of checking their stoppers, until his train is announced and he has to slam shut the case so that the vials rattle like beer glasses on a waiter's tray and run to the platform where the train to Edinburgh is waiting. He finds a seat in a compartment with two other people, a smartly dressed woman with a boy who looks to be about thirteen, just a bit older than David, and he stows the case in the overhead rack.

'What's that smell?' The woman glances up from her magazine, wrinkles her noise.

Herman keeps quiet, he knows very well what the smell is. The boy says nothing. In fact, he is oddly still and although his hands are resting in his lap, the knuckles are tensed.

Someone opens the door to their compartment, spots the remaining unoccupied seats and bellows over his shoulder, 'Down here, lads!' before making a face and hastily withdrawing.

The woman raises an eyebrow, 'A useful smell.'

Herman grins before he notices her white shoes. And he freezes. Just a few weeks ago in Moscow, after returning from the lab one night, he found the door to his apartment swinging open and a book splayed on the hallway floor. As a scientist he's not given much to contemplating symbolic gestures, but even he was capable of recognising the meaning of the book's spine broken in two. When he backed away from the book to the window he spotted in the evening gloom a man, almost invisible except for those white shoes. The man standing in the shadows did what all such men do, he waited for Herman to notice him before he walked off against the slipstream of Moscow workers hurrying home from the factories.

White shoes are like the white eyes of an artificially mutated fruit fly; they're a sign that someone is able to manipulate the world around them. Now, in the train to Edinburgh sitting opposite white shoes seems a bad omen, not the new start he desperately needs.

Because Herman is fed up with zig-zagging around like a fly. He had to leave both Texas and Berlin on account of his political views; the University of Austin and the Nazis taking exception to his being a socialist, in the latter instance quite violently. What seems unfair, not to say ironic, was that he also had to leave the Soviet Union on account of being a socialist. He agreed with industries being nationalised and farms being collectivised, and thought this would be an ideal country to put into action his plans for improving human beings themselves, making them more resilient to their surroundings. But it turned out that Stalin genuinely believed biology only applied to animals and plants, and not to people. Took extreme exception to it being suggested otherwise. So, after a short interlude serving on a battlefront in Spain to prove his 'true' socialist beliefs – thus avoiding a longer interlude in a Siberian gulag – Herman has had to move on yet again.

As the train slides away from the station and past row after row of little brick houses the same dark red as the eyes of a wild-type fly, he tries to relax. Perhaps white shoes are popular here. How should he know, he hardly knows anything at all about Britain.

Later, they're passing through a field, the engine's noise disturbing a flock of sheep and scattering them in all directions, when the woman says, 'Cheviots.'

'Excuse me?' says Herman.

She nods towards the field, 'A skittish breed. They always run.'

'Are you some sort of – sheep expert?'

'Huh!' Her reply jolts Herman. 'If you mean, do I know how to be midwife to a ewe what's been labouring too long, or how to keep a newborn alive when his mum don't like the look of him, or how to dig out a flock buried in a snowdrift, then yes, suppose I'm an "expert".'

The boy blinks, apparently surprised by this discussion of animal husbandry. He's not with her, then. A bit young to be travelling by himself, surely? He does look superficially like David, but his manner of holding himself very still while constantly glancing around as if checking for signs of danger, is, as far as Herman can remember, nothing like David's cheerful disposition. But Herman hasn't seen his son for four years, and a lot can happen in that time.

At the next station there is a muffled tannoy announcement, like a prompter off-stage, listing all the future stops. It means nothing to Herman but the woman sighs a little and produces a handkerchief from her handbag, wiping her mouth clean of scarlet lipstick. Then she pulls down her own case from the rack, and exits their compartment into the corridor of the train.

Fields and hedges continue to trundle past the window, and the boy remains silent and hunched in on himself. The door to the compartment opens and the woman reappears, like an actress changing outfits between scenes; she's no longer wearing that city-woman skirt but trousers much worn and used for physical work by the look of them. Her smart hair-do's hidden beneath a scarf and even the white shoes have been replaced by dark boots. Her outfit is first cousin to the clothes worn by Russian peasants in the fields outside Moscow.

After she sits down she appears puzzled, her eyes darting around the compartment as if she's watching a small, active ghost, before she leans forward to look out of the window. Perhaps she's interested in the squashed-together houses and distant church spires. No, she seems to be looking at the window pane itself, before she lifts her hand and—

'Stop!' cries Herman. Fortunately his jeweller's loupe is in his coat pocket. He peers through the magnifying lens at the fly moving here and there on the glass. It's a bar-eye, one of the more difficult to create mutants.

Now, for the first time since the beginning of the journey, the boy stirs. He too leans forward and scrutinises the fly before he stretches out a finger and the tiny creature walks onto it, and settles there.

Herman inspects his case; sure enough flies can be seen crawling over the handle. Some escapees are inevitable but even so, he'll have to check the vials yet again. He opens the case, and holds the first glass tube up to the light.

'You keep *flies?*' asks the woman.

Herman nods.

'Why?'

'I want to understand how animals pass on physical characteristics.'

'You want to live on a sheep farm, then.'

Herman laughs but she doesn't join in, just pats her head to make sure the scarf's secure.

'What about your nails?' Herman gestures at her pearly finger tips.

'Oh no,' she starts to scrape off the varnish, 'they don't understand. They wouldn't even recognise me if they saw me in London. Out of them all, it's only the dogs that I'm really looking forward to seeing again. And the sheep, I miss them too.'

The train clanks to a stop in a cavernous station.

'Well, this is me,' says the woman, 'think of me up to me ears in muck, in no time at all,' and she's out of the door before Herman or the boy can reply. On the platform she's approached by a dog who jumps up at her with obvious delight.

'Where are you headed?' Herman asks the boy.

'Edinburgh.' It's not much more than a whisper, and he's staring out of the window as if he too is watching for white shoes.

'Same as me!' Herman knows nothing at all about Edinburgh except for one hastily gleaned fact from an encyclopaedia he found in a Moscow library, 'They say it's twice the size of Houston.'

'Hooss-tonn?' the boy repeats.

'You know. The city in Texas.'

The boy shakes his head, but he's unwound a little and he glances at the case which has Herman's surname stencilled on it.

'Muller,' the boy reads, pronouncing it the way Herman's grandfather used to pronounce it. The grandfather who escaped from Germany after 1848 and the revolution that was supposed to bring democracy and make everyone equal, but failed. Fruit flies don't fight or create social hierarchies, in fact they're the most egalitarian creatures Herman has ever encountered. Perhaps that's the real reason for his interest in them.

'You're from Germany?' Herman asks.

The boy tilts his head up. Herman is trained to notice small gestures, and sometimes it doesn't matter if you're looking at flies or humans.

'What are you planning to do in Edinburgh?'

The boy shrugs.

'Your family moving there, too?'

The boy looks down at his hand. Perhaps the fly is still sheltering there.

Dumb question, Herman realises. 'Listen—' but what can he tell the boy? That everything's going to be OK? From his own experience he knows this is not true. 'Well, *I'm* going there because they've offered me a job and I needed to get away from Stalin—' at this the boy is visibly startled, *Stalin?* Herman continues, 'My family's in Texas but I can't go back there.'

The boy looks at him as if to say, and that's why you breed fruit flies? To make up for your absent son, whom your estranged wife took when she left you in Moscow and returned to Texas, knowing you couldn't follow them because you'd get arrested there?

How many flies make a family? Herman has 250 vials of mutated flies in his suitcase and each one owes its existence to him, and will enlighten him about how life is capable of adapting no matter what it's faced with. Every mutant quirk - whether it's curly wings, or yellow bodies - will reveal something, because sometimes the truth is very small indeed, smaller even than the body of an insect.

They're finally rumbling into Edinburgh, and when Herman lowers the window to release the door catch, the air seems to have a distinct tang to it as familiar and as yeasty as the flies' food. The train slides past a large building with a sign reading 'McEwans Brewery' and the smell gets even stronger. Nobody is going to complain about the flies here.

The boy's looking hunched over again, so Hermann sticks his nose in the air and hoots 'What's that *dreadful* smell?', managing to provoke a laugh. Two women are waiting at the end of the platform under a banner announcing help for refugees, and the boy's still smiling when he shakes their hands.

MARK VALENTINE

LAUGHTER EVER AFTER

Cogenhoe always associated double decker buses with town streets, so it seemed odd to him to be on one travelling through the narrow lanes of an empty countryside, especially as the number of passengers it carried from village to village never seemed to amount to more than about a dozen or thirteen. Yet though it was incongruous, it also seemed curiously comforting. He enjoyed the slow, chugging pace. And what might have been dull and monotonous was enlivened a little by a brisk breeze. The bus swayed and creaked in the wind as though it were a sailing ship. Why it was that the Combined Counties service had selected this great green galleon from its fleet for the journey he could not say. It must mean at least, he reflected, that there could not be any low bridges on the route.

He stared out of the smeared window from his top deck seat. The grey haze from his cigarette seemed to sympathise with the scudding grey cloud outside. Through this drifting, the flat fields that passed beneath his gaze were a sodden dim green. The trees, he noticed, had relinquished their dry leaves early, as if resigned already to winter. No-one, he supposed, ever came to this part of the world for pleasure, unless it was pleasure of a peculiarly perverse kind. It might be said, he decided, that pleasure was what drew him here, but it felt more of a necessity, as it often is for the fierce collector.

The bus stopped at what looked like a disused toll house, octagonal and with a conical roof and pointed-arch windows. It had once been painted mustard yellow but now the condiment had congealed. The driver turned off the engine and waited, presumably to stick to his timetable. Nobody got off and nobody got on. The sudden silence that descended was brittle. It was soon filled. A passenger further back stirred and coughed, as if he did not like the silence. Outside, leaves crept furtively along the road and jackdaws cackled. There was a weather vane on top of the toll house and Cogenhoe had a good view of it from his lofty vantage point. The restless black arrow was veering about from North to East. Scatterings of hail rattled on the bus windows. After a few minutes the engine started up again with a hoarse lurch, like a burst of laughter.

Nobody could call the town, when at last they got there, notable, but it was, Cogenhoe decided, tidy. They had pulled up in the market square. The driver stared indifferently before him as they all got off. This was where the journey ended, though not for him: he would be taking the bus back. The square, which wasn't square, had a war memorial, and black and white bollards like a row of art deco salt and pepper pots. Cogenhoe could see a pale town hall that looked like an attempt at a Roman temple, and a chapel in red brick Gothic. There were a lot of benches, as if people mostly spent time here waiting. A newspaper stand promised the results from the local Cribbage League.

Things seemed neat here, squared off, like a draughtsman's drawing. And now Cogenhoe felt doubtful. His real reason for coming, he began to realise, would be an intrusion into such a place of quiet, subdued civility. He hesitated, and himself took a seat on one of the benches. There was a smell of diesel oil from the bus and into this there emanated the fumes from a fish and chip shop. He gave the matter some thought and decided to offer, if asked, a version that would be more acceptable.

He went over this again as he sat in his hotel room with its mauve candlewick bedspread and its monochrome prints of scenes from *Pilgrim's Progress*. The fact was that he had come here in search of a pamphlet. Nobody else had a copy, not even the British Museum, nor the great collectors and finders: not Dolby, the eminent editor, not the great collector Latcher, nor the ingenious bookdealer Oggeling. It was, of course, the sort of thing that would be hard to find. Pamphlets hide on the shelves, caught tight between the books, or they lurk in boxes of ephemera, with guides to ancient monuments, theatre programmes, old street maps, official brochures for long-forgotten regeneration projects. This one, anyway, had never yet turned up. It was known about only by rumour, a passing reference in a study, with an evasive footnote, and a doubtful entry in some guide issued by an obscure publisher up in the wilds of Yorkshire. To tell the people here that he had come all this way in quest of a pamphlet would be to invite incredulity, he felt sure, especially as what it was said to contain was a ghost story.

Cogenohe was an assiduous collector of ghost stories. Not, he would always patiently explain, the anecdotal, supposedly true sort: no, the literary. It was an art not disdained by the distinguished: Kipling, Buchan, Greene, Spark, among many others. And the pamphlet was supposed to be of that kind, a work of fiction. But he thought that if he were to explain this, it would make him even more culpable in the no doubt polite but nevertheless perturbed judgement of the good burghers here. And for another thing he did not want the townsfolk to know that the little publication, said to have been issued by some local society, had any great value: he must not arouse suspicion. Perhaps he might even secure a cache of them in some long-forgotten stock room, and then be able to sell them off carefully, gradually to his rivals.

Fortunately, there was a better reason for his presence, one which had the advantage of being linked to his real reason and therefore half-true. And this aspect at least was plausible, since it concerned the town's most famous son, and would be sure to appeal to civic pride. Cogenhoe remembered hearing him on the wireless in childhood, rather too often, indeed. He had found out about his local connection when he had been looking into the history of the town to inform his visit.

This was Charles Penrose, a music hall entertainer and comic turn who had had an enormous success with 'The Laughing Policeman', the entire point of which was summed up by its title. It was certainly jolly, in a sort of forced way, and Cogenhoe kept an affection for it, despite its ubiquity. He had felt mildly shocked then, though, by a line which urged the listener, when he encountered that eponymous official, to 'shake him by his fat old hand' and 'give him half a crown'. Policemen, he had thought then, were not supposed to take tips. Admittedly the song was just a fantasy, but still, it did not seem correct.

Penrose, he had learnt, had been obliged to follow up this roaring success with similarly mirthful other roles: including as a Laughing Curate, Golfer, Major, Typist and Lover. Imagine having to laugh on cue all the while, on stage, in the recording studio, and no doubt for your friends and fans too. Surely, thought Cogenhoe, sipping at a weak tea made from the dusty tea bags on the hospitality tray, this must be at the very least trying, and perhaps much worse. You must lose the ability to really laugh, in an unpremeditated way, to be caught joyously by something genuinely funny. He would not be at all surprised if Penrose had been, like many comics, secretly melancholy.

The collector had decided to say that he was in the town to research Penrose for an article and perhaps even a book. The performer's father, he knew, had been a watchmaker and jeweller here: the family had lived above the shop at no 1, High Street, then in other places around the town as the business had prospered. And, since the story in the pamphlet was apparently also about Penrose, that would provide slyly the necessary link to ask about it. It could scarcely be about anything else, he thought, since nothing else seemed to happen here.

Cogenhoe had first been told about the elusive story by a collecting acquaintance of his, Michael Essendine, and he had been wary, sceptical even. This fellow was known to have a peculiar sense of humour, and sometimes invented things. It was even said that he spread news of fake rarities in order to distract attention from his quests for real ones. On the other hand, some of Essendine's tips had proved undoubtedly true, and timely. He had got Cogenhoe onto Fraser, for example, and Houghton, well ahead of the crowd, or at least the coterie, and so had enabled him to pick up their titles before they rose in value: no doubt only after he had got all *he*, Essendine, wanted, but even so. And the thing was, you could not risk missing out. Besides, Cogenhoe liked the chase, the game that was, at its best, like a detective story, and also in its way like an enigmatical supernatural story, a de la Mare or an Aickman, where you never quite knew where you were or what was to happen, or even what *had* happened.

Well, he certainly knew where he was now, he thought, as he put the vague tea in its blank white cup back onto the tray. In Biggleswade, Bedfordshire. It was time to explore, if that was not too grand a word for a perambulation of the predictable streets. He made his way down the stairs to the lobby, where the receptionist was studying a ledger and ignored him.

The clocks had gone back some time before and even though it was only early evening the dark had descended and the shops were closed. In the dimness of their various window displays he could see floral-decorated crockery, fawn corduroy jackets, faded magazines, gifts that nobody had chosen. The bustling wind seemed to encourage him along the High Street, though there was nowhere much beyond it that was worth more attention, so far as he could see. He stopped and cupped his hands to light a cigarette under the earnest glow of a streetlight. The fumes were seized and wafted away like a handkerchief in a conjurer's trick. He inhaled gratefully and considered what to do next. He ought to be after something in particular, he thought, to give his wanderings a goal, a purpose. Well, then, what was it that he ought to be after?

The likeliest places to find the pamphlet, if it was to be found, would be the library or a bookseller. He had no idea where either of these were, but at least he could now stalk the streets looking for them. On the other hand, it was to be presumed that other assiduous collectors had already tried these, so perhaps what he should really be looking for was the *unlikely* places. In his collecting he had sometimes found things where you would least expect them. At a shop in Radnorshire with rows of china dogs there had been a shed round the back with piles of damp books, well worth foraging in. In a supermarket foyer in a small Norfolk town there had been boxes of fat paperbacks on sale for local causes, but somebody had donated a dozen first editions of RC Hutchinson, a once-respected but now neglected author.

He remembered also a pub that had lined its walls with old books bought by the yard simply to give a quaint effect. He had not been able to resist studying them, of course. And there had been a Francis Brett Young title, not a particularly scarce one, but even so. He had said to the young waiter who had brought their food, 'Do you mind if I steal one of your books?' The haughty youth had not been discountenanced: 'I could not condone it, sir,' he had replied. Cogenhoe had enjoyed the Jeevesian phrase, and repeated it to himself now, with a gentle laugh. And so he hadn't got the book, though it would not have been missed. He himself could not condone it either, he had found.

Where were the unlikely places here then? Well, you couldn't work it like that. The very point of the unlikely places what that you didn't expect them. They were only found by chance, by putting yourself in a slightly abstract state of mind, wandering around as it were aimlessly, giving chance a chance. So that is what he would do. And he would let his thoughts drift too.

The ash from his cigarette flew in fragile grey specks, and the wind seized his coat flaps, blowing them out like beige wings. Penrose, he now remembered, had been interviewed in the Nineteen Thirties and, contrary to Cogenhoe's own theory that he must be lugubrious from all that laughing, had seemed quite contented and still fond of his home town. Still, that might have been just the public façade.

Penrose had been apprenticed to his father's clock and watch trade and remembered in particular an eccentric old lady whose grandfather clock he used to repair and maintain. It was her habit to go about the town with a wheelbarrow and, when she felt like it, to set this down and sit on it. She would then commence a lively patter of jokes and commentary, followed by a swirl of dancing and some boisterous singing: passers-by would give her money, though she did not ask for it. Perhaps her example, that had caused good-natured laughter to echo through the streets of Biggleswade for some years, had influenced Penrose to earn his own living from comic repartee and song. She was a 'character'. She had also been superstitious, especially when the clock stopped unexpectedly: there was a suggestion of the fortune-teller, even of the sorceress, about her.

The wind had now risen further and there was a spattering of rain in it too, which rattled rhythmically. A shred of newspaper scampered like a creature across the street, wrapped itself around his shins for an instant, and then darted off, as if expecting him to chase after it in some happy game. He stared at it, wondering if he should. He rather wanted to. And – there was a sudden lunge in his thoughts – had it been, definitely been, just a piece of newspaper? Could it have been a pamphlet? The thing was still tumbling down the street, alternately seen in gloom and amber as it passed into and out of the beams from the street lights. Every so often it would pause, caught in something, or resting in some temporary lull in the wind, but to Cogenhoe it seemed as if it was waiting for him, summoning him, daring him to join in its race.

It was absurd. Of course, it wasn't a pamphlet, and certainly not *the* pamphlet. It was just some bit of yesterday's paper that had leapt out of a waste bin or been thrown down by a loafer after he had studied the racing pages, or detached itself from fish and chip wrappings. It was being followed now, he saw, by scutterings of gold, copper and bronze leaves in an insistent susurrus like half-concealed sniggers, no doubt at his own delusions. And they were not pamphlets either, though they were strangely papery-like. After all, what colour was the cover of the pamphlet? He did not know. Was he quite sure they were all leaves?

He shook himself. It was time to go back. Tomorrow he would conduct proper research, get at the facts. That was what mattered. He would interview the librarian, find out what civic societies there were, or had been, go and see their secretaries. There was the town clerk, the bookshop proprietor, the postmaster or postmistress, the history teacher at the local school. One of them must know something. Thoroughness, that was it, a calm, careful, logical approach. By the time he left he would know for sure. Either it was there or it did not exist. And of course he would question them about old Penrose too, to keep up the idea of the supposed reason why he was there. Maybe even about that eccentric old lady also, to show he had already done his background work. Besides, she was interesting. There was something there, about the way Penrose had told of her, that hinted there was more to be told. The same could be true of the town itself. Could any place that could harbour two such curious individuals really be so prosaic? He laughed softly to himself as he thought of a pamphlet that he could produce, with some such title as *Secret Biggleswade*. Well, why not?

But as he made to turn, he found that the strong gusts caught him and carried him, not quite against his will, along the road. And everything else seemed in movement too. A bin lid clanged in the gutter ahead of him as if a mad cymbalist was marching about, shrubs swayed like green drunkards, and there was a roaring like a never-ending chant. The town, that he had thought so trim, seemed to squirm: the houses and shops were like rippling painted banners. And ahead, just at the farthest distance that he could see, there was still the pale shape of the piece of paper, gilded now by a light that seemed brighter than any streetlamp could cast.

Then he found himself spreading his arms wide and letting the wind fill his sails, and he joined his roar to the wind's roar.

It came to Cogenhoe, when he let himself go fully into the gale, that this was life as it should be, this wild rush, this hectic dash, this exhilaration, this ecstasy. His spirits soared with the wind, and he wanted to run with it for ever, panting, joyous, heedless of where he was going or what happened next, hoping in fact that there was no next, except this and this and this. And as he ran, he heard through the booming a great laughter, over and over, a whooping, swooping, cacophony of bellows and guffaws, laughter, laughter, laughter, laughter ever after.

DAVID BEVAN

HELIUM

ON SUNDAY MORNING he went for a walk. He went the way they'd always used to go, up the steep rutted track, past the farmhouse to the moor gate. The house was long abandoned. In the hollow socket of the downstairs window the remains of the staircase hung swaying in space.

In all the years he'd walked that way alone, he only remembered seeing the old farmer who lived there once; cutting rushes in the marsh, scything the light, his long coat aflap in the wind. We live our lives a flicker. He'd read that somewhere. It came back to him then, recalling the old farmer, his fleeting memory of him.

Through the moor gate he followed the path along the drainage dyke. Up ahead, near the firing range, some people were walking their dog. He didn't want people. Crossing the dyke he cut a diagonal up through the dead bracken and heather, past the old quarry to the open moor. The sky was white, gauzy with mist, the moor rusted and blackened, soaked full of winter. He followed sheep trods 'til they petered out, stepped over bare bones, listened to the damp concussions from the firing range. After an hour, he stopped and looked back the way he'd come: moor and marsh, a kestrel bent on the wind, a solitary car moving slowly along the valley road. Something welled in his chest. If she'd had have been with him they wouldn't have come that way. They'd have stayed on the lower path. She would have spoken to the couple with the dog. It doesn't cost us anything, she would've said. 'Hello,' he said aloud. A grouse leapt from the heather and throttled away in protest.

He hadn't been expecting her. The long bitterness of his parents' marriage had haunted his childhood. As a younger man, its inheritance had undermined his own relationships. None ever lasted. He'd lost count of the years he'd spent alone, had just assumed he always would be.

They'd met at a volunteer tree planting across the other side of the valley. He'd kept to himself throughout the morning, working away from the main group. When the lunch break was called, he'd walked further up the slope they'd been planting to take in the view from the gritstone escarpment. She hadn't followed him there, rather, it seemed that they'd had the same idea. When she arrived on the escarpment a few moments after him, it would have been more awkward for her not to have sat beside him.

It had begun there, her polite request to join him, the scudding moorland light, reflected in her eye. It kindled slowly. They shared a passion for nature and landscape, the urge to walk. She'd been married, divorced, had a grown-up daughter, a grandson. They lived far away, and secretly, he'd been relieved to hear that. From the beginning, she'd met his reticence and quietness with generosity and warmth. For a time it lifted him up, allowed him to hope that he might become different, bigger somehow.

When he arrived at the trig point, he moved slowly among the solemn gritstone boulders gathered there. Like hunched druids they stared over the miles of emptiness, their backs bent and hollowed by centuries of wind. Turning to the West he watched a hailstorm push its white fist up the valley. For a long time it was far away, then, quite suddenly, it was all around him. He lifted his hood. Like hurled grit, the hail rattled into him. He heard her voice then, 'You'll be OK,' she'd said. They'd been in his hallway when she'd said it. She'd just taken her coat from the extra hook he'd hung for her a few months before.

The hail storm passed as quickly as it had come, diving off the escarpment, leaving an ionised taste in the air. He pushed back his hood, sniffed sharply, raised a knuckle to his eye. Moving away from the trig point he headed in the direction the storm had come from. As the ground steepened, for a time he fell into a long, loping stride, chasing the windblown swells through the russet cotton grass. In that moment he felt light, uplifted even. It did not last. With no one to share the feeling with, it seemed to slip through his fingers. Ten minutes later he met the Pennine bridleway. To the left the path led up to the moor gate and beyond that the road. To the right, it led down to the small reservoir at the valley's head, perhaps a mile away. In the distance he could see it, a slash of mercury in the rusted blanket of the moor. Slowly he began to walk that way.

After a hundred yards, he stopped, cupping his hands around his eyes. 'What?' he asked aloud. On the far shore of the reservoir, there was a beckoning figure. From head to toe they were dressed in bright metallic silver. Something in the way the figure moved was strange. For a moment, it seemed, almost, to be dancing. A shiver moved across his scalp. Who was this? A pilot bailed out from a crashing aircraft? A fireman suited up to tackle a moorland blaze? He scanned the landscape, muttering. There was no smoke, no burning wreckage in sight. There was nothing, just the vast empty moorland, the reservoir and the distant figure waving at him. Whoever it was, they must be in some sort of trouble. Tentatively, he raised a hand to return the wave, then he continued down the track.

After just a few yards, he stopped again. The figure's movement *was* odd. One moment it was upright and beckoning, the next it was crouched low, creeping amidst the tussocks. As if it was hiding, as if it was teasing him. A feeling of growing unease began to peck at the back of his neck, like a crow over roadkill.

In that moment, a torn fragment from his childhood floated back to him. Coming home from school, the bedroom curtains drawn in the daytime. The card he'd made for her. Get well soon. The silent desperation in her eyes. Later, seeing his card in the kitchen pedal bin, food scraped over it. His father's voice: Your mother doesn't need your sympathy, boy.

The sudden yelp of a goose directly overhead brought him back. Harsh, like a warning shout. It undid him. Fear came then, strong and visceral. He no longer wanted to help. He wanted to turn and walk away, to go back the way he'd come. In the act of turning, he heard Helen's voice again, soft, inside his head. 'What are you afraid of?'

They'd been together nearly two years that February. Quietly, he'd felt proud of that. That he could achieve such a thing with her. She'd made it easy for him, allowed him the space and time he was used to. She came over at weekends, brought food and wine. They would do the same things, talk, walk, sleep together in his single bed. Though he'd fretted over the thought of their becoming intimate in that way, she'd made that easy too. They weren't kids, she'd said, they could take their time. That weekend she'd brought flowers too, daffodils. He'd wondered if they might be for Valentine's Day. He'd wondered if he might try again, to find the courage to tell her how he felt about her.

'What's the occasion?' he'd asked, glancing at the daffodils she'd brought.

'None special,' she'd replied, 'perhaps the return of another spring.' He had no vase. She'd put them in the pint tankard he'd been given on his retirement from the railway, set them on the kitchen window ledge. After dinner, she'd asked him again, if he would come with her to have lunch with some old friends of hers. It would mean a lot to her, she said. It wasn't the first time she'd asked it. Other times he'd pretended that he hadn't heard her, or he'd found a way to change the subject. Those excuses had now run out. Still, he couldn't admit the truth. Tell her that he dreaded it. That he would have nothing to say, nothing to contribute, that before meeting her, he'd been like an empty jar, that loneliness was the only life experience he'd had. Of course, they would see that, her friends. Afterwards, they would call her. Ask her in a kindly way, what was it she saw in him? No, he couldn't confide any of that, so he'd lashed out instead.

'Are we so bored already then?'

'Bored? I don't understand?'

'Of each other, I mean.'

'What?'

'Well, we've said all we have to say to each other now, haven't we?'

'What are you talking . . .'

He hadn't let her finish. He'd learned from his parents that negativity was something you built, like a wall. 'Yes, we're just repeating ourselves now, aren't we? Telling each other silly fairy tales about our late-middle-aged romance. No doubt, they're the same silly stories you've been telling to these friends of yours.'

'What are you afraid of, Joseph?' She'd asked it quietly, given him the chance to climb down from the wall he was building. But he did not take it.

'Nothing, boredom, didn't you hear me?'

'What are you afraid of ?' Her question shamed him then. Of course he couldn't turn away. Whoever this mysterious silver-suited figure was, they needed his help. Lifting his arm he waved again, this time more purposefully, 'I'm coming,' he said aloud, then strode on down the track. At the near shore, he stopped once more. The figure was still some distance away across the water, perhaps a hundred metres. A moment ago, when he'd waved, it'd been upright, beckoning once more, now it was hunkered down again, somewhere near the narrow channel of the inlet stream. For a long time then, he stood staring across the wind-broken surface of the reservoir. When, eventually, he dropped his gaze, a murmur fell from his mouth.

Grey waves clapped against the embankment wall as he walked across it. On the other side, he stepped down to the marshy grass running along the far shore. At first, the figure was nowhere to be seen. As he approached the inlet stream a gust of wind moved through the grasses, lifting the string of helium balloons that were snagged on the broken fence at the stream's edge. Suddenly, the ethereal figure was conjured anew. The letter L upraised, a beckoning arm and shoulder, the letter O outlining the contours of the head and torso. Two more letters twisted below.

Crouching to the broken fence he untied the string. It was, perhaps, one of many flights of balloons that would have blown across the moor that Valentine's weekend. At the edge of the reservoir, he stood for a while, the wind tugging insistently at the string in his hand. When a stronger gust came, he slowly opened his fingers and watched the bright reflection race away over the peat-stained water.

ROSE BIGGIN

THE ICE TIGS

ONE OF THE most interesting facts I was ever told is the human body does not know its temperature. It can only detect when there is a *change* in its temperature. This is why, on a lovely spring morning for example, getting steadily warmer as the sun rises may result in a delay to opening the window or removing the jumper until long after it might comfortably occur - but leaving an air-conditioned building during a city heatwave will knock one's breath out with the force of sudden heat. This fact (which I'll admit I haven't researched further following its acquisition one evening in a pub, due to how satisfying I find it) is of particular interest to me because I have, since childhood, suffered from a particular affliction of the fingers and toes. The issue concerns my circulation, and the rapid withdrawal thereof. Put simply, in the cold there's a high chance my fingers will ache and go numb suddenly, then experience a strange tingling, before finally a distinctive paleness - the ghastly yellow-white of a long-drowned corpse - appears in blotches proceeding to spread from the fingertips down, until all are uniformly that same awful colour, in which state I cannot feel them and can hardly use them. What puzzled me as a child was this unpleasant occurrence was just as likely on a perfectly hot and sunny day. I now realise it would be because I was in a place of high wind, or somewhere (the shade of a tree, say) that hadn't felt the sun at all. Conversely, sometimes a day is ghastly cold all the way through and my hands remain unaffected. Since learning it is not the temperature of my fingers *per se* but a rapid change for the colder that triggers the phenomenon, I have been able to understand why in some circumstances but not others my circulation will, as it were, panic and withdraw. It has made it easier to manage.

I have always thought that this peculiar phenomenon of mine could make an interesting mechanism for fiction. A ticking-down timer of suspense, as it were, present within a character's very person, seems to me a device that could work well to embody tension in a story. A detective, say, enters a frosty crime scene and immediately senses the tell-tale chill about his knuckles, and knows he only has a number of minutes to examine the evidence, decode the clues, unlock the safe, restrain the suspect, reload the gun and so on before his fingers will be not only in pain but utterly useless to his needs. I continue to hope to see my affliction represented in the narratives of others, of which the above example is one of surely a great number of possibilities, but I have yet to satisfactorily include it in a story of my own. What I can offer however is the following true account, of an incident that has changed, ever since, how I feel about the condition.

I recently obtained a contract of employment at a respected establishment of higher education. An administrative position in the History department, the role was obtained on an ad-hoc basis, paid at an hourly rate, and contracted for a dozen weeks or so, applying to the first term only. Even though the university was in a city quite some distance from where I was living at that time, promises were made during my online interview of a large office space with hot-desking opportunities, which might (I thought) be preferable to my own working conditions every now and again (although working from home was, of course, acceptable, even encouraged in the admin department), plus I would have access to all the library resources. So I went in the week before term began to meet my head of team and be shown around.

The leader of Admin & Admissions met me by the large glass lobby, which sat like a frozen bubble against the brickwork of the building proper. He greeted me enthusiastically and proceeded to offer a tour of the place as if it were his own. Since this was the main reason I had come in, it was with some amusement that I agreed, but he didn't appear to notice this. He had a friendly air, if somewhat ramshackle, and always seemed a little distracted, as if he were listening to music in one ear while talking to you. Brian (I'll confess to changing his name) began by pointing out the river, which certainly did draw attention.

'We're famous for that,' he said. 'So I'd better start the tour with it!'

It was indeed a dramatic sight, flowing closely past the building as it did. I'd walked over the picturesque wooden bridge (recognisable from the university website) on my way in, which had been lovely, through all the gorgeous autumn sunshine.

'It's very striking,' I said, looking again at the river. Brian nodded.

'Lots of maintenance of course,' he said. 'They're forever dealing with damp in the ground floor seminar rooms. But that's nothing, I think, compared to how lucky we are to have this right on our doorstep.'

My attention was drawn to a spot in the water near the far bank. 'High maintenance,' I repeated, feeling unsure about something but not knowing why.

'Oh yes,' said Brian. 'There's always something going wrong with it. Frankly it's strange you're here on a day where there's nothing happening in the water!'

'I think there's somebody dredging it right now,' I said.

He frowned. 'Not at all no, why? Not until much later in the year.'

'But aren't those bubbles?'

'What? How do you mean?'

'It looks like somebody's scuba diving under there.'

He squinted out towards the river with his hand over his eyes like a great explorer. 'Whereabouts are you looking?'

I pointed, but after a moment's peering he only shook his head.

'Looks normal enough to me,' he said. 'Perhaps I can't tell where exactly you're seeing. Anyway: let's go in and I'll show you the offices and so on.'

I was shown empty classrooms, a staffroom containing one threadbare settee, and a cupboard-cum-kitchenette where a single empty jar stood haunted by the ghost of instant coffee. All the while Brian told me about the workings of the place, and I was re-acquainted with things that had been covered during my interview with the added enrichment of his own perspective. I learned how the department of Arts & Humanities ('sounds like a tautology to me but there you go') was increasingly driven to compete for dwindling funding and resources with the smaller but sleeker Department of STEM & Social Sciences ('I always call it STEMSESS in meetings like Gollum, they don't like that') and I learned the university had a long and respectable past ('they should make me an honourable History prof., to be honest I've started thinking of myself as one') – this seemed to be his favourite topic and his enthusiasm greatly increased when he got to it.

'Well of course we go back hundreds of years, many centuries if you count the initial charter, established this place as a site for apprenticeships to the wool-makers and the dyers, if you include all that sort of thing, well, we're more ancient than some of the oldest universities there *are*, that's what I say, but because of having this vocational emphasis in our background, it sets us apart so it's good but we do get treated differently, prejudice you know, not seen as "proper" until more recently, but of course we've always been able to give the redbricks a run for their money and that's what really counts, in fact speaking of our competitive edge we could give anyone hell in a boat race I don't mind telling you – do you row yourself?'

'I'm afraid I don't,' I said. (It wouldn't be good at all for my fingers.)

'We've got an active Society. Discount lessons and so on. Could be an opportunity to learn, eh? Anyway, Admin's just down here...'

We were reaching the darker rooms at the back of the building and his talk turned to the latest financial troubles. 'Things are a bit on edge at the moment. Nothing we haven't gotten through in the past and worse, but with one thing and another it's very difficult in the teaching sector and that's putting heavy pressure on us in dusty Admin as well. We need all hands, all the hands we can get; yours will come in very useful! Had to beg to be allowed to hire you, mind.'

'Really?' I perked up, feeling I might be seeing the glint of a deeply sunken compliment.

'I don't mean you personally,' he said quickly. 'I mean every time we want to hire *anyone* it's a struggle. Management always say we've got an admin person, but it's me, so come on! They let us bring two aboard this time so now it's me, Moira who helps out, and you and Vince: have you met Vince? Ah, you should have come in together. Why didn't Moira arrange that? Anyway, what this means is you increase the team by... a large percentage! Can't do the sum, I'm not STEMSESS.'

We went on, through the remnants of History and towards the Admin offices, when my attention was caught by a large old photograph in a tarnished frame, taking up most of the wall. Clearly vastly blown up from a smaller print, smudged and distorted in places, it was a group of Edwardian-looking young men whose dignified facial hair didn't hide the boyishness of their features, standing in sepia-toned seriousness outside the same building we currently occupied (albeit without the glass lobby).

Brian stopped and pointed at it proudly. 'That's our first cohort in history, that! In the History degree I mean, ha-ha. They're standing outside the building – you'll see it when you leave, if you look back, that's the front door you came though, without the lobby obviously – don't they look impressive? In those days they had to wear uniform hence the robes very serious and scholarly looking isn't it, I think, not like these days, have you seen some lecturers they're bringing in now, supposed to be teaching History? How are you supposed to cultivate a respect for the dignity of the past if you can't bear to put a suit on? I've seen members of staff in *leggings*, I ask you.'

I looked at the past students again, standing before the wisps of ivy which at that time were making a creeping way up the building's walls, but had since been pulled down, perhaps during construction of the lobby. I had to admit, their dark jackets and smart ties did have a certain weight to them. Although his ire seemed specifically aimed at teaching staff who chose to sport such offences as leggings, I was very aware that I was at that moment wearing them myself, so I made a non-committal noise of support to my line manager's comment and we moved on.

Finally we went up a narrow staircase into a room with a plastic sign on the outside reading: A - - - - R A T I O N. The door opened with a heavy sound and he had to push with his shoulder against some invisible resistance.

Inside was a large, dark room lined with desks and dozens of flat computer monitors, the blank screens coated with dust from disuse. The ceiling was painted dark grey and its pointedness showed we were up in the roof of the building. There was a small window in one wall, through which could be seen a view of the university grounds with its close-passing river.

He stood in the middle of the empty room with his hands on his hips, as if inspecting it for potential DIY. 'You're welcome to come and work up here as often as you like,' he said. 'Normally we . . . there used to be a booking system but as you can see—' he gestured around at the army of unused computers, 'you'll hardly be fighting to get an hour with a screen, so you can just come in, there's no need to email ahead. There's always someone in the lobby who will let you in and it can be nice to not work from home sometimes, can't it? You get that collegiate feel, batting ideas around in person, nothing like it.'

'Do you work in here?' I asked.

'God no, I've got an office down on the same floor as the department heads.' He looked at me with slightly narrowed eyes. 'You're not from nearby are you, I'm guessing?'

I shook my head and named the next-but-one city over.

He whistled. 'How long does that take you then?'

'It's about an hour twenty on the train,' I said, by now well used to saying it. 'Plus getting to and from the station, so, about two hours' commute overall. Two and a half.'

He paused a moment, sombrely, as if paying respects to my lost time. 'And this isn't a permanent job you'd consider moving closer for, no, I think that's quite true, we get that a lot.' He sighed. 'I ask because it would be nice for the department to feel like a team effort again. What with only hiring people a term at a time, it has knock-on effects, gives us trouble convincing people to stay on. I don't mind telling you we have a high turnover of admin staff.'

I put my bag down beside one of the computers, hoping to evoke the spirit of spreading a towel on a beach chair, although I had already noticed this room was considerably colder than the others. 'It's a difficult time for the sector,' I offered.

He nodded. 'We get through it together, eh? Well, I'll leave you to get settled in.'

At the door he turned back. 'Oh, and I recommend not using *that*.'

I followed his pointing finger down to the small metal bin, over which a clear plastic bag was stretched to precarious thinness. It was empty except for what appeared to be a Pret receipt and a single wad of used chewing gum, the weight of which pulled the bin's lining downwards until it resembled the gravitational map of a black hole star.

He looked back up into what must have been my questioning gaze, and explained: 'They don't have anyone coming in to empty those any more. It's a cost-saving measure. You should use the communal bins in the corridor.'

When he had gone, I turned on the computer and waited a few minutes as it roused itself into life. During this time I tried to make the light switches work, and found they did not. I returned to the desk defeated and listened to the sound of the antique computer still starting up, a noise I hadn't heard for years, not unlike a roach trying to escape from a matchbox. It had been a long time since I'd used a desktop and my fingers moved the mouse with some nostalgia. On my fiftieth attempt to enter my login details (which the IT department reassured me, days before, would be functional when I came in) I decided I would never again attempt to work in the Admin office. Not only was the blank judgemental gaze of an army of unused computers off-putting in itself, but the room's darkness was oppressive without a working mechanism for the strip-lights, and most of all, the room's coldness in comparison to elsewhere in the building had intensified, and my fingers were quite quickly (as soon as Brian left, in fact) experiencing the unpleasant feeling of steady freeze I have already described as being the precursor to the more serious stages of my circulation problem. I picked up my bag, noticing it left a shape in the dust, and decided to have a quick look out of the room's small window before I exited the office for good. The view was nice, it must be said, giving a wide aspect of that famous river, as it wound through the city to pass the university and fill the view from this uppermost window.

My fingers were now cold all over and the ache had set in. It wouldn't be long before whiteness began appearing; I needed to get somewhere warmer. I was rubbing at my knuckles to delay the condition, but it wouldn't do for long. Still, not being very good at giving up on things, I returned to the ancient computer for one more try at logging into the system.

I placed my hand on the mouse and immediately recoiled as my fingers shot with pain. It was the same sharp pins-and-needles as touching something cold with my condition at its worst, as if my fingers were already numb and yellow-white all over. (Hence I wear thin cotton gloves to go through the freezer.) The feeling was unpleasant as well as painful, as I'd had no reason to expect it.

'Jesus Christ,' I said out loud: and I intended to continue, perhaps with something redundant like *how cold is that mouse?* – but I did not get so far, as I stopped and instead stared at my breath coming visibly out of my mouth as steam, sending *Jesus Christ* up into the ether. *'Fucking hell . . .'* I whispered, making more steam, as I stood, hooked my non-painful hand onto my bag and exited the office at pace. I sped to the staff toilets (having noticed the signage on my tour which had otherwise not included them) and spent a good ten minutes running my hands under the hot tap before the flush of my own skin colour came creeping back into the white. The taps required a new push every time I wished to conjure a second and a half of water flow, and the overall activity put me in mind of churning butter by hand or making toffee, not that I have ever engaged in either.

Returning to the autumnal air outside the university building I began to rub the knuckles of my right hand again, and prepared to begin the long walk to the train station. I felt a hand on my shoulder. I'm not sure why I jumped as much as I did, but when I turned around it was only the Head of Admin.

'Finished everything you needed?' he said. He sounded almost hurt to see me leaving so soon.

I nodded and muttered something about the office being a bit cold.

'We do have problems with the air-con. It's unlivable in the summer. Sorry it's uncomfortable now, might be trouble adjusting as it's getting into winter, still autumn for a while though, please say it is, we've got all term to get through . . .! It's something to do with circulation of air I think? Are you walking back to the train station? Lucky you, going back over the river. The best view is from the bridge – I always watch people taking their selfies there, it's the spot for photography it seems. Speaking of being cold,' he said, 'want to know something interesting? In the olden days the river used to ice completely over. Fully thick and solid you could walk on it. They used to have activities on there, games, stalls to shop on, that sort of thing. Talk about your ideal Christmas market! Doesn't happen any more of course.'

'That's a shame?' I said politely, still rubbing my knuckles.

'It's climate change. The river doesn't freeze up as consistently as it used to. So no frozen-over markets since . . . well, it's a good thing of course, according to some! But listen to me wittering on while you're wanting to be headed off. Let me know when you're next coming in, won't you, and I'll see you at our next online – end of this week, is it? Thursday. Pleasure to meet you! Any questions email.'

On the train home, with little better to do on my phone once I'd completed the usual round of thoughtless app-checking, I searched for images of the river and its famous freezings-over. It was a romantic idea, and I hoped pictures of the old winter fairs might be interesting. I found an article that seemed pulled together from various sources with little adherence to grammar or sense, and, if I closed enough pop-up ads, had some old photographs of the river with wooden market stalls on it and people clustered around, standing in groups on the ice. I began following links, exploring. (My data was always patchy on trains; buffering and refreshing the page can safely be excluded from the narrative.) I read an article about how to cook the famous ice fair roasted chestnuts, and I even paid attention to the biographical yarn at its beginning. Then, at the bottom of this page, in the grid of spam and algorithmically generated articles clustered together like a gallery of rogues, I saw one image, among the squares of otherwise nonsense, that I recognised. It was a moment's thought to place where I had seen it before: the photograph on the wall of the History department. It was one corner of that cluster of young men, all in the dark-ish uniform. The caption said: *You'll never believe what happened at the last ice fair!* 'When she saw it, she screamed . . .' – I will reiterate the sheer length of the train journey to justify why I tapped on it and read.

Surprisingly the article I was taken to seemed real, perhaps plundered from some digitised archives somewhere. It described an accident that had befallen what turned out to be the final year of revelry on the frosted river, which was in the mid nineteenth century just as my line manager had told me. The ice had cracked beneath a chestnut stall which quickly expanded to a fatal flaw in the ice, into which a dozen revellers slipped and fell, pulling each other in with the panic. Following a frantic rescue all but one got out; one young man, a student of the university, drowned in the ice-cold water. After this tragic event the community lost their taste for the fair, but in any case the author of the article estimated future events would have been on increasingly thin ice anyway, with the gradual warming of the waters due to ongoing changes in the climate, so it was all to the good there hadn't been one since. I scrolled up again and tried to press my finger onto the name of the student who died, since it seemed a different colour to the other text, a dull shade as if it were a link I'd already clicked on. Nothing happened but I made a note – the student's name had been Edward Tilling – and resolved to see if he was among the young men in the photograph.

Although I wished to see the photograph again at some point, I then spent a long time not going into the university. Since we were welcome to work from home, and the office was at least as cold and dark as my own desk situation, this was what I preferred to do. I did not meet my admin colleague Vince in person but was introduced via email from the head of the History department Moira James, a professor who specialised in political cultures of the long nineteenth century and who took on a lot of Brian's duties as he tended not to do them. Once term began the workload was an avalanche, with endless confusions across every single aspect of the department; every email I sent conjured a dozen more. Halfway through term a few weeks were disrupted due to industrial action from the teaching staff, in solidarity with which I will not narrate events.

The first day back after the strikes we had an online meeting to bring Moira up to date (since she was a member of the teaching staff, it had been left to myself and Vince to battle the tide of errors, queries, clashes, bookings, admissions, readmissions, complaints, conversations, meetings, meetings, meetings, meetings).

Moira came into view on the screen first, her bobbed hair a shining halo in the glow of her ring-light. I will confess to envying her professional set-up, but Moira was an in-demand guest on various history podcasts and other media.

'Morning everyone,' she said. When the various signals had calmed down she continued, realising it was just me: 'How has it been?'

A few words into my answer, I was interrupted.

'You're on mute . . .'

I made an exaggerated grimace of embarrassment and turned on my microphone. I could suppose the efficiency of Moira had knocked my confidence although that wouldn't explain why I always forgot to unmute myself on other occasions.

Two more pictures flickered into life and myself and Moira were pushed into quarters of the screen instead of sharing it between us. I was, frankly, glad to see the other two were, in terms of quality of broadcast, closer to my own standards. Brian joined from his downstairs office in the building, the bulb illuminating his face so closely he looked set to tell a thrilling ghost story, and there was also a new face, in a white T-shirt and thickly-rimmed glasses, in a somewhat pixelated environment I believed I could nonetheless identify. I asked Vince how on earth he'd gotten things working in the admin office.

'I didn't! I'm using my own laptop,' he said. 'I was in town today, so,' he shrugged; at least I believe he did, the white pixels of his shoulders moved up and down blockily like a space invader. 'I hadn't actually been on site yet, so Brian showed me around and I thought I'd try joining from here, see if it's workable. Can't get these computers to log in but my laptop managed. Signal's shit though.'

Moira moved the conversation on to an overview of this point in the term. Having experienced this meeting once already I've no wish to relate too many of its details and shall move swiftly to a moment near its end.

'All okay on forthcoming exams?' said Moira. 'Where are we there?'

I opened my mouth to respond since I had main responsibility for this part of the workload, but to my surprise Vince spoke up instead.

'Can I just flag something quickly?'

'Go ahead,' said Moira.

'I've been getting these continual requests through the QueriZone portal,' said Vince. 'Since I logged in before the meeting started. And while I've got you here I thought I'd mention it. I think it's a student who's confusing admissions with, like, submissions?'

'What do you mean?'

'As if they submitted an essay, or they're waiting for exam marks. I thought it was a system error but it's happened a few times: a request for E. Tilling's final results. I deleted it the first time because as I say, I assumed it was a bug or some weird error. But more are coming through, while I've been sitting here.'

'Are you sure it's not somebody looking for results? From last year, say, or if they need a transcript for an application . . .?'

'I'm positive, because I've looked and looked, and there's nobody of that name, staff or student, on the system.'

'Really?'

'Absolutely positive; I just checked twice.' There was a pause and the sound of frantic typing. 'Right, so, I've just replied to the second one: SINCE IT'S START OF TERM THERE ARE NO RESULTS TO DISCLOSE, SORRY. They'll know I'm onto them now. Sorry about that everyone; didn't want to interrupt the meeting, I thought I should mention it in case anyone else in the admin team gets a similar contact and we can put together if it's real, or not, or what. Excuse me one more moment, I've got to put a jumper on.' The head of Vince dipped below the range of his camera and for a moment his dark square remained empty. Then the blocky representation returned to his quarter of the screen, the lower half in pixels of a darker hue.

Moira nodded slowly as if considering news of great import. 'If it's a student with a genuine query we'll hear from them again,' she said. 'Are you sure it's not a name we have on the system? I ask because as you'll remember we had an awful time getting everybody signed up at the start of the term, it wouldn't surprise me if someone slipped through the cracks. Only students access the query portal so in any case it seems an odd sort of fun to me. Could you let me know if it happens again, Vince? Agh, his screen's frozen. Never mind, perhaps my voice is still getting through. In the meantime we can catch up on the rest – only takes the two of us, doesn't it? – for the admissions stuff . . .'

Myself and Moira managed the rest of the meeting between us and I was able to close my laptop only half an hour after the intended end time. Just before we said goodbye, the otherwise silent and non-contributing Brian sent me a semi-colon and a closing bracket in the private chat box.

As the term went on the workload, already unmanageable,

somehow contrived to increase. There were problems with every module the department ran and some it was only thinking about running, issues of staffing that never went away, room bookings that *did* go away, every flickering strip-light and patch of damp mould seemed to need to be reported to me. Each email I dealt with was replaced by twenty more, with eighteen of them marked Urgent. The difficulty of facing each day was rising at an exponential rate not least since I had now taken over Vince's duties as well. Moira forwarded to me anything he would usually have been expected to cover; I was getting more emails than usual since he had stopped answering his.

The end of term was in sight, and with it the end of my contract, when Moira sent me an email (not marked Urgent, thankfully) asking if I wouldn't mind taking a quick phone call. My heart was in my throat as I put my phone to my face and heard her voice.

'Do you live locally?' she said, shouting if she were battling high wind. 'I think you don't, is that right?'

I told her I wasn't local at all, and began to explain the length of the train journey.

She interrupted. 'I know this is all a bit last minute and I'm terribly sorry to be asking this, but I've had an emergency come up and you'd be doing me the biggest favour. They're doing an episode of *In Our Time* about the Luddite uprising and one of the guests is testing positive; completely wiped out apparently they can't even speak to do it remote. Problem is, I'm supposed to be attending the upper-management meeting at the same time, on the admin side. It's got to be in person because the VC doesn't like to do things online . . . anyway, Vince has gone AWOL as we know, and Brian never bloody does anything. It doesn't require you to do much, it's just about being present at the meeting and reporting back.'

I felt a great reluctance to return to the university building that I am still at a loss to explain. 'Are you sure Brian can't do it?'

'Very sure, he's taken some last minute annual leave. I swear he keeps some in reserve for meetings he's forgotten about.'

'I don't get annual leave,' I said, automatically. 'Sorry. I don't know why I said that.'

'You should shout about it! But for now, yes, as you say, you're about and there's no-one else. You'll have to come in, would you mind? We'll see if we can get your train expenses on the books or something. Do you have a railcard?'

While microwaving my dinner that evening I endeavoured to reconcile myself to the positives of the situation. This was my opportunity, I reasoned, to search the old photograph for the poor fellow from the ice fair. I had done more digging since conducting my initial research on the train, following Vince's mention of his mysterious marking query. My current role gave me access to a range of databases and old records and I tentatively searched the student's name across various systems. I didn't find any more versions of the photograph, but I did eventually locate one mention of an '[?]. T[??]ling' in a digitised newspaper, a century-and-a-bit-old article in tiny typographic letters with a dense paragraph of student names, one of which seemed to be (for the scan was imperfect) the one I was looking for. This was from a report on the creation of a Modern History degree at the university. Assuming he was there to read History, I put the years of that first cohort against the dates of the city's last ice fair. If the earlier establishment operated with anything like the current timetable, the accident of the frozen river had occurred after final exams had taken place, but before the students received their results.

Since we were nearing the end of term, although it was still midafternoon when the train pulled in, the light had already begun to fade and the weather was bitterly cold. As soon as I left the train I could feel the familiar chill creeping over my hands. Walking quickly, I kept them balled into fists inside my gloves, but by the timings involved I knew I would need a hot tap on arrival. I could feel my fingers succumbing as I walked, head down and hands scrunched, towards the university building.

I reached the river and something caused me to stop before stepping onto the bridge. I looked across the surface of the water. In spite of the icy air the river was dark and quick, and it was impossible to imagine it entirely iced over, never mind the site of a stall for roasted chestnuts. I took off one of my gloves and massaged the knuckles, attempting to get some circulation going. The condition had worsened as I'd been walking, and all the fingers of my right hand were now completely white, bloodless and numb. If I rushed, I could get to the sink in the kitchenette and commence the uncomfortable process of scalding my hands back to life, and be able to attend the meeting I'd come all this way for with digits that at least resembled those of the living.

I put my hand down onto one of the wooden bridge posts and started at the feeling of sudden pain all over my fingers, as if I had placed my hand on a piece of ice. I looked down and saw, between my hand and the wooden post, another hand, upon which my own was resting. Its fingers were the same shade of whitish-yellow. Indeed, that colour had spread as far as the wrist, which was all I could see. It did not resist or seem to react to my touch but, as I have mentioned, it must have been freezing cold, for it caused at the touch a painful sensation all over my fingers, an unbearable discomfort almost like burning.

I pulled my hand back and clutched it with the other, and with my eyes squeezed closed heard myself cry: 'You passed, you got a First, I saw it!'

After a few seconds' remaining still as a statue I opened my eyes and looked again at the bridge post. There was nothing but wood.

I do not remember the journey home, or how I managed it. I can only recall the moment I realised why I hadn't been able to see any skin beyond the wrist, which was because it had been covered in heavy dark fabric, sopping wet.

The last week of term was disrupted by further industrial action and in any case I did not return to the building. I will mention one incident that took place on what would have been results day since it briefly became a talking point (you may have heard of the incident). A sudden volley of hailstones, some the size of a fist, pummelled down over the picket line, causing injury to those who did not have a placard to shield themselves. A video of the incident went viral online and the whole thing was interpreted as one of the ongoing freakish weather events characteristic of continued disruption to the climate. It seems to me the presence I encountered on the bridge would support a picket, representing as it does an embodied resistance to the act of crossing over, so I am inclined to think the climate explanation is the most likely in this case.

I wish I could say that when my contract with the institution came to an end I stopped suffering from the phenomenon in my fingers. But the condition pre-dates my working there and still appears when the temperature cools with adequate rapidity. What has changed is I am no longer confident, regarding the exact cause of the chill.

BARET MAGARIAN

THE PORTAL IN LISBON

PETER WAS BUOYANT by nature, but everything had gone wrong lately. It started in Paddington when his scooter burst a tyre and he skidded and crashed into some railings. Luckily, he had his helmet on, but he still got a nasty knock on the head and a bad case of whiplash, and emerged with bloodied hands and elbows. After waiting for five groggy hours in the Accident & Emergency Unit of St Mary's hospital he was finally seen. They gave him a chest and neck X-ray and told him he didn't have any fractures, but that he should take it easy for the next few weeks and stay housebound. He was given a neck brace and discharged.

The next day bruises appeared along his chest like rotten fruit and he felt dizzy whenever he stood up. He managed to take two weeks off work – he was a lecturer in English literature – and upon his return learnt that the students preferred the substitute teacher. Then he was pickpocketed in Soho. The thief got away with about £200 and with one of his mother's most treasured possessions – a rare 1840 Two Penny Blue stamp. Peter had lost his mother six months earlier and he had nursed her selflessly through the devastation of dementia and horribly painful arthritis for years. He managed to stagger to the end of the semester and then resolved to get away. The British summer, true to form, was proving to be rather wet, so he decided he would book a flight to Lisbon – a city he had always wanted to visit – and try and recover his energies after all this grief and trauma, on his own, and in the sunlight.

Lisbon in June was sweltering, but the city was ventilated by cool breezes from the Atlantic. Peter found the old town comforting, almost familiar, as he wandered slowly through its side streets, quaint shops and cheap but excellent fish restaurants. At moments he felt he had gone back in time or that Lisbon existed in a parallel universe untouched by mobile phones and the shrill voices of modernity.

As he walked Peter was sometimes struck by the impoverished state of the houses, with their shutters and visible cables and their drying, swaying laundry hanging out on lines; but every now and then some marvellous bit of blue ceramic fantasy on one of the facades caught him off guard and he gazed into it, transfixed. Then he would walk into a cafe and order a coffee and a pastry and watch as tram number 28 chugged past, sometimes chased by laughing little boys. He climbed onto the tram after he had finished his coffee. Once inside he was filled with the notion that life should be improvised, could be made up on the spot, was as freewheeling as the tram. The tram made him think of a box of matches, a doll's house, his mother's china tea cups . . . and then he remembered her face in the last weeks of her life, ravaged, weak, but filled with a new love for him, miraculously unveiled after a lifetime of remoteness.

The tram slowed and he jumped off, finding himself in the tightly packed Alfama district. The afternoon sun was blazing, and it seemed that its intensity would never ease. That day there was no breeze. Everything was heavy with the etched stillness that is an effect of overwhelming heat; it was as though cotton wool or plastic had wrapped itself around all matter so as to deaden sound.

He walked in the direction of a piece of graffiti – a vase of flourishing, multi-coloured flowers whose petals eventually terminated in diamonds and emeralds. His eye found an ancient poster below it that seemed to have fused with the wall upon which it was glued.

FADO A LISBOA
TEATRO DO PASSADO
BECO DOS LOIOS, ALFAMA, 19h

Peter peered closely into the poster and looked in vain for some sign of a date. He remembered something that he had read about Fado in his guidebook: *A type of Portuguese singing steeped in longing for the departed . . . For the sailors who had vanished into the distant, icy Atlantic . . .*

He searched in his rucksack for his sunblock, decided against it, preferring the unfiltered heat, which he felt was burning out all the poison of the last six months, and he would have liked then to have spread out on the ground, naked in its recalibrating rays. He glanced at the graffiti and thought of his potted plants in his tiny Paddington flat and hoped they were fine. His neighbour had promised to water them. But they needed *his* love. The only things that relied on him, now that his mother was gone. One by one Peter's friends had all married and deserted him, or they had clashed and the jealousies that emerge in middle age had driven a wedge between them.

Peter wished then he could have spent more time with his mother at the end, with the beautiful, mild woman she had become.

He entered the cafe theatre shortly before 7 p.m., after admiring the glorious blue ceramics of the entrance which depicted four troubadours around a table, one of them strumming the Portuguese guitar. Peter had to descend some steps to reach the basement theatre. He purchased a ticket and sat down, waiting for the show to begin.

The small black stage was pierced by spotlights whose essences mingled, distorted by red and blue filters so that the stage appeared foggy and indistinct. The dimensions of the auditorium were more or less indiscernible as hardly any light reached it, so the patrons existed in a collective, borderless tenebrosity. But after some time, as Peter's eyes grew accustomed to the dark, he could discern more clearly the other guests seated next to miniature side tables barely wide enough for a glass and bottle of wine. The musicians walked onto the stage one by one without a word: the Portuguese guitarist and a classical guitarist. Then the singer, a regal-looking woman swathed in black, stepped up and without any introduction began to sing *a cappella* in a voice that faltered. The audience shifted uncomfortably in their seats and poured themselves wine.

Finally, the singer stopped altogether. The resulting moment of disconnect seemed momentous. It felt like the breaking of the music, of the show's continuity, shattered some great certainty. Or as though the rhythm of the heart had been thrown into a wild arrhythmia. Peter glanced around at the faces of the other members of the audience. They too seemed to have frozen, feeling pity and embarrassment for the poor *fadista*. A strange claustrophobia permeated everything. He had the feeling he was no longer in a theatre, but in a mining shaft or oven. The crowd were still . . . then abruptly they began to stir and chatter, and clap to encourage the unfortunate woman. She apologised in Portuguese, spoke a few words to her musicians and then they began the song from the top, playing together. This time her voice was startlingly assured. But Peter could not rid himself of the impression that reality had somehow changed in the interim, that some fundamental pattern had been re-configured, as though a photograph had been subtly doctored, manipulated . . .

He didn't like the sound of spoken Portuguese that much; he found it dissonant, but now that the language had been melted down into music, rendered fluid, continuous, its harshness had coalesced into something richly sonorous. He didn't understand a word and nor did he want to. He just wanted the music to make him insensate or to restore some spark of life after all the bruises and loneliness life had bequeathed him. He wanted the loneliness he sensed in the music to render himself devoid of loneliness. He wanted a deluge of sadness to make him so sad that eventually the sadness would build him a tower from whose heights he could discern a land across the borders that was happiness. He felt protected in the theatre, safe from the world's descent into full-blown psychosis, he felt the stirrings of a camaraderie among souls he didn't know.

Peter felt that it was not merely the singer's lungs that generated her voice, but her whole body, each organ, each limb, which was igniting this conflagration of music. The painfully exquisite pathos of the Fado punctured Peter's self-possession and a tidal wave of emotion crashed out. His mind filled with figures from his past and the dying face of his mother and the last lucid words she had uttered: *be kind to everyone you meet.*

The music no longer seemed to him to be music. Peter could feel his field of vision trembling, his forehead sweat. He glanced at the audience – they seemed fine; rapt, entranced, but fine. He was filled with sudden fear that the pain in the singer's voice would cause her mind to break . . . The theatre was poised between two worlds, one fixed, the other indeterminate, and Peter straddled both. Was the theatre a bridge, a penumbra, a portal?

The singer stopped and acknowledged the enthusiastic applause smilingly. She took a moment to recover her energies. Peter began to imagine that all the friends he had lost or argued with or been betrayed by or had himself betrayed were slowly filing into the theatre, that the little cafe theatre was filling with all those lives that he had touched or been touched by. They would all return, and all the sorrows and losses of his life would be erased . . .

Now the singer's voice was rising and fluctuating like flames. The voice grew more and more tragic, freed, finally broken by the full flowerings of pathos, then abruptly ceased. Before the audience even had time to draw breath the classical guitarist launched into a solo, strumming and plucking the strings, slowly at first, then with ever greater force, and Peter could hardly believe that one instrument could draw forth such density of sound. The *fadista*'s now fluid, now corrugated voice became entwined in the guitar's exploding arpeggios; the extemporisation rose to a climax, subsided, then died away at last into an echo, an icy, distant memory . . .

Peter stepped outside into the mild Lisbon evening and walked towards the main thoroughfare. Little children were playing on the steps leading to a church; some were humming, their little hands outstretched as though trying to catch imagined petals drifting through the air. There was a line of people waiting at the nearby tram stop. Peter took out his phone to check the time, but the battery was dead. He glanced at the people in the queue and one or two of them smiled at him. Peter asked a man with a moustache the time. The man told him, in very good English, wanting to show off his skill, that it was just coming up to seven o'clock.

'Seven o'clock? I thought it was more like eight. The fado concert lasted an hour, I think . . .' Peter pointed in the direction of the street he had just come from.

'The concert? Senhor, but there are no longer concerts in the *Passado* . . . it is only a museum.'

Peter hardly seemed to comprehend. He was on the point of saying something when he thought better of it. The tram rounded the corner and came to an exhausted halt. People bundled on. Something about the tram seemed to be inviting Peter to climb on as well, though he knew it wasn't going in his direction.

The man looked at him with concern. Not knowing how to express it, he asked abruptly: 'Do you need directions? Do you know where you are going?'

Peter stared into space, hesitating. Time slowed.

A blanket of serenity seemed to descend and envelop the world.

He scrambled on board the tram, then called out through the open window, 'Yes, I think so.'

The man watched the tram trundle off, then recede from view. Everything was flowing, swirling with joy and colour.

SIMON OKOTIE

WHEN VIEWED FROM THE HEAD RATHER THAN THE FOOT

YET AS SHE rolled from her left side onto her back by pressing, with her right hand, on the internal rear façade of that eight- or twelve-sided three-dimensional enclosure and, at the moment her centre of gravity passed to the right beyond the base formed by that left side, simultaneously removing that right hand and retracting her right arm, initially by, as it were, folding that arm around its elbow and then, as the hand passed to the right of her torso, unfolding it again around the same joint and revolving it progressively around its shoulder-, elbow- and wrist-joints, such that the hand was in a position to land to her right on the base of that space and act as a shock-absorber for the remainder of her body as the latter revolved, clockwise when viewed from the head rather than the foot, which is to say, when viewed from a position on the superior side of a transverse section through her body, under the force, now, entirely, of gravity, towards a supine position, she found that, rather than being able to adopt a position whereby, through bending her knees, she could place her feet flat such that, by subsequently exerting a force through the soles of those feet, she would be able to raise her torso from that base by arching her back, her feet and shoulders acting as the 'bridge piers', if that's the correct term, such that she would finally be able to release her left hand which, for now, remained trapped beneath her given it had been behind her when she'd been in that recumbent position on her left side, with this manoeuvre being, in fact, a mere staging post en route to her ultimate objective, which was to move forward within that space, which is to say, to move to her right towards the front of that space given that that eight- or twelve-sided three-dimensional enclosure was conveying her from left to right from her perspective, this being the most likely façade, in her estimation, from which to effect her eventual release therefrom, she found that, instead of her heels moving towards her, which is to say, instead of moving towards her backside such that the angle subtended by the upper and lower legs would progressively decrease in proportion to that decreasing distance, and I could hardly avoid being implicated, she thought, given our multiple mutual entanglements, the equivalent angle between feet and shins increasing accordingly as her toes moved towards the ground or base of that space, they remained resolutely in place, which is to say that her heels made no movement, implying that, despite the signal having been sent by her, so far as she could tell, urgently if unthinkingly, in the usual way, for this manoeuvre to commence, which is to say the movement of the heels along their, and her, resting place towards her buttocks, this latter word preferable to her than the previous way in which she'd referred to this three-dimensional region – the 'backside' – in that it was, she thought, both more specifically technical – less colloquial – and more evocative of the fleshy parts of its counterparts, the heels, as well, of course, as being pluralised like those counterparts, which is to say that it evoked and, to some extent, paralleled the shape and relative fleshiness of the latter, not, of course, that she blamed me exactly, she thought, for her predicament – that wasn't what we were saying – perhaps unsurprisingly given the shock-absorbent function served by both zones or regions, one pair in relation, of course, to standing, walking and (dare she say it) dancing, the other in relation, primarily but perhaps not exclusively, to sitting, that the signal had, somehow, gone unreceived or unrecognised, meaning, in short, that she was literally and metaphorically powerless and in the hands of others, at least, that is, in relation to the lower limbs, the upper being, so far as she could tell, still capable of receiving her volitional transmissions, the right arm, of course, being the one best suited to testing this hypothesis in that it was relatively unencumbered, as it were, by the rest of the body, remaining, as it was, more or less free in its articulations as her right hand approached the base of that enclosure to the right of her torso, meaning that it, at least, was available to assist her in moving in the manner described, which is to say, to assist her in moving towards attaining a position whereby she would be able to release her left hand from beneath her such that she could use that hand with its counterpart to manipulate further the remainder of her body, through whatever means, in such a way as to adopt a posture within that enclosure whereby she might eventually effect her release therefrom, a strategy and approach that she decisively, now, modified, given not only that her right hand had finally touched down upon the base of that space to the right of her torso, but also that the space itself, as though in response to this additional contact, had started to tilt backwards, consistent, that is, with it having started up a ramp in a forwards direction, such that its leading edge had gained elevation in relation to its trailing edge, with this development being, of course, contrary to her aspiration to move forwards within that space, as though through as it were placing her therein, she thought, I had this indirect control over her on its part – given, that is, that her body was arranged laterally within it such that a backwards – or upwards – tilt objectively translated into a leftwards tilt subjectively – thereby opposing, or resisting, the clockwise revolution around her longitudinal axis when viewed from the head rather than the foot, which is to say, when viewed from a position on the superior side of a transverse section through her body, that she had so long aspired to, leaving her wondering why it was that, rather than actively resisting this motion on her part, which is to say, actively resisting the motion induced, or potentially induced, in her by the front of that eight- or twelve-sided three-dimensional space elevating itself consistent with it entering upon an upwards ramp in a forwards direction such that this would induce in her a counter-clockwise revolution around her longitudinal axis which would serve to send her back to the position of resting on her left side from which she had commenced this whole manoeuvre, this resistance taking the form, for instance, of her placing her right hand, which, remember, remained at liberty and available to her, unlike its counterpart, the left, back upon the internal rear façade of that space, and applying an equal and opposite pressure to that being applied upon her by the increasing elevation of the front of that space in relation to its rear, which is to say, the counter-clockwise revolution around the space's rear axle when viewed from the right of that space as it moves from left to right in front of us, this equal and opposite force being just sufficient, by definition, to resist the counter-revolutionary force being applied by that space upon her in the manner described, there being no reason, of course, on her part, for her not to increase the force that she could apply in this way such that she would, in fact, continue in this manner to revolve clockwise around her longitudinal axis when viewed from the head rather than the foot, which is to say, when viewed from a position on the superior side of a transverse section through her body, as she had been hitherto, not, of course, that she would need to initiate this resistive force until that space, whose front was still in the process of elevating itself in relation to its rear, had attained a certain angle, which is to say, a certain degree of steepness, given, that is, that the breadth of her body (and that of most human and even humanoid bodies per se) was proportionately much greater than its depth, meaning, in short, that in circumstances in which it was arranged in a supine position, a steep angle would be required to tip such a body from its back or, were it arranged in a prone position, from its front, onto one or other of its sides, such that she decided instead, instinctively and immediately, and despite now removing her right hand, or, more specifically, her right palm, from the base of that space, actively, in fact, to accentuate rather than to resist the counter-revolutionary force that continued to be induced in her by the front of that space elevating itself, or being elevated, in relation to its rear, by leaving her right elbow in situ on the base of that space to the right of her own supine torso, with the deployment of that vertex designed to enable, in short, greater leverage on her part, given the ongoing non-responsiveness of her lower limbs, in relation to the counter-clockwise revolution around her longitudinal axis when viewed from the head rather than the foot, which is to say, when viewed from a position on the superior side of a transverse section through her body, and which she now initiated by applying a force through it that was sufficient, despite the mismatch in the aforementioned relative dimensions of her body – despite, that is, its breadth being so much greater, relatively speaking, than its depth – decisively to switch the polarity of revolution in her body, to initiate, that is, this counter-clockwise revolution around her longitudinal axis when viewed from the head rather than the foot, which is to say, when viewed from a position on the superior side of a transverse section through her body, a motion she further accentuated by moving her right hand counter-clockwise both around the equivalent elbow – when viewed, that is, from her right – and around her longitudinal axis when viewed, as before, from the head rather than the foot, which is to say, when viewed from a position on the superior side of a transverse section through her body, such that it traced a curved trajectory around her torso, thereby shifting her centre of gravity slightly to her left, which, with the addition of the still-increasing backwards, upwards, or, from her perspective, leftwards, tilt of the space itself meant that she found herself on the brink of another tipping point, albeit one whereby her centre of gravity shifted from the infinite three-dimensional volume to the right of her base when viewed from the head rather than the foot, which is to say, when viewed from a position on the superior side of a transverse section through her body, to the infinite three-dimensional volume to its left, which, incidentally, removed, once again, the pressure that had been placed on her left hand and arm given that, in this transition, the right-hand side of her torso had, of course, elevated itself, or been elevated, such that that left hand and arm, which remained behind her, were no longer bearing that part of her body, with the pressure on her left shoulder increasing accordingly, at which point she was literally and metaphorically in a position to remove her right elbow from the base of that space, which is to say, literally and metaphorically to transition back from using her right elbow to apply thrust to the base of that space towards using her right hand to apply thrust to its internal rear façade, with the relative dynamics within that space, in this interim between force applications upon surfaces that were, of course, at right angles to one another, being sufficient, she judged, all else being equal, to maintain her counter-clockwise angular momentum, which is to say that, despite being literally and metaphorically in no position, during this interim or hiatus, to use her right elbow or hand to apply pressure upon any of the internal façades of the eight- or twelve-sided three-dimensional space, given that the right elbow and hand were, as it were, then free-floating within that space – as that hand transitioned, that is, through the arm's straightening around that elbow and the wrist's bending in the process, in preparation for the contact of that hand, in the form, perhaps, of its palm or fingertips, with the internal rear façade of the eight- or twelve-sided three-dimensional space once again, just as it had transitioned previously, albeit in the opposite direction – although she found, as she judged her right hand to be approaching that surface, which is to say the internal rear façade of that eight- or twelve-sided three-dimensional space within which she remained, for now, enclosed, that the trailing edge of that enclosure actually commenced elevating itself – or being elevated – not though in relation to the leading edge, but rather in a way that was consistent with the continued increase in elevation of that leading edge such that both edges, now, were engaged in increasing their absolute elevations while maintaining, between them, a constant elevatory differential so that, as far as she could tell from her compromised and constrained vantage point within that mobile enclosure, the space's trailing edge had – perhaps inevitably – now entered, in a forward direction, upon the same upwards ramp or slope that its counterpart, the leading edge, had been occupying and ascending ever since her right palm had first touched down upon the base of that space to the right of her torso as a form of shock-absorber for the remainder of her body as the latter revolved clockwise around her longitudinal axis when viewed from the head rather than the foot, which is to say, when viewed from a position on the superior side of a transverse section through her body, although she still judged, despite concerns to the contrary, this abrupt elevatory action on the part of the trailing edge of the space to be, in fact, insufficient to prevent her from reaching her revised goal, given, that is, both the proximity, now, of the fingertips of her right hand to the internal rear façade and the angular momentum still available to her from both the force she had applied via her right elbow to the base of that space and that of gravity supported by the ongoing angular disposition of the space itself, which remained, of course, broadly supportive of the counter-clockwise revolution around her longitudinal axis when viewed from the head rather than the foot, which is to say, when viewed from a position on the superior side of a transverse section through her body, in which her body continued to engage, despite that angular disposition no longer, now, increasing, such that she felt certain she would eventually turn fully to face the space's inner rear façade again, her right hand placed upon it, with the latter having traversed that inner volume via a series of swept paths resembling, if not replicating precisely, the mirror image, rotated through ninety degrees, of the route it had taken from that façade, the hand, wrist and elbow, in these trajectories, acting, she thought, like the weights at the end of a series of connected pendula to effect the aforementioned motion, and she would continue rolling towards the rear of that space until, that is, she found herself, as she did now, back in her starting position, resting on her left side facing, at close quarters, the inner rear façade of what she regarded, now, as the relative safety of that dreadful enclosure, a stasis she monitored and maintained by ensuring that her right hand not only stayed in contact with that façade but, in addition, remained poised to increase, reduce or remove accordingly the force she had at her disposal, in response, that is, to the changing dynamics imposed upon her if not by me then by some unnameable – and seemingly unassumable – presence that is, perhaps, despite its rigours, worthy of preserving in its undifferentiated, non-subjectively inhabitable, non-objectifying, non-automated, unfocalised and fully unaffiliated combinatory form.

HANNAH HOARE

FLIGHT OF THE ALBATROSS

THE VAN WINDS up the hill swinging round one broad S-bend after another and Perran's stomach lurches at every one. It's partly motion-sickness, but it's nerves too. He's been doing this for more than a year but his intestines still get tangled before a flight. The radio plays some American pop music which he doesn't recognise, and anyway the lyrics are drowned out by the hubbub of conversation. He never joins in with the banter but prefers to sit quietly and focus, running through the take-off in his head. He calls to mind the feeling: the moment the wing rises and stretches above him; the moment he feels the pressure of the wind through his brake-lines; the run, always awkward with a passenger, and then that breathtaking moment when he steps into air. He always pedals his legs a few times. The others laugh at him but sometimes the wind is tricking you and you dip back down and need to push off the mountain again. If you're not ready ... well, he's seen many pilots bump down on their backsides and mess up a take-off like that.

It takes twenty-seven minutes to get to the top and by the time the van comes to a halt Perran's butterflies have settled. He steps out of the warm, plasticky fug and breathes in the cool scent of salt and cedar. Cloud hangs on the mountain's shoulders, but it will lift soon enough. Perran lights a cigarette and walks to a broad, concreted patch of slope. Plenty of room, though it'll soon be crowded. There are always dozens of people elbowing for space at take-off, mostly tandem pilots, like him, with jittery clients. Paragliding is big business here; a twenty-minute flight over the bay is a once-in-a-lifetime thing for most people, something to tick off the bucket list. He still can't quite believe he gets to do it as a job. He always thought he'd work with his father, driving an airport taxi, ferrying tourists into town. He rode along with Baba now and again when he was a small boy and the memory still causes him to glow with pleasure. He'd wave maniacally at aeroplanes roaring upwards, never dreaming he would one day look down on the world himself. He'd listen crumple-browed to incomprehensible foreigners who never spoke a word of Turkish and usually over-tipped Baba because they didn't have a clue how much the lira was worth. In between trips, while they waited for the next flight to arrive, there were endless games of okey and glasses of sweet tea at the café behind the taxi rank. The men smoked black tobacco and moaned about the price of petrol, and the waiter slipped Perran an extra sugar lump. Baba still drives his taxi, and bores every passenger with a sales pitch. 'Best thing to do in Turkey,' he says. 'Very excellent, very beautiful. Ask for Perran, my son.' He taps his chest proudly. 'My son. Flies like . . .' He pauses. 'What is your favourite bird?'

Swallow, they might say, or blue jay. Or eagle.

'My son, flies like eagle.'

'Let's have a smoke, Perran.' It's Temel, bumming a fag as usual. Perran tosses him the packet and his lighter. He's known Temel since they were at school; he's a couple of years older and it was he who taught Perran to fly, and got him this job. 'Flying is good for your soul,' he used to say, 'but also for your head. It's about decision-making. Do you want to sit on your arse your whole life and grow a belly like your father's, or do you want to use your brain?' Temel can have as many cigarettes as he likes. They smoke in silence. The hill slopes steeply away below them, the concrete take-off quickly giving way to scree, then boulders. To their right a huge spur juts out. It's mostly hidden by cloud now, but Perran knows every contour. When the time comes, he'll fly out well clear and turn to pass it, and a few seconds later he'll be able to see the bay. He remembers the first time he saw it from the air. A huge horseshoe gouged out of the coastline, a perfect inlet. He was so high that the wide, curved beach whose gritty sand was always spattered with leather-skinned sun-bathers looked empty and pristine. A different planet. And beyond . . . that was what was so enthralling: the stretch of the ocean seemed infinite, a luminous stripe of reflected sunlight pulling him towards the horizon. But then Temel was there, carving a tight three-sixty around him and waving towards the beach. When they landed a few minutes later Temel was shaking with anger and fear. 'Are you crazy, Perran? There are no thermals over the ocean. Once you go too far, you'll never make it back to land. And if your wing goes in it'll fill with water and drag you under. You want to die? Fly out to sea.'

The metallic growl of a van door sliding open snaps him back to the present. Ozan is here with the clients. Eager, excitable, babbling tourists. Perran braces himself. He speaks pretty good English but he has a thick accent which foreigners find hard to understand, especially if English isn't their first language. Talking is tiring. Today the clients are Japanese; seventeen of them, boys and girls. They look like teenagers but they could be in their twenties. A holiday after finishing university perhaps. Ozan starts allocating each of them a pilot. Temel clocks the prettiest girls and cajoles Ozan to pair him up with a beauty. 'Give me that tall one with the pigtails and I'll make sure she comes back for more.'

It's the same every trip. Sometimes it works and Ozan seems to take pleasure in handing over a stunner to the twinkling Temel, right under the nose of her queasy-looking fiancé. But often Ozan's got a beetle up his backside and is in no mood to be playful. Today is one of those days. Temel gets the chubbiest of the Japanese boys, easily ten kilos heavier than any of the others. Perran winces as Temel rolls his eyes dramatically. It's so rude. But the boy doesn't seem to notice. He beams and makes Temel pose for a selfie. Ozan approaches Perran, propelling a slender girl who looks as though she'd rather be at home with a book than preparing to fly off a Turkish mountain.

'This is Perran. My best pilot. Just for you.' It's Ozan's standard patter; he's said it to every other client this morning, about every other pilot.

'Hello,' says Perran.

'Hi.'

'First time paragliding?'

The girl smiles politely but looks blank.

'First time fly?' He points at the sky.

She twigs, and nods.

'Don't be nervous.' Perran speaks slowly. 'You'll love it. Ozan is right, I *am* the best pilot. My father says I fly like a bird.'

She smiles again, more broadly. 'Yes. Bird.' She flaps her arms.

A breeze tickles around them; the cloud is disintegrating into wisps. The girl's smile fades, and she shivers. She's wearing a T-shirt the same sharp blue as the sky, with a pair of cat's eyes and some whiskers on it. And a tiny pair of yellow shorts.

'Here . . .' Perran reaches into his bag and pulls out a black sweatshirt. 'Put this on.'

It won't make much difference. Why Ozan doesn't make sure people dress better for this is anyone's guess. It's sweltering down in the bay where the hills stand guard on three sides, cutting off the wind and bouncing heat back down to the beach. But up here, six thousand feet above the shops and bars and ice-cream stalls, the breeze is cold. And when they take off and push out over the turquoise water it'll be freezing. The sweatshirt reaches almost to her knees.

'Okay, let's get you clipped in.' He helps her into the harness, slipping straps over her narrow shoulders, and fastening clips at her chest and legs. He pulls them tight and checks them. 'Don't touch these,' he says. 'Very important. Only me.'

'You,' she says. 'Best pilot. Bird.' She's smiling again.

He grins. She's very sweet. And behind that goofy pair of Hello Kitty glasses her eyes are dark and earnest.

There's a cheer. The first pilot takes off, his red-and-blue-striped wing fluttering as it fills with air and surges off the mountain. The passenger squeals with delight and mock terror, and her friends wave and take photos with their phones. Another brightly coloured wing pops up, then sails off the hill to another chorus of encouraging shouts.

'See,' says Perran. 'Easy. Come on.' He finds a clear spot and rolls out his wing – corn-cob yellow vivid against the dusty ground. A network of thin lines runs neatly to two fat karabiners on his harness. He shrugs on the rig, snapping buckles and tugging at each one, double-checking they're fast. Then he clips the girl's harness in front of his own, pinning her to him. Once airborne she'll sit comfortably between his knees, but on the ground they're clumsy and embarrassed by the closeness. Her hair smells of coconuts. 'Ready? When I say run, you run. Okay?'

'Ouch,' she says, fiddling with straps digging into her thighs.

'I know,' says Perran, 'but it will be fine once we're in the air. You'll sit in the harness and the straps won't bite anymore.' Out of the corner of his eye, Perran can see the chubby boy coming towards them with a tiny video camera. 'Okay, here we go. Your friend is filming. Smile for the camera.' He tugs at his lines and deftly spreads the wing across the ground. It catches the breeze and begins to inflate. He loves this moment. His wing is suddenly alive; no longer an inanimate bundle of cloth, but a breathing being. It quivers impatiently. 'Yes, here we go, my friend,' he murmurs.

He lifts the risers and the wing arcs joyfully into the air. Perran tries to run. The girl does not run. She sits. Perran takes a few steps down the slope, and staggers. Even her small frame is too much dead weight. He pulls the brake-lines and the wing collapses around them, disappointed. The girl looks confused.

'Sorry, but I can't take off if you sit down. You have to run until we are in the air. Understand? Keep running. Don't sit till I say. Don't worry, we can have another go. Go back to the top and I'll bring the wing.' Perran releases her harness from his, and points back up the slope. Temel comes to help gather up the glider, once more inert and unwieldy.

'Come on, Perran. No time to fluff today, the wind's picking up.' If it gets too windy to fly Ozan will have to give refunds, and Ozan hates giving refunds. And if you fluff your launch twice, he'll dock your wages. They carry the wing to the top of the take-off, and Perran hitches the girl's harness to his again.

'Okay. Better luck this time. But keep running, yes?' He cycles two fingers in front of her face.

She smiles and nods, and blushes slightly. 'Yes, run. Okay.'

Perran takes a deep breath and lifts the wing above their heads once more. He feels the pressure, and runs. And this time the girl runs too. A few steps are all it takes and their feet are off the ground. Perran lifts one knee to nudge the girl gently back into her seat. And in that instant, everything changes.

She slips. Perran's butterflies come crashing back. Not fluttering but pounding their wings in panic, thumping against his insides. She's not clipped in. She should be snuggly secured in front of him, but instead she has slipped down almost to his ankles, her legs dangling in nothingness. One arm is caught over the front strap of the harness, her elbow bent awkwardly, her hand gripping so hard her knuckles are turning white. He grabs for her but she's out of his reach and in trying he just yanks the controls. The glider veers wildly towards the craggy, limestone spur. He's never been so close to it - pale and pockmarked, every rock poised to shatter bones. Instinctively Perran turns his body away, shifting his weight and steering the glider out to the valley. He flails his legs, trying to loop them round her, trying to grip her somehow, anyhow. But he can't get purchase and all he does is kick her. She starts to cry. Perran wants to cry too. He should speak; reassure her that this often happens, that he'll have it sorted in a jiffy. But he can't form the words. How is she not clipped in? He checked. He always checks. Did he? Their second take-off, did he check again? The straps were pinching her; it would be the most natural thing in the world to undo them as she walked up the hill. Did he not check? He forces the thought away. Temel's voice is loud in his head. 'Paragliding is all about making decisions. Use your brain.' Use your brain, Perran. Think. It will take at least ten minutes to fly out and spiral down to the beach... can she hold on that long? Probably not. Her fingers are going blue. He swivels his head, craning to see in every direction, searching for somewhere to land. The mountainside is a hundred feet below, giddyingly steep and chaotically strewn with rocks. And then he sees it. The ocean. That glimpse of the bay he always loves. Of course. He must try and make it out over the ocean. How long will it take? Six minutes maybe? Five? It'll be a hell of a drop but landing in water is surely better than hitting the ground. His heart lifts. He's got a plan; it's going to be okay. If she can just hold on.

She can't. She makes no sound at all as she falls. All Perran can hear is the blood in his own ears. He can see no clawing hands or wild eyes; just a baggy, black sweatshirt billowing slightly over a pair of thin, pale legs. For a delirious moment he thinks it's slowing her fall like a parachute. But then it sags as it hits the ground and the legs flip up, cartoon-like, and swing to one side, pulling the sweatshirt after them. The bundle tumbles once, twice, and abruptly stops against a boulder the size of a washing machine. The legs stick out at odd angles.

Perran circles above. He tries to remember his last moment of happiness. The surge of dopamine as his feet danced off the surface of the earth. But try as he might to crystalise that split second of joy, to cast it in amber like a mosquito suspended for eternity in a dollop of golden sap, he cannot hold the memory clear of the horror that came next. The shocking jolt as the girl slipped, and scrabbled, and whimpered. Never will he have one without the other.

So many lives have just been cracked apart. He thinks of Temel, standing on the mountain, watching his protégé, his friend, do the unthinkable. Did he see the girl drop? Perran hopes not. He can't bear to share such a shameful, sordid thing with anyone. But of course people saw. He thinks of the chubby boy with his video camera. He'll have more than seen, and he'll carry his terrible souvenir home to the girl's family. Perran never even asked her name. He thinks of his father. He remembers how nervous he was telling Baba about his job as a paraglider pilot. He'd braced himself for that disappointed frown, the one he used to get when he'd dropped a grade at school or kicked a football through a neighbour's window. The other boys got the belt but Baba never did that. Just frowned and smoothed his big moustache, and shook his head. Sometimes Perran thought he'd have preferred a beating. But when he broke the news that he wouldn't need the second-hand taxi Baba had saved up for because he'd got a job flying tourists off the mountain Baba didn't frown; he threw his arms around his son and gave him a hug that squeezed the air out of his lungs. Then he kissed his cheeks and said he was so proud. 'My son, flying like a bird . . . who would think? Who would think?' Perran knows he can never again hold his father's gaze. He looks out to the horizon. There's no trace of the morning's cloud and it's impossible to tell where the sky stops and the water begins. He leans to the left, curling his glider around to face the ocean, and starts flying out to sea.

A year to the day later, a taxi rounds a bend and the young couple in the back get their first view of the bay. The water is every bit as blue as the brochure and out of the perfect, cloudless sky bright paraglider wings zigzag their way to the beach.

'Oh my god, Jules, we gotta have a go at that. It's gotta be *so* awesome to see the world like a bird!'

'You know my favourite bird?' says the driver.

'I'm sorry?'

'Albatross.'

'Uh-huh,' says the girl, crossing her eyes at her boyfriend, who whistles softly and taps his temple.

'Albatross can fly forever. Never comes to land.'

'Um . . . I'm not sure . . .' The girl catches sight of the driver's face in the rear-view mirror, and reads such sorrow in it that the smile is wiped from her own.

'Albatross flies for joy and finds all he needs up there. He sees the world below and knows he cannot be happy down here. Albatross flies forever. My son,' the taxi driver says, laying his hand on his chest, 'flies like albatross.'

IAN CRITCHLEY

GHOST WALKS

'WELCOME, WELCOME, COME nearer, don't be shy. Call me Ishmael. Or Bob. Whatever takes your fancy. How many of us are there? One, two, three . . . nine, ten, eleven, twelve. Thirteen, including me. Unlucky for some.'

Sarah rolled her eyes. The guide was tall and dressed as an undertaker, top hat and all. Despite the mizzle, his umbrella remained furled.

It was Tom who'd seen the sign earlier that afternoon, soon after they'd arrived in the city: 'Come and be terrified by ghostly tales of terror.'

'Might be fun,' he'd said.

They'd gathered at dusk by the minster's west front. Arc lights illuminated the statues and the gargoyles. Beside Sarah stood a family of four, the kids no more than five or six. A group of women – a hen party? – giggled into canned cocktails. A couple, teenagers maybe, held hands, their eyes shining bright in the darkness. She and Tom had been like that once.

Ishmael/Bob brandished his umbrella like a sword. 'The minster. Built on the sweat and the blood of hundreds of workers. Stone by stone by stone. Tough work. Physical work. Stressful work. Two of the builders, John and Joseph, were sworn enemies. John was a craftsman, Joseph a labourer, and Joseph believed that John looked down on him. One night, driven to fury by John's condescension, Joseph took up his hammer and brought it down once, twice, three times on John's head until John stopped talking, and moving.'

Sarah glanced at the children, a boy and a girl. Was this really suitable? They seemed to be lapping it up, though.

'But what to do with the body?' the guide went on. 'There was one very simple solution. Joseph bricked John up in the walls of the half-built minster, where he lies to this day. Sometimes, on still nights, you can hear a voice on the wind. "*Help me,*" it cries. "*Help me.*" He held up a finger and they listened for a moment, but all Sarah could hear was Tom rustling in his pocket and then blowing his nose.

'Onwards!' cried the guide.

Away they trooped down one of the narrow streets leading away from the minster. Nothing looked familiar to Sarah, which maybe wasn't surprising, given that the only other time she and Tom had been to the city was more than thirty years ago. They'd stayed in a tiny B&B, their first weekend away. First time they'd slept in a double bed together. First time she'd slept in a double bed full stop. They'd barely left it that whole weekend. Though there was that strange moment when she'd stood at the window and seen a woman staring up at her. Thinking it must be someone she knew, Sarah raised her hand, but then the woman stepped back, into the road, and an oncoming car had only just stopped short of hitting her.

'Come closer,' the guide beckoned. 'Are we all here? One, two, three . . . twelve, thirteen, plus me. Have we gained someone along the way? Never mind, at least we haven't lost anyone.'

Tom slipped on a cobblestone and Sarah shot out a hand to steady him. 'What would I do without you?' he said, gathering himself.

The street was so narrow, the buildings on either side almost met above their heads. A solitary lamppost illuminated the gloom. Sarah wrapped the darkness around her like a blanket.

'A tunnel runs under here,' Ishmael/Bob said. 'Some say it

stretches from the minster to the river and was a route for smugglers. But it was closed up and for centuries nobody could locate it. On a night very much like tonight, three lads newly turfed out from a tavern spotted a doorway, just here, that they'd never seen before. The door was unlocked, the hinges creaking, creaking as they pushed it open. Darkness, complete and utter.'

He paused. The kids were rapt. The hen party swayed, and the young couple kissed, half hidden by a raised umbrella.

'But one of the lads wasn't afraid,' the guide went on. 'He laid a bet that the doorway led to the old smugglers' tunnel. He'd go down and report back. He had with him a penny whistle and bade his friends follow his tune from above ground. He disappeared into the black, tootling his tune. His friends followed the sound, twenty yards, thirty, but the sound grew fainter, then stopped.'

'Did he die?' the small boy said.

'Who knows?' the guide replied. 'For he was never seen again. One of the friends fetched a lantern but when they returned to the doorway, they found no trace of a tunnel ever having been there.'

The boy shrank back into his mother's midriff.

'Let us continue,' Ishmael/Bob said. 'And as we do so, we should remember this: Wherever we go, whatever we do, we leave an impression, an imprint for later generations to see. Like footprints that never get washed away. Some say that this is what ghosts are – echoes of what came before . . .'

'That's what we'd have ended up doing if we'd stuck to the acting,' Tom said later as they studied their menus in the Chinese by the castle. 'Cheesy ghost walks.'

'It's a living,' Sarah said. She meant it as a joke, but Tom didn't laugh.

After ordering, they sat in silence. Someone had told her once that this was the sign of a strong relationship: the ability to be comfortable in silence. But she was not comfortable, and it didn't look like Tom was either. He pulled off his jumper and draped it over the back of his chair. He rolled up his shirt sleeves as if he was about to punch someone. A sheen of perspiration formed on his forehead. She had loved the way his fringe fell almost into his eyes, but when he pushed it back now it stuck to his forehead.

They'd almost got through the main course when Tom said, 'Listen, I'm sorry. I really am. I don't know how many times I have to say it.'

'You don't have to keep saying it.'

'But I don't feel like you've forgiven me.'

'It's a lot to process,' she said.

'That's understandable.' He gulped at his wine, leaving a vampiric stain on his lips, then said, 'I thought maybe coming back here would be a good way of reconnecting us, you know? Reminding us of happier times.'

Happier times. She wondered if that was true. It *seemed* true. They had been hungry for each other. They'd had dreams, ambitions to make it big, turn their drama degrees into gold. But she remembered an overwhelming urge for the days to pass, to hurry up, to get to the future. She'd longed to be older.

He was on a roll now, asking if she remembered that time . . . that time when . . . when we did . . . Do you remember? He scattered a whole host of memories around her, hoping perhaps that some of them would take root.

But there were alternative memories. She could have countered his with some of her own. Do you remember when you did that? Do you remember when you . . .

Do you remember?

Back at the hotel, she filled the roll-top bath and slipped down into it. It was almost too hot to bear, but she made herself stay in. From the bedroom came bursts of tinny laughter, a choir singing, two men arguing, more laughter. Her body turned an angry shade of red.

The scar on her abdomen remained white, though. She fingered the ridge of it, then ran her hands up and down her belly. She wondered how many layers of skin she had shed over the years. Her young skin gone, replaced by something drier, baggier. She kept renewing herself, but how long would she keep on doing that?

When she went into the bedroom, towel wrapped tightly around her, Tom was lying on his back, eyes closed, breathing softly. He was still fully dressed. She was glad she hadn't washed her hair as she didn't want to wake him by using the hairdryer. The towel dropped away and she stood naked in front of him. He didn't stir. She aimed the remote at the TV, turning it black. After putting on her pyjamas, she slipped carefully under the duvet. Tom shifted and she held her breath, but he settled again. She switched off the light and blinked into the darkness.

She woke briefly in the night and found the other side of the bed empty. Tom did that sometimes, got up and wandered around when he couldn't sleep. But where was there to wander in the hotel room? The bathroom light was off, so where was he? It didn't matter, she didn't really mind, and she was too drowsy to puzzle it out anyway. She soon fell asleep again.

Next morning at breakfast, Tom said, 'Thought I'd do one of the history tours today. Fancy it?'

What was it with him and tours all of a sudden?

'You go,' Sarah said. 'I'll look round the shops.'

The streets seemed even narrower in the daylight, perhaps because they were even more crowded. She stepped off pavements, bumped into people and got bumped into. Apologies were mumbled or shouted. Her breath clouded in front of her, mixing with everybody else's. All this breath, hanging over them like a miasma. At least it wasn't raining.

She was soon lost. She turned a corner and barely registered the sign as she passed. Doubling back, she took a second look: *Bed and Breakfast.* Something caught her eye in one of the windows above: a young woman wearing tartan pyjamas. Sarah couldn't see the woman clearly. Was she waving? Sarah pulled her hand out of her pocket and raised it in reply. It wasn't really a wave, more a mirroring gesture.

A car horn blared behind her and only then did she realise she'd stepped back into the middle of the road. Now she held up both her hands to the driver. For a moment, she thought he was going to shout at her, but he drove off. Sarah looked back up at the window, but the young woman was gone.

Sarah saw the minster over the roof of the B&B. She made her way towards it, keeping it in sight, until she found herself in familiar streets again. Soon she was back at the hotel. In the room, she stood at the window, but nobody waved at her. She packed quickly, not bothering to fold her clothes. Downstairs, she left her key with the receptionist, but didn't explain anything and the receptionist didn't ask.

Out in the city for the last time, she set off for the station. She thought of the builder buried behind the minster wall, the whistle player in the tunnel under her feet. Trapped.

Her phone buzzed but she ignored it. *Happier times*, she thought to herself. *Yes.*

IAIN SINCLAIR

UNDER THE FLYOVER

Dwarf angels, wing-clipped, retracted necks, nicotine-yellow beaks and claws, occupy crawl space abandoned by feral pigeons: a flightless owl cabaret under the flyover. A mute chorus appeased by the 24-hour thud and thump on concrete; acoustic footprints of heavy-metal freight, folk memories of community rock festivals. Gentle carbon flake snowstorms. Birds are the only surviving witnesses to a newsreel parade of civic shame. Feathers singed from smouldering balconies. Eyes burnt black as olives. The ghosts of themselves. Talking to themselves. Homeless at home. And forbidden the streets.

The English have never 'got' surrealism. Even Londoners – especially Londoners – all of whom, signed up to the entropy tango where the bad stuff arrives first and is road tested to oblivion, with acceptable and irreversible collateral damage, are proud, card-refusing, sexually plural, pan-global, pre-traumatic, post-truth immigrants. Lost souls from elsewhere busking it: bravely or bitterly sea-shaken. Frozen from padlocked containers. Undeceived by experience. Abdicated from the potentialities of new worlds. Welcome to Rwanda! Politics is what happens when surrealism atrophies.

The scapegoating of the migrant falls across the city. Especially on me, boasted Norton, a border-jumper from the far west, taking chapel prophecies personally as always. And hiding his face behind a painted goat mask. Every stalled vehicle in the hobbled dance of our punishment transport system, every phone-swipe cry for assistance, is an affront. Bed blockers over forty-years-of-age should know better than to quit their burrows. Every bruise and bump and botched hip replacement gifted by the peloton of entitled – and don't they know it – super-cyclists and electrified beat-the-lights Deliveroo maniacs in black Lycra with no lights of their own. Every ramming from behind by supercharged disability rafts. Every considerate construction pit and tall crane pendulum swinging ominously in the Sahara dust agitated by twelve-storey microclimate whirlwinds. Pollution you can taste. And enjoy.

'Wanker!' Screamed at the slipstream.

'Come back and have a *proper* discussion.' Howled at a safe distance. Fists raised. As useful as a ski resort cease-fire debate. Or private jet climate conference in Switzerland.

The City. How we live it and love it.

Norton registered this comprehensive catalogue of insults as a programme of torments conjured overnight by the Secret Lizard Masters of Californian Cyberspace, in order to thwart his lack of purpose, while he tramped his demented nocturnal circuits like Poe's 'Man of the Crowd'. Pricks of malfate, he conceded, were contrived for the promised enlightenment he resisted with every last fibre of his immortal but clapped out soul.

That was always the deal. The game. The final contract. And it was weird, delusional. He didn't accept or believe one word of it. But it was never 'surreal'. Or 'iconic'. Or a 'direction of travel'. In radio speak: 'How do you feel?' After the killing of your special child. After the upgraded bronze butterfly medal. After your dog howled in tune through the national anthem. 'You know what? Surreal! Didn't sleep a wink, know what I'm saying? Totally surreal.'

None of that blustering froth, and none of the self-seeding street signage with instantaneous spray-can improvements, none of the fake news from cosmetically enhanced, lectern-elbowing bullies with big flags, none of the identity theft scams, video porn decapitations, none of those cute furry animal hits pimped on antisocial media, the four-legged chickens and obscenity-shrieking Amazonian parrots, *none of it*, drumming through the auditory ossicles of Norton's middle ear, had any kinship with classic Parisian Surrealism.

In fact, that ship had sailed. Sunk. Or been very expensively converted into a floating prison or experimental incubator for interesting new viruses. The only acceptable European imports waved through without paperwork.

The foot-foundered walker seethed and swore, and lost the narrative thread, every time he was assaulted by yatter from some ayahuasca-enhanced game show looped on an unquiet TV screen in a favoured breakfast café. Interrogated sportspersons, coached in clichés, frozen in front of a backdrop of corporate logos. Award-snaffling fame junkies greeting every ordinary, mundane escape from a two-goal deficit or the undeserved presentation of a gilded dildo: 'Surreal! *Totally* surreal.'

Beyond amazement. Out of this world. Surreal: meaning its polar opposite. Without vision. Without mystery. Linguistically bereft. Dead in the mouth. Dulled by common usage. Locked in secure files by the academy.

Surrealism, said the last English poet, is 'the cuckoo's egg laid in the nest (whose brood is lost) with the complicity of René Magritte'.

'Magritte' as in a museum gift shop postcard employed as bookmark in a Jeffrey Archer paperback in a uncharitable charity pit in St Leonards-on-Sea. Windows boarded over, spider-webbed by universal protesters: climate change, second-home DFLs, closed banks, threatened post offices, Brexit, animal testing, inappropriate dog shit. And red-eyed patriots staggering from the Old England pub on London Road to stomp deviants. NO MORE CHARITY. Further donations refused, bursting bin bags heaped in piss-stained doorways staked out by rough sleepers at the rough end of padlocked local conveniences.

Marine watercolourists identified a whiff of France, somewhere out there, in the innocent evening hours, overriding sewage outflow inflows, fish fries, spitting batter baths, and the regularly replenished guano layering of the Goat Ledge gull dormitory. It's a long swim to abroad. Keeping your head above the 'May Bloom' that smells like rotten lizards wintering in a sock. A couple of drunken lads have abandoned a swan pedalo mid-Channel. But it's still not surreal, it's sixty seconds on the teatime East Sussex news.

In the watchful torment of another sleepless night, Norton admitted to his covert surrealist pantheon that memorial obelisk from Abney Park Cemetery, Stoke Newington. The dwindling column topped by a single severed hand, digits parting the clouds, pointing towards the dereliction of heaven. Odd, certainly, and singular enough to stall a rambling tourist, but *surreal?*

Here, in this root garden where Edgar Allan Poe and Arthur Machen promoted something authentically uncanny but still in nature, freakish exhibits were no more disruptive to a map of congenital English banality than a margarine light bulb, an avenue of decapitated angels, or a sprawling lion with its polished nose sniffing at the sepulchre of its trainer. Or even a football-sized pot of Marmite left on the steps of a war memorial. *Any* pot of Marmite (outside Burton-on-Trent). There is a rational explanation for every quirk and folly: the pointing paw on the obelisk is the missing hand chewed off by the hungry lion. Fill in the blanks and it makes perfect sense. Stoke Newington intellectuals, determined to upgrade their cemetery park, are formulating post-doctoral theses proving that Machen, in giving his support to Franco, was a fellow-travelling Golden Dawn surrealist. 'They walked the same forgotten streets by night,' said one of them, 'without remarking each other, but navigating by the same constellations on their curious adventures.' Abney Park made informal (and rejected) overtures to Buttes-Chaumont.

Watch out, before anything else, for heritage dowsers, blue plaque vandals, copywriters of local particulars: colonists of history. And be wary of those caves beneath railway arches, where they have dumped the Vietnamese boat people finessing MOT certificates and upgraded to poodle parlours, ethical coffee connoisseurs, bare-brick fusion dining rooms. And dripping caverns where influencers dressed as NHS nurses from 1970s television lead their tame clients into quilted pods where they can access alternative lives at one flash of tablet credit.

'Surreal! Totally surreal. A groovy time trip that is sure to become a Hackney habit,' reported one gratified punter on his/her (their) digital survey form. After twelve minutes on a paradise atoll, a pink coral reef spared from climatic predations and the half-life devastation of atomic bomb tests safeguarded with plastic spectacles. 'Totally surreal!' To be walking with wombats, wind-surfing salt deserts, coupling in non-judgemental sexual bliss under a weightless waterfall, swooping like a killer drone through the private apartments of the Vatican, under stupendous ceilings manfully toshed into a steroidal superhero drama by Michelangelo.

Norton trembled at the offer, which was more of a non-refundable curse, and accepted immediately. He mimed an air gesture of credit transference, as if he really did have a phone in his hand, and was not simply glad to be getting out of there. The woman in question, appearing from a sulphurous kitchen zone, set down the heft of a murderously generous shovel of actual and simulated pigmeats, pink, purple, black, with morbidly swollen mushroom pelts and a reflux of sun-lamp beans, on a ceramic platter like a souvenir Jubilee shield muddied with a puddle of Daddies Brown Sauce. The starred item on the allday breakfast slate was still the Olympic Special. (Not to be confused with the Special Olympics.)

The accosted client took a speculative pull at his brimming mug of cooling coffee substitute, checking for undissolved sludge. He needed a moment to steady his nerves. Here, inside the perfumed maternal clout of this woman of the Estuary, was the agent of oblivion Norton had been waiting to meet for most of his conscious life. Why else would he wander these trackless purlieus? Mme Mephistopheles in wrappings of pubic pink at his elbow.

'Your lucky day, mate,' the apron said. 'And just in bleedin' time by the sight of you, no messing. Day release? Or was you flushed out with the smelly stuff?'

A bog standard visitation brought on by riding ticketless anywhere beyond Barking.

'You familiar with Ford Madox Ford's little punt on "The Future in London"? How'd you like to trade some of that old bollocks for a working pair of your own?'

Planting her vividly lipsticked cigarette butt in his discounted Andrew and Fergie wedding mug, the good wife of Tilbury Town continued, unabashed.

'London, old Fordie's London, 'astings to 'arlesden, Oxford to Oxshott, all yours, mate, any period what takes your fancy. But you never quits those 'allowed 'amlets, one whoppin' great sixty-mile sweep of Billy Blake's compass, from Aldgate Pump and the bleedin' bell foundry they done over as a smart little gaff with a rooftop swimming pool. You should try it. Soon. I'll gift you the soap.'

The downriver vision took. It was grafted and permanent like a crow tattooed across the meniscus of the eyeball. Prisoner of geography, man in the goat mask, one-name Norton, era-hopping tourist, had become an inducted participant in whatever he chose to read: he was there, *but only there*. He could beat the bounds of London but never break them. 'How do you feel?' Frightened, emasculated. Up for it. And terminally tired. Like all the rest.

When the request arrived by electronic Wells Fargo snailmail from Texas, referencing 'the 100th anniversary of the Surrealist Manifesto', Norton struck out, without hesitation, capitalised offprint in his zipped pocket. After the substantial hallucination in the Tilbury café, he acknowledged that the gift of temporary immortality – the immortality of new-build brownfield estates in chalk quarries – came with certain responsibilities. And could be withdrawn as swiftly as a Tesco's special offer. Solicited commissions from legendary headbangers of solid repute (and rumoured generosity) could not be refused. Instinct carried him west, like soap factory pestilence from the Lea Valley, towards the square of the *Greater London A-Z* where he had last encountered the editor of this anniversary collection. A cultural sentimentalist in good standing. That man remembered everything. Performed or imagined.

'Under the pavement, the beach,' they used to say in Paris. And tried to prove it by digging up cobbles as potential projectiles to hurl at the shields of shock troops.

'Under the flyover, trash,' was the London translation. And Norton was there to confirm it, at first light, every Friday, trawling, with no great expectation, where deceased or liberated flotsam spread out over rags and tarpaulin like conceptual art without a sponsor: single shoes, institutional forks, hair curlers, cans without labels, amputee dolls, dud batteries, unsafe razors, dog collars (hairs included at no extra charge), padded scrum caps for post-operative brain surgery survivors, sawdust cigarettes, unspooling cassettes, unpopular paperback bestsellers from yesterday. He swooped, a starving heron, on something like one of his own visions of those flyover angels disguised as uniclaw pigeons: a fabulous contrivance in dazzling colour.

Take care!

Here was authentic cover art. Soft pearly-grey birds, coupled, and rubbing necks in monogamous bliss. Alongside a diminishing perspective of Masonic handshakes borrowed from memorials in Abney Park. 'SURREALISM', the designer boasted in brick red capitals. A drawing credited to Max Ernst. 'A SHORT SURVEY' accomplished by David Gascoyne.

Watch out! Poetry alert!

'What was once considered the ravings of a few hysterical lunatics, has become of international interest.'

1936. The tall young English poet, a regular Channel hopper, Dover to Calais, smuggled the implications of this subversive movement into London. He took part, as amiable altar boy to the high priests of Paris, in a sensational exhibition. Gascoyne had endured, with fortitude and clots of apocalyptic imagery, curses of his own. He had given everything, gone through the fire, in pursuit of language. 'Entrance,' he wrote, 'has generally been supposed, up till now, to be the sole privilege of poets and other madmen.'

Purchase made. Item carried away before the trembling, junk-sick vendor can complete his well-honed Ancient Mariner confession, the justification for parting with a holy relic. Book in hand, Norton's breath fails and our story begins. Notting Hill: the waiting room of Dr Bluth, artists and poets enduring sonata assaults as they wait for a shot.

The critic asserts that Dada and Surrealism are not art movements, they are religions. They have their cardinals, their hierophants. Their pronouncements are studies in controlled hysteria. In approved delusion. Gascoyne summoned the Battle of Cable Street. He tracked his attendance back to meetings in a comfortable bourgeois house on Blackheath. As an amateur Marxist and Mass Observer, his presence was required on the streets. In the affray. But not *inside* the actual violence, the bicycle chains and the razors. The improvised weaponry of the Aldgate spielers, the drinking dens. Bad boys coming good when it mattered. Gascoyne spoke about all that on Sunday evenings when his wife, Judy, was in church and he enjoyed a free run at the telephone. Surrealism was the smokescreen, a cult for initiates. The British thought it belonged in Blackpool.

'Rimbaud was a surrealist in life and elsewhere. Swift in malice. Poe in adventure. Jarry in absinthe.'

Handling the poet's dazzling book, in the fug of the Tilbury café, on his return to the end of the line, there was no immediate transformation. Norton was not stepping into the Tardis or being beamed up to a space cruiser of leisurewear freaks lost among future galaxies. A time-travelling induction by way of the chosen volume, the one he hardly dares to open, takes a considerable leap of faith. And who, after all, was doing the choosing?

He does not move through the years, but a previously unsuspected and unemployed empathy gland, stimulated by whatever the witch in the refuelling pit slipped into his coffee, causes him to accept his role as silent witness to the behaviour of the cast of whatever volume he happens to be perusing. One book at a time.

This is how he understood the mess into which he had blundered, the one he had been flirting with since his adolescent arrival on the wrong side of the river. The woman who plonked a laminated menu down on the yellow formica, like a set of tarot cards customised by Alan Moore, said that books were his karma. Tracking them through London's suburbs, street markets, and boxes dumped on the pavements of compulsively recycling boroughs, had allowed him to scratch a living. But that was all over. Now he was being granted the honour, more valuable than a Fellowship of the Royal Society of Literature, of becoming what he read, entering the narrative in some modest fashion, swelling a progress, nudging the odd rib, picking a pocket or two.

The price was nothing, a token: he would never leave the limits of the capital city, London Nation. The get-out clause being that those limits had never been adequately described or confirmed. The orbital motorway, turning octopus sprawl into a traffic island, was elastic. Sometimes stretching to accommodate a pregnancy of private estates and revamped asylums, sometimes biting hard like a whale-bone corset.

The dark-wigged fortune-telling gypsy of Tilbury Town in her starched apron, was more Peggy Mount than Marlene Dietrich in *A Touch of Evil*. But she knew, better than anyone, that Norton's future was all used up. 'Go home.'

1936: surrealism came first. July, silly season, West End gallery. Street politics followed in October: immigrant quarter, blackshirt marchers halted by housewives, Hoffman pressers, market traders, bakers, card-carrying activists.

'It is the least caprice of Marcel Duchamp,' Norton read. 'It is the struggle of Alberto Giacometti with the Angel of Invisibility who has made an appointment with him among the blossoming apple-trees.'

The library-haunted hedge scholar carried his trophy, the book from under the flyover, rubbery pages saturated with yellow smoke and airless cupboards of dead overcoats, to the unregarded Wellclose Square orchard. Blossom time, abundant and ignored. 'White curtains of tortured destinies.' It was beginning to work, this equation between stop-framed text and neurotically revised London territory. Norton understood: when Gascoyne's higher self evolved, or raced off in a rush of amphetamine conviction with involuntary chasers of eidetic imagery – YES! – crimson sun burning to golden aureoles of pollen vortex in close-cropped urban parks, so the seduced reader yielded to the vision. And lost the privilege of anonymity as man of the crowd. The power of the poet's words, published to inform and engage, faded into hardened grains of the ground to which their subtle cadences, the clink of spade on broken sod, had carried Norton. Failed detectorist! Voiceless hack doomed to fulfil an unwritten commission.

There were the inevitable conferences, art magazines, suicides. Dali read his poem 'I Eat Gala' with the promise that he would 'manipulate a strange living body'.

'Surrealism,' Gascoyne concluded, 'cannot be limited to any one particular time or place . . . No longer does a surrealist await the message or the image to arise from the vast unconscious residue of experience; he actively imposes the image of his desires and obsessions upon the concrete, daylight world of objective reality; he actively takes part in "accidents" that reveal the true nature of the mechanism that is life far more clearly than "pure psychic automatism" could.'

The poet had provided Norton with his escape clause. 1936 was uncomfortable, he had not yet been dropped into the world; blue, clenched, and refusing to draw breath. Being in company with Gascoyne, and somehow knowing how it ended with a stair lift on the Isle of Wight, meant that the system was not fully functional. They were together at the crossroads of Cable Street and Cannon Street Road, in a seething crush and still able to whisper, with the poet asking Norton if he'd ever had a shot at translating Rimbaud.

Gascoyne had no books left. He was going nowhere. But he still possessed a photograph album through which he could travel to the frozen days of a volatile life. There he was, and Norton with him, in New York City with Allen Ginsberg. There he was with the band of English Surrealists, making their new worlds from rationed paper. 'All the dark rooms are moving / All the air's nerves are bare.'

The system was in meltdown. Place overwhelmed persons. The time-traveller's library had spilled into the streets. *A Short Survey of Surrealism* became a compendium of madness, ticks, twitches, fevers and frighteners. There is a translation from Benjamin Péret: 'Work on the land the streets the docks / and sow there what you will / paving-stones smoke or bottles / but work like a lunatic / and dung the stones.'

He dunged. Norton dunged when he worked the land, when he broke from his dock labours. In bushes. In parks. No breaks but smoke. Old Holborn roll-ups and shreds of black tobacco stuck between the broken tines of rabbit teeth. The interlude of the orchard. *This orchard*. In the book rescued from beneath the flyover, Norton finds a grey reproduction, like aerial surveillance of an ancient camel-route city flattened in the desert; drone-dispersed, returned to sand. A horror of grey with mounds and pits and sudden revelations of skeletal mosques and hospitals. But this is just Man Ray's photograph of a detail from a Marcel Duchamp painting: *The Bride Stripped Bare By Her Own Bachelors*. Glossed as: 'unfinished'.

The creeping horror now, as the man with his back against the apple tree, last ribbons of mortality spent among shivering blossom, realises that one book is never *one* book. That it enfolds multitudes. Within young Gascoyne's prodigious survey there were many yelping, jabbering, overconfident heads: all trying to seduce an imagined audience, that solitary reader by monkish candlelight, *the special one*. The one who truly *understands*. And approves.

In the place where Norton sat, scratching his hidden parts and calling up the derision of Mosley's blackshirt legions when they attempted their abortive invasion of this sacred territory, the planting ground where the living bones of the Swedish scientist and mystic, Emanuel Swedenborg, once lay. A head, more monument than man, once buried, twice stolen. And even now, those thin lips, stained with bitter coffee, mumbled about the well-endowed man of mud, the giant Jewish revenger, conjured from sediment in Wellclose Square by Rabbi Falk. Conjured by demons. A legend told and retold. Drowned by the dull keening of a buried bell. Posthumous warnings from yesterday's river. The Golem, in its summoned visitation, turned back the dark forces of the fascist marchers. But the sound of tramping boots continued. Out into Essex. Zombie knives on safe suburban cul-de-sacs.

Norton wakes to a sharp crack across the shoulders, as he swerves away from the Cossack sweep of the knout wielded by the black rider on the great white horse. Cable Street had become the entrapment of

Grosvenor Square; those sing-along masses, the war protestors and the anarchist shock troops assaulting the embassy, hammered back by police cavalry. Medieval absorbs contemporary: newsreel violence with a sting puts the real into surreal. The client state kettles and stampedes, protecting a cliff of aggressive architecture.

1968 to 2018: Norton's London shatters. It is hard to tell the sponsored artwork from the detritus of illusion.

An antique television set, thick as a butcher's safe, and leased on instalment in a spasm of national pride, in order to experience some national catastrophe, coronation or football championship, has been repurposed and stocked with monster goldfish, their heads orientated to the east, where a pale sun is expected. The fish share their tragic rectangle with a slime-coated Buddha. Water has frozen overnight into a block of ice. The placement is specific. Across the road from the four short steps where a working man, returning from his favoured boozer, and carrying a replacement chair leg wrapped in newspaper, was gunned down by an atypically prompt tactical response unit. Responding to a bad joke by fellow topers, fools with an idiot phone.

An old white woman, of Balkan origin, has adapted the remnants of a tartan rug to form a rudimentary shelter between the trunk legs of the wide open stance of a giant black statue, one of a pair positioned outside the proud frontage of a Town Hall from some discontinued civic era. History-improving sculptures referred to by police-on-special-measures and politically incorrect cabbies from the forest fringe as 'The Muggers'.

MONDOSURREALISTHOXTON ©. DADADUMPBIN.

A hulking alpha ape, a Kong in bronze, palled with a basset hound, up on its hind legs, stares upstream. They are brandishing long-lens cameras. Witnessing the steps where the body of a suicided acid-attack-killer would be beached.

Brightly painted Day of the Dead carnival masks attached to a brutalist concrete hulk. Accidental art.

A 1600-year-old tree stump from Aleppo has been returned to life – emerald-green roots, black buds – in an unoccupied development nightmare of reflective towers.

Politics is surrealism from a rejected manifesto. Craters in the road. Mysterious mounds crafted from Super Sewer landfill. Yesterday's culture abandoned against a coherent programme of resistance. Budgeted and explained. Mansplained. And loudly forgotten. Julian Assange pens handed to highway pedestrians outside Belmarsh Prison. With free chocolate biscuits. To compose poems of protest.

'ROUSSEL is surrealist in the anecdote, etc., etc.' The Revolution is over. Status quo confirmed.

Surrealism was once a valid thesis, a utile outrage belonging to its deniers, its outliers. Buñuel, in his Paular Hotel fugue, waiting for a beam of sunlight to penetrate the green glass of his ice-kissed gin. *Sister Vaseline.* 'The bourgeois,' he said, 'revolting against the bourgeoisie.' And he chewed his foul cigar. And grunted at the approval he did not require. Antonin Artaud, hair on fire, crawling over a mountain of black shoes, acknowledged that the centre of gravity had shifted to Mexico. Mexico and Spain and the Aran Islands. His hatchet-carved cheekbones and furious intensity confessed Jeanne d'Arc. Prepared her for the coming barbecue. And his own sessions with the rubber gags and electricians of Rodez. 'Surrealism has never meant anything to me but a new kind of magic.'

To have witnessed and experienced, without leaving his cave, so many dramas, historic, post-historic, or entirely fabulous, drained Norton of the will to walk and wander. What if he *had* been present when Henry James was plugged, midflow, by the sudden insertion of a supersize cheeseburger? What if the warnings of the Tilbury witch were meaningful? And he was what he read. Nothing less, nothing more. What if he had been on his way to report on a whale washed up in Deptford when he eavesdropped on five different versions of the death by blade of Christopher Marlowe? What if he dropped a scatter of brown coins into the claw of Hugh Boone, the Man with the Twisted Lip, as the economic migrant squatted, cross-legged like a Whitechapel tailor, stock of wax vespas in his lap, at an oblique angle to the terrible wall that encloses Threadneedle Street? What if Neville St Clair, Boone's better self, on his evening commute to a respectable villa in the marshes of Kent, flurried the horse that threw the sister of the friend of Vincent van Gogh on Blackheath? Murder by mind game. Was he responsible for a report he had not written? What failure of nerve stopped him from intervening when the quorum of racist thugs launched their attack in Eltham? Neville lived seven miles out and remained within the iron rule of London.

By torchlight, Norton scoured his groaning shelves for guidance, for already composed instructions that would help him to plot his escape, his conclusion. The only duty of the writer, he knew full well, was to assist the imaginations of the dead. To extend or refine their unfinished paragraphs.

'Norton was evidently an important factor ... He was a lawyer. That sounded ominous.'

So the later and lesser Norton read, his chapped finger tracing the letters across yellowed paper. Conan Doyle composed these words for *A Scandal in Bohemia*, the first tale in the haunted man's copy of *Sherlock Holmes: The Complete Short Stories*. A fat volume, small print, yellow dustjacket, published in 1928. Is that where Norton belonged? Where he came in? An invented or documented spectre, a literary conceit? Everything is predicted if you know where to look. Fate spelled out in the speech bubbles of a graphic novel.

'It was a delicate point, and it widened the field of my inquiry.'

Irene Adler, the only female Holmes spoke of as *the woman*, married Norton. 'The photograph becomes a double-edged weapon.'

Male costume was nothing new to Irene. She had her walking clothes at the ready. And her newly scripted Norton husband. She could stride away from mere fiction.

In his introduction, Conan Doyle quotes a 'witty' critic: 'Holmes may not have been killed when he fell over the cliff, but he was never quite the same man afterwards.'

Doyle's Norton, a minor plot contrivance, dismissed husband in a frequently republished story, a different man at every degraded iteration, absorbs and overwhelms the current Norton, the cursed London writer. The hollow revenant fated to walk the night playing at detective. Digressing in pursuit of every abortive clue in some feverish sickbed tale of mystery. Stiff white sheets up to the throat.

'Ten papers were taken from Woolwich.' Norton was already after them, the Elizabeth Lane a gift to spooks, laying out a topographic structure, the limits of imaginative fiction.

He was mad as a felt-curer; a medieval hatter swooning deliriously on mercury vapours. Lost down a Barking outflow rabbit hole. Doomed for a certain time to keep company with a mentor shade, with David Gascoyne, the visionary poet championing surrealism on a bus to Twickenham. As Norton's rational boundaries burst, in sympathy with the poet's torment, he suffered the sharp prick of cold new stars registering their predictive power over a frozen river. Frost fairs in summer. Rain always.

'You've 'eard of libraries? Them book bazaars we uster 'ave?'

Sage advice offered with the same chipped and unrinsed mug of coffee substitute, back in Tilbury Town, now deader than Deadwood. And amputated by railway.

'Give it a bleedin' spin, mate. Borrow two, get one free.'

The wise woman in the apron slid another brimming plate, with great delicacy, hard against the glassine spine of *A Short Survey of Surrealism*. Not a mark made. While the deluded bibliophile of the Estuary, connoisseur of breakers' yards, took the hint. *Man's Life*

Is This Meat. Allday breakfast flesh, pink and glistening, was once alive. 'Shoeleather covered with the vomitings of hedgehogs.'

Norton had only to return the Gascoyne production to its place of origin, the carpet under the flyover, and he was done with imported surrealism. With police horses and truncheons. With ignorant armies clashing by night.

The Portobello vendor was at his post, a sanctioned grunge-dandy, colour-copied from Jerry Cornelius. His pinstripe flares flapped around wasted limbs. His riverboat gambler's silky waistcoat had buttons like silver skulls. His canines were gold. He accepted, without comment, the rare and coveted 1936 volume, with its distinctive smell, paper made from old raincoats soaked in aniseed. And he allowed Norton a single paperback in exchange. Something more comfortable with the territory, the malformed condition of pre-Thatcher England. Something from another era, admittedly, but still novel, still fresh, with unbroken spine. And spirit. Unsullied by previous owners. Unread. It even boasted in black lettering of representing NEW WORLDS while doubling as THE ASSASSINATION WEAPON. April 1966.

Norton remembered a time when he was still capable of remembering (or reading about) all that. London on the cusp: prefabs still in occupation, vacant lots tolerated, fortunes to be made parking cars on bombsites. Coppers and criminals shared a convivial pint, putting the world to rights, by getting hammered in the same pubs, before driving home, full throttle, without tax discs or seatbelts. Transatlantic visitors were stirring the pot. And promoting new ways of staying ripped. 'God bless you Mr Vonnegut,' said one *New Worlds* review. Another one, from a Brighton bookman, celebrated William Burroughs, in residence a spit from Piccadilly, and looking for the right bar. 'His life is ordered, material for his books is kept in a series of files of photographs and clippings which usually travel with him.'

Weary from his tramp across town, dowsing the heat of the latest underground investment, massive excavations, monumental enclosures, fantastic futures and tamed pasts in buildings that would never be built for people who would never draw breath, Norton carried his paperback prize to an offensively beige refreshment kiosk, sanctuary for humming laptops, where he sniffed at a thimble of iced coffee conjured entirely from ethically sourced oats and grains. He broached the *New Worlds* warning that 'most people are unable to detach themselves from the particular mood of their times'. The author had a familiar name. Norton knew from experience how this person was both saturated in his moment and capable of voyaging, at the first touch of the keys, to a paradoxical past, both actual and improved. Or a future more imminent than anything previously known.

It worked!

The featured item, 'The Assassination Weapon', credited to JG Ballard, cut the time lines. Norton's oat coffee turned at once into a chamber pot of builder's tea, with the sort of greasy film that gifts working drinkers a Mexican moustache at no extra charge. The toast was thicker and sturdier than the book. This was more like it! That *New Worlds* era, Norton appreciated, reeked as much of damp wallpaper, launderette soap powder, fags and chips, as of patchouli and cannabis. Ordinary people still took buses and paid with coins for tickets that coming generations would mysteriously collect.

But being on the street early, with the traders, in spring sunshine, new days on Portobello Road, was a hit Norton would never forget. Or forgive. The optimism. The innocence. The way crowds sashayed in 8mm home movies.

'All the images that fill the mind of modern man are seen through the eyes of a fictional spiritual descendant of Eatherly – the landscape of a nuclear explosion, flyovers, advertising hoardings, oil derricks, radio telescopes, and wrecked and abandoned machines,' the magazine's editorial concluded. Summoning the karmic residue of the clinically obedient pilot of the aircraft delivering the atomic bundle, destroyer of worlds, as portal to a listing of prophetic elements and objects. The debris of surrealism is the aftershock of the burning instant when occulted poetry imploded from the state-approved machinations of military-industrial physics. Relativity bursting its cage.

'Ballard's fusion of fact and fantasy succeeds in creating a kind of reality far removed from the "reality" of the events reported and analysed in the popular press and elsewhere, but in our view he comes up with a far more real view of these events than has hitherto been published.'

Was he *here*? This man, Ballard. Ever? As reported? Was Norton? Ballard visited Burroughs without penetrating the alien aura. He knew him well enough through publications and pronouncements. He tracked the shifting cut-up narrative, and his own relation to it, from the first lines of *Junkie* in 1956. That sensational B-feature cover!

'My first experience with junk was during the War, about 1944 or 1945. I had made the acquaintance of a man named Norton who was working in a shipyard at the time. Norton, whose real name was Morelli or something like that, had been discharged from the peacetime Army for forging a pay check, and was classified 4-F for reasons of bad character. He looked like George Raft, but was taller.'

1944 or 1945, that was around the time that the biological Norton, whose name had never been Morelli, got his start in the present cycle of reincarnation. When the other Morelli was still the one who tried to take over Hay-on-Wye, the unlikely Cemetery of Dead Books on the Welsh borders. He had a collection of passports in many colours. But the name of Norton was not to be found on any of them. Ghosts from the time of the Morelli consulate stopped Norton on Hackney streets to show him copies of his rarest publications, long since reforgotten: they always boasted of finding them, for less than fifty pence, in Morelli's container-stacked former cinema.

Pavements trembled. Stalls of sanctioned junk, displayed and burnished for sale, shook and faded. As if the conviction of the London set didn't hold. Hallucinations were cheap, gifted from passing strangers on the nod, prominent thyroid cartilage bandaged in silk scarves. And scuttling amphetamine crabs, muttering and cursing in the perfumed air. Norton did not belong here the first time, those communal rooms where explainers, high for days, tried to say the unsayable, while assorted bodies huddled under Moroccan blankets. They were on the edge of diminishing revelation. If the absolute *had* been revealed, they would have closed it down. Now he was here again, expecting to encounter his earlier better self, jaunting towards accident, between imported films and Dylan from open windows.

He grips his paperback like the last testament. If he lets it go, the famous morning was all for nothing. He staggers into a doorway and flicks the pages. Arson is a topic. Light glints on the eye of a Cyclops. A youth in a tenement near the Old Kent Road will pick up on that clue and let it fester.

'I can start fires but cannot extinguish them.' That sentence recalls the period, the hair, the beards, the hats in photographs, the drawings by Mal Dean. The way Moorcock collaged absurdist news clippings into his post-surrealist prose riffs. Into the real dreams of the only day.

The editor/author improvises: 'I glare at the books. Voltaire, Dickens, Dostoevsky, Shakespeare, Conrad, Hemingway surround me, glaring back, mocking me. Their works will last, they seem to say. Mine is finished.'

He was of the Fellowship, this Moorcock. He says that his anger set 'tongues of flame writing around the books'. It was the resolution of the space traveller condemned to the wrong universe, condemned to write his way home.

Ballard, it appeared, took a different route. Eavesdropping across the sump of mass media noise, he isolated the crucial dramas and made them into gigantic billboards to be scanned and forgotten from the speeding taxi to the air terminal at the limits of every serious city. He filtered the hurt, the looped imagery, back into a semi-detached riverside retreat. The Victorians understood that mania, heavenly visions, non-conformity and premature pregnancies, were a contagion. They should be expelled to the final fold of urban civilisation, one day's walk from the centre. In Belmont Asylum psychosis earthed universal pain and edited it into marketable prose. 'In the mirror of this swamp there are no reflections.'

Fire again. Flames everywhere. Fire spreading its tendrils over high-rise tower blocks and pre-wilded concrete islands. 'Bonfires of Jackie's face burn among the reservoirs of Staines and Shepperton ... At night he sleeps beneath an unlit bonfire of breasts.' The surrealism of the hoarding brings forth demons. Paperback in pocket, Norton, elective vagrant, bibliomaniac, knows what must be done. Where he must go next in pursuit of disappearance.

Holding to false memories, cinema implants from forgotten nights in suburban palaces, under a curtain of smoke, Norton decided to make his approach by way of Staines. He liked the name. And its implication. The suggestion that something of importance had leaked away, leaving its sticky residue. He liked the point of confluence of Colne and Thames, where he had once witnessed the ceremony of Swan Upping. He liked the dancing play of light in the elegant sweep of the arched bridge supporting the orbital motorway, the ripples in the moving water he watched for hours at the time of some now obliterated book.

According to the Tilbury witch, he would never escape the gravity of London and this was where it ended. What if he walked through the bridge to the far side? The country from which no mortal returns. Would concrete crumble or would he? Dust in the water. He took out the *New Worlds* paperback and thumbed the loosening pages looking for inspiration. A contribution called 'The Ruins' caught his eye. The prose had the authentic flavour of the editor, filling up empty pages under a pseudonym. Norton was reminded, he couldn't recall where he'd seen it before, or what happened after he broached a guerrilla raid on that scenario, of a composition by a respected Liverpool poet and academic.

'I taught the poems, the legend, and a novel based on the hoax,' the Scouse scholar said, 'because they raised interesting questions about literary intentionality and value, the ethics of signature.'

What a title, what a prompt: 'The Ethics of Signature.'

Norton slumped on the gentle slope between water and overarching concrete span: he basked. He ripened the moment, the golden morning, by reading a few lines of this tale by a person who didn't exist, a signature of convenience.

'Was he some kind of outcast? He couldn't remember. There had to be some reason for his being here. Someone had put him here? People from the city had taken the trouble to transport him here.'

Had Norton scratched that out himself, in the old days, which were the only days? Was it Beckett in reverse translation? What was he waiting for in Staines? It was surely time to follow the Martian invaders of HG Wells to Shepperton. Direct quotation was illegitimate, unless he dumped his *New Worlds* for old ones. Wars of the Worlds. Didn't the river run red? Like a plague of Egypt. This bridge was a temple lacking gods but thick with echoes.

If those Notting Hill conspirators, in their heated arguments, their jealousy and their mutual support, had suffered from Norton's pathology, travelling through aeons of crowded shelves while sticking to their caves, could he break the causal chain by challenging one of them in the house where he was reputed to have hidden away?

But before he can move, the shape of the words on the cover of the paperback, JG BALLARD, in sunflower yellow, calls up the recused privilege of working days, out in the air. Of poets labouring alongside certified and toothless madmen, released on licence into a community that has no place for them. And how the not-yet-writer has to locate an ethical signature and do justice to the annoyance of the seer's rant. The madman whose madness is the higher poetry, the higher cost: the Artaud contract. What the poet takes home, beyond a few sentences to knit across a ruled page, is the conviction, on a hot July day in 1966, that a voice has spoken as he takes a rest from cutting grass outside the Carshalton Steam Laundry. And that his 'vocation' is confirmed. As one of the elect, the damned. So he hopes. So he honours with lifelong poverty and labour. So it is.

Nerve failed on the approach to Old Charlton Road. Norton could have settled here once, along the river reaches, among weekending Edwardian pleasure-seekers. He could have tried to make his new world in an old place; a place tried and tested and already claimed by a writer who understood the perverse ambivalence of suburbs. Commuter trains stopped at every hamlet, giving undecided travellers time to change their minds. And step down. To repent of their foolishness. And return to waiting London pits.

'At present,' the Shepperton sage wrote, 'people can at least exist in the gap left between the past world and the world to come. *But wait until that gap is closed.*'

Tongue loosened after weeks of silence, Ballard advised disciples who found their way from California to his Shepperton den, with recording devices, to put a brick through the window of any enterprise offering cappuccino-and-croissant. Stop the rot at source! Old Charlton Road, he boasted, was 'the real psychic battleground'. For many decades before it actually happened, the visionary author relished the dominant mode of airport culture, as it flattered rational spasms of barely managed terror. Dead-eyed drifts of digital zombies, animated by the battery cells they carried in clutching hands, while processing through endless corridors, up and down escalators; navigating structures dedicated to suspending flow: the congealed queues, no beginning, no end, of illegitimate document holders. And hard benches designed to deter the wrong sort of sleeper. Faster and faster, the stateless fed their treadmill, devices in ears, blocking out the first intimations of the century roar. The bursting of permeable bounds. The overwhelming of river barriers. The tumbling of towers. The dying of species. The scorching of crops. The beaching of whales.

Of all the new worlds Norton had visited, this was the worst. Such faith, such hope. So many loves. With the certain knowledge that it would all go. Ash in the fire. A suicide pill. The black heart inside the heart of darkness.

He came to the front garden where a solid British Ford, crumpled but unbroken, was up on bricks. You might have thought, arriving here by way of some eco-warrior new puritan podcast of the next century, that the garden was a suburban experiment in giving nature its head, bringing back native vermin. Grass like mattress stuffing was unmolested by mower, no special status for magnolia or box hedge. Windows in the speculative villa were uncurtained. Affording a view of deckchair and tin palm tree. A peeling door yawned. The property looked unoccupied, but it pulsed with life. With an active intelligence at work: a whisky-sipping Prospero hunched in concentration over a manual typewriter. The keys rattled like teeth in a drum.

But Norton was not going inside. Coverless books had been flung into the undergrowth. As a gesture towards premature compost. It wasn't that Ballard had been brought back to life. Generally speaking, as Artaud noticed, the dead do not return. They don't have to make that tedious journey. They never go away. They become an emanation of place. And we, stalking our confused circuits, are *their* ghosts. We are doomed material beings. Norton was reluctant meat. He squeezed a thin wrist in proof of that alarming proposition. The keys hammered upstairs until the windows shook. Ballard was writing Norton into his story.

'A typewriter with half the keys missing (he picks out fragmentary sentences, sometimes these seem to mean something).'

And sometimes not. The delirious percussion stops. Norton turned away, as a figure in uniform shouldered past him, as if he wasn't there. (He was *and* wasn't. Like that rhyming apparition on the stair.) The householder, tieless, in casual wear, unbuttoned faux Hawaiian shirt, is irritated but civil, prepared to engage in brief badinage with the familiar postman. (Remember them?) He accepts a bundle of taped packages, books for review. And sorts them faster than any machine. He sorts them by weight. Thinner ones and big fat numbers that might be art picture books or Helmut Newton, he accepts. 'Hampstead fiction', as he calls it, and polite supplement fodder, goes straight into the bushes. Let stalking beasts sharpen their claws. Let magpies pad their nests with bubblewrap. Let foxes lick the glue. Norton is shamed at witnessing these intimacies.

An hour later he is still at the gate when Ballard reappears. 'It's not imagination that falters, but the *will*.' To wake from a posthumous dream is rejuvenating. There is a cat. Norton is convinced that if it so chose it could talk. 'It's not mine,' Ballard said, 'she tours.' She is supple and slow and courteous enough to stretch and yawn and lick her privates in a warm pool of weak sunlight.

The Shepperton writer strikes off in the direction of the river. It is the hour of his constitutional. 'Must be the period when he lost his licence,' Norton thought. A year of learning to use his legs again, letting the topography of film studios, reservoirs, business park and motorway, sing to him. Drifting in the slipstream of Ballard's drift, bowed under the screeching flight path, Norton was in his element. As a potential escape route, he had stuffed a hefty lump of paper from the Old Charlton Road garden, book ballast, into his rucksack. If this migraine coming at him in waves of electrified and dancing prose, with light surges like the immediate aftermath of hammer blows, didn't let up, he would have to broach a different textual source. *New Worlds* was transformative, but you can't fall into the same multiverse twice: that would be greedy.

'The Water World: Moving through darkness along the causeways between reservoirs. Half a mile away the edge of the embankment formed a raised horizon, enclosing this world of tanks, water and pumping gear with an almost claustrophobic silence . . . He disappeared down a stairway.'

The inevitability of that which is written swallows not only the author but also the reader. Revising, editing out, skipping, improving, we fit whatever is offered into the bardo of our established fantasies.

Ballard faded. An outline absorbed into the lurid and disnatured green of the motorway meadows, the farmlands and market gardens stolen for airport expansion. Disposing of the vast and still provocative enterprise of *New Worlds*, news that stayed news, in one of those book swap bird boxes that had appeared overnight across the most unlikely of edgelands, Norton reached blind for his new biblio-portal: *London, City of Disappearances.*

Instinct had him striking north towards the ring of decommissioned asylums shadowing the orbital motorway between Watford and Shenley. It was time to beg for sanctuary, to turn himself in. But what was this volume? The pages his trembling fingers picked out were floating over the ground where he was already walking. 'I found that this alluvial plain, with its ditches and hatches, had the feel of another country.' The uncredited reporter, explorer of margins, had discovered 'a colony of derelict smallholdings'. 'For years,' he wrote, 'this little enclave of farmhouses remained hidden beneath the Heathrow flight paths.'

The troubled but eloquent advocate of this ground confessed to being an archivist of ruin, 'retrieving letters, diaries and borough guides from these unofficial time capsules'. The trash found in abandoned cottages and shelters. In full De Quincey fugue, out of time and in place, the electively disappeared scribe spent many nights under the stars, in water towers, signal boxes and fake villages built to be bombed. He outperformed Norton by becoming the thing he described and using the energy of previously unnoticed plants and highway interventions, scraping the scarp, to launch a tidal wave of words hinting at a better life. He got the courts, prisons, asylums and addictions done before he launched his life quest.

'A white police van drove southwards along the Perimeter Road ... We tumbled down the slope, rehearsing our explanations.'

But there are never adequate explanations. Norton interrogated the silence of margins for the sound of sirens. 'The police were waiting for us. They were armed.'

They take photographs to compare with other photographs already in the files. They want to erase this nuisance from the virgin ground of the latest grand project; the millions due to be written off when overweening promises are cancelled by the incoming administration. The cameras were black and digital. Hi-spec tools for idiots. Self-operating and impatient of bungling thumbs. Content providers for new fictions. Suitable for light 'editing' by a royal princess with time on her hands. The writer was ordered to stay out of the territory. Which was like advising him to wake up tomorrow in a newer and cleaner skin, his 'impressive' record of misdemeanours forgiven and forgotten.

The 'disappeared' reporter in the fat book never returned, in person. But the story of his return did not fade. It was the beacon of hope that lit Norton on his tramp north, when there were no more pages to prod him towards an unwritten destination. All these scattered settlements will disappear too, the prescient junk-accumulating writer warned, 'swept aside by the urge to find depth and richness elsewhere in the world. Always elsewhere.'

ALISON MOORE

THE JUNCTION

HE EXPECTED TO be home by six, in time for the evening meal. He preferred to eat later than that but while he was under his mother's roof he would respect her rules.

He had only been away for a week and yet it was strange to be home, or not quite home. It had been disorienting to hear English on the plane, and to leave the late-summer warmth of Paris and return to this chill and a feeling of damp in the air. It didn't help that a diversion was now forcing him to take an unfamiliar route.

There was a tin of shortbread on the passenger seat, which he had bought at the airport so he'd have something to give to his mother. She had little appetite these days but she liked sweet things. As he drove between the airport and his mother's house, he had to resist opening the tin and eating one biscuit after another. He would have liked to have the radio on, for company or background music, but it no longer worked.

His small suitcase, full of neatly packed dirty laundry, was stowed in the boot. He travelled light, avoiding baggage reclaim and goods to declare.

Now he was on country lanes, driving cautiously around the bends, conscious of the statistics, of country lanes being the most dangerous of roads. Coming to a junction, he paused at the white line and looked both ways. The road was quiet. His stomach growled and he glanced down at the shortbread on the passenger seat, and when he looked up again there was a Volvo, in his rear-view mirror, coming too fast to stop. He'd never been in a crash before. The impact took his breath away. It shunted him over the white line and across the empty road. The tin of shortbread was flung from the passenger seat into the footwell, and though the lid stayed on, he could just imagine the devastation inside.

The Volvo driver was the first to get out of his car, holding his neck as he approached as if he were holding his head on. He bent down to say through the window, 'I didn't see you.' He stepped back so Paul could open his door. 'My mind was on other things.'

Paul climbed out, waiting to feel any pain in his body, but there was nothing. He went around to the back of the car, which was his mother's car. The damage was bad.

'Are you hurt?' asked the man.

'I don't seem to be,' said Paul. 'How about you?'

'Ah,' said the man. 'It's nothing. Are you insured?'

'Yes,' said Paul.

'You're not from round here.'

'No.' Paul looked out at the hazy moorland. He was some way from home and none of this was familiar. He told the man where home was, where he was going, and the man whistled.

'You can't drive your car now,' he said. 'Not all that way, in this state.'

Paul sighed, nodded. 'I guess the insurance company will send a tow truck.'

'I guess so.'

'We should swap details.'

'Yeah, yeah,' said the man. 'Look, I live just here. Just down there.' He pointed down the road and Paul looked for a house. 'You don't want to be standing waiting out here in the cold. We'll go to mine, I'll put the kettle on, and we'll do what needs doing from there, all right? You can drive that far, can't you?'

Paul was not sure what he was supposed to be looking at. He could see some trees, a sprawl of hedges. But yes, he thought, beyond the hedges there was a roof, a chimney pot, puffing out smoke, perhaps the edge of a village.

'I'm Neville,' said the man, holding out a hand for Paul to shake.

'Paul.' He took Neville's hand.

'Just down there,' said Neville, gesturing again into the distance. 'Follow me.'

Paul got back in the driver's seat. He lifted the tin of shortbread back onto the passenger seat, wincing as he righted it and heard everything inside shifting, resettling. He pictured his mother opening a tin of broken biscuits, a tin of crumbs and dust.

Neville returned to his Volvo and steadily reversed, and Paul imagined the impact itself being reversed, the damage undone, the metal uncrumpling, the lights unbreaking.

They set off. Paul drove gingerly: something was dragging on the ground; something had come loose. As they made their way down the road, an opening in the hedges revealed itself, a gravel driveway into which Neville turned, and Paul turned too. There in front of them was the house with the smoking chimney pot: a semi, with its twin on one side and an adjoining garage on the other. Neville parked close to the garage door, and Paul's car fitted snugly in behind. The house was not dissimilar to Paul's mother's house, and he thought of her in her kitchen, chopping something on the chopping board, warming the oven.

Getting out of the car, Paul sank slightly into the gravel. He looked up at the ivy-clad face of the house. 'Nice place,' he said.

'Well, it's home,' said Neville. He crunched over the gravel, towards the front door, and Paul followed. There was a sign in the window: BEWARE OF THE DOG. 'Don't worry about that,' said Neville. 'There's no dog.' Nevertheless, Paul found himself looking out for one, coming at him with its teeth bared, as they made their way into the house. He could smell the coal fire. 'Shoes off.' Paul, removing his shoes, placing them neatly beside Neville's, was glad his socks were decent. 'Follow me.'

Neville put two cups of tea on the kitchen table and sat down, gesturing to Paul to take the other seat. 'You want my details,' said Neville, finding a blank scrap of paper and a pencil nub. He wrote in tight little capital letters. 'And you give me yours.' Neville passed the paper and pencil across the table to Paul, who wrote his own information underneath Neville's. And there were no witnesses, so that was that. He tore the page in two and gave Neville his half.

Neville spooned sugar into his cup and offered the bowl to Paul. 'When you've drunk your tea,' he said, 'you can make your phone call.' They both took their tea hot and sweet, and Neville said, 'We needed that,' as if the crash had happened to himself as much as to Paul, as if he were not responsible for the collision. He had not said sorry. But then, you were not supposed to, Paul knew that.

While Neville washed their cups, Paul phoned his insurance company. He gave Neville's address: the house had a name but no number, but Neville said that was enough, and Paul supposed it was that sort of place, a small community, where no one locked their doors. 'It's not hard to find,' said Neville. 'There's only one road.' Every line of the address was something strange and pretty; when Paul read it out, it sounded like an incantation. He was told he could expect the recovery service within the hour.

'Another drink while you're waiting,' said Neville. 'Something stronger.' He reached into a kitchen cupboard for glasses and poured two measures of sloe gin. 'I make this myself.' He carried their drinks to the kitchen table and they sat back down in their places. 'The berries grow in my garden.' He raised his glass to Paul, who lifted his own in response and took a cautious sip.

'That's nice,' said Paul. 'Quite sweet.'

'Aye,' said Neville. 'It is sweet.'

Paul glanced at his watch. 'I should still be home before it gets dark,' he said, though the evenings were getting shorter.

'And what is it you're getting home to?' asked Neville.

'My mother,' said Paul. 'And work, though I'm in between jobs. I'm a librarian – *was* a librarian, for nearly twenty years. But they've closed my library down.' He had been looking at vacancies but had not applied for anything.

'Everyone around here is redundant or retired,' said Neville, 'or dead.' He leaned forward to top up their glasses. 'Seeing as you're not driving.' He sat back again, undoing the top button of his shirt. 'I keep myself busy though. I have hobbies.'

'I used to make Airfix models,' said Paul. He remembered the patient, careful work, the smell of the glue, the smell of the paint, the satisfaction. He listed, for Neville, the finished models he still kept in a cabinet in his bedroom in his mother's house. She used to tell people he played with toy cars, which made it sound like he wound them up and made them go, but they weren't that sort; he kept telling her, they were models, they didn't go anywhere.

From time to time, while Paul talked, he went to the front window to look out, and each time he came back, Neville said, 'Nothing?'

'Nothing,' said Paul.

The hour went by. 'I'd have been home by now,' said Paul. 'My mother will be worrying.' She would be eating alone, or else waiting, the welcome-home dinner going cold.

'So call her,' said Neville.

Paul nodded. He would have to tell her what had happened to her car.

While Paul spoke to his mother – *I'm miles away, Mum . . . I'm being looked after . . .* – Neville took their glasses out to the patio. He said, when Paul joined him, 'We can still hear the door from here.' They sat on matching deckchairs, enjoying another inch of sloe gin in the evening light.

'How long have you lived here?' asked Paul.

'I've always lived here,' said Neville. 'I hope I'll die here.'

'It's nice,' said Paul, admiring the garden: the orderly vegetable patch, the colourful berries on plentiful bushes, the apple tree, the neat dry-stone wall, beyond which was the moor. 'All that,' he said, 'on your doorstep. How big is the village?'

'There's no village here,' said Neville. 'There *was*, at one time, but it was deserted centuries ago. None of the original buildings are still standing. There are houses, of course, here and there; there was a community of sorts, but we've been dwindling.' He watched a fly land on the back of his hand. 'So what brings you here?'

Paul recalled the quiet road, the junction, the shock of the impact. *You brought me here*, he thought. 'A diversion,' he said. 'I was just passing through.'

'Have you been somewhere nice?'

'I've been in France,' said Paul, 'with my fiancée, Paula.' People had always commented on that, Paul and Paula, saying it was romantic, that they belonged together, or else finding it funny, as if it were a joke. 'My ex-fiancée,' he added. 'She broke it off.' He lifted up his empty hands.

I don't think . . . she had said. *I'm not sure . . .* It had been brutal.

Neville nodded. 'And where is she now?'

'She's still there,' said Paul. 'She lives there. She's a schoolteacher, a maths teacher.' She and her young pupils were familiar with concepts that Paul had either never known or had forgotten. She had introduced him to perfect numbers and happy numbers. He had explained these things to his mother, but his mother had never heard of them either and refused to believe there was such a thing as a perfect number, a happy number.

They drained their drinks and Neville said, 'I don't think they're coming.'

'They're bound to come eventually,' said Paul. But after a while he phoned, to see where they had got to. He stood at the back door, on hold. Occasionally, he rolled his eyes at Neville, who only smiled. Finally, he got through to someone, who told him that the recovery vehicle would be there within the hour. When the hour had passed, and the sun had sunk, he called again, and was assured someone would come within the hour.

'I'm hungry,' said Neville. 'I'll make us some supper.'

'I don't want to put you to any trouble,' said Paul.

'It's just leftovers,' said Neville, fetching a tub from the fridge.

Paul hadn't realised how hungry he was until the smell of the warmed-through leftovers reached him and drew him to the hob. 'That looks lovely,' he said to Neville, who was stirring a bubbling stew.

'I've got some wine to have with it,' said Neville, picking out a bottle and uncorking it while the stew simmered. He laid the kitchen table and told Paul to sit.

'Thank you,' said Paul, 'for all this.'

Neville passed him a glass of red wine. 'Sloe wine,' he said. 'I made it myself.'

Paul took a sip. 'That's nice,' he said.

'It goes well with the stew,' said Neville, taking two bowls from a cupboard and filling them from the pan.

Paul picked up his fork. 'I haven't had a hot meal in days,' he said.

'No?' said Neville.

Paul shook his head. He had been living on crisps and crackers.

'You've not been looking after yourself.' He topped up Paul's wine. 'These vegetables are from my garden.'

'They're beautiful,' said Paul. Everything was very soft. He thought of Paula, who carried raw vegetables in her bag, crudités in plastic tubs, so she wouldn't have to stop for a meal; she was always on the move, always on the go, walking fast, talking nineteen to the dozen. *Slow down*, he kept telling her. *Wait.*

'Crumble,' said Neville, reaching for Paul's empty dish. 'And then a little glass of port.'

'I've probably had enough,' said Paul.

'Just try it,' said Neville.

Paul tried to think what he'd had: a glass or two of gin, a glass or two of wine. He didn't feel too bad.

'Apple and blackberry,' said Neville, putting a bowl of crumble and custard down in front of Paul. He gave him a spoon and watched him start, watched him taste the fruit. 'The fruit's from my garden. The berries last for months in the freezer, for a year or more. I've got a chest freezer full of them in the garage.'

Paul, through a mouthful of hot apple, said, 'It's good.'

With one hand on his stomach, he phoned again about the recovery service, and was told it could not reach him that evening but that it would be with him first thing in the morning. 'In the morning?' said Paul, widening his eyes at Neville. What was a person supposed to do, he said after hanging up, what was a person to do, abandoned with a broken-down vehicle, left at the side of the road all night?

'But you've not been left at the side of the road,' said Neville. 'You're here with me. You can stay the night.'

'You've been very kind,' said Paul. He would have to call his mother again, let her know not to expect him.

'Now,' said Neville, when that was done. He was holding a bottle whose contents were almost black. 'Sloe port.' He filled two glasses and passed one to Paul, and watched to see how he liked it.

Paul took a sip. It was very nice, he said.

'You could get your car fixed here,' said Neville.

'I have to use an approved garage,' said Paul, 'for my insurance claim. The recovery vehicle will be here in the morning.' He didn't mean to sound ungrateful. 'Thank you though, otherwise.'

'Well,' said Neville, 'now you're staying you'd better fetch your things in.'

'Yes,' said Paul. 'I'll do that.' There was not much. He moved languorously, full of dinner, full of sloes. In the hallway, he eased his feet back into his shoes and went out into the world, out into the night. The air was still and cool. The stars, in the port-coloured sky, were astonishing. He stood gazing at the constellations, by which men used to navigate; he tried to remember what was what.

There was nobody out, no traffic on the road. The adjacent house was quiet: there were no lights on, no signs of life.

His car looked strange in Neville's driveway - this familiar thing in a strange place, his mother's car in this stranger's driveway. Paul waded through the gravel, going around to the boot. Every movement, every action, seemed so noisy: the shifting of the stones, the unlocking of the car, the opening and closing of the boot and the passenger door. He carried his belongings to the house. Neville met him at the door and brought the suitcase in. 'Is that everything?' he asked, holding on to the suitcase and nodding at the tin.

'That's everything,' said Paul, closing the door behind him. 'It's quiet out there.'

'It always is,' said Neville.

'What are your neighbours like?' asked Paul.

'Your guess is as good as mine,' said Neville. 'There's no one nearby. There was a family next door but they've gone now.' He started up the stairs.

Paul followed, carrying the shortbread with care.

There were three closed doors on the landing. 'That's the bathroom,' said Neville, pointing to the far end. 'You'll be wanting a warm bath after your journey, after the day you've had.'

'That would be nice,' agreed Paul.

'And this—' said Neville, opening the door at the top of the stairs, '—is your room.' He showed Paul into a bedroom - a neatly kept guest room - with oatmeal walls, oatmeal bedding. He put down the suitcase. 'I'll fetch you a towel.'

'Thank you,' said Paul. 'I'm looking forward to a good night's sleep.' He felt shattered, and grateful for Neville's hospitality. He was almost glad it had happened; he was glad he was here.

'Me too,' said Neville.

'I've put in a bath bomb.' Neville, with his shirt sleeve rolled up, tested the water. 'One of my wife's. My late wife,' he added.

'I'm sorry,' said Paul.

Neville read from the discarded packaging: 'Sweet vanilla.'

Left to undress, Paul rid himself of his travelling clothes and lowered himself into the scented bathwater. He could see, for the first time, his vivid bruises; he could feel some tenderness when he pressed them. He rested his head on the rim of the bath and closed his eyes. He could hear Neville moving about downstairs, clearing the table, washing up, opening and closing doors, stirring the fire.

Paul was in danger of falling asleep, drifting off in the warm water. He felt as if he had been on the road for days, but only that morning he had been in Paris with Paula. He'd had a bad night though; he'd had a series of them. Paula had been different, distant, in the days before dumping him. It had affected his sleep, and his appetite. That morning, he'd woken early, got dressed in the dark and left Paula's flat before dawn, slipping out without saying goodbye.

He opened his eyes and sat up. The bathwater had cooled around him. He rose heavily from the vanilla-scented water and reached for the towel that Neville had provided him with. It was comfortably big enough, if somewhat old and thinning. With the towel wrapped around himself, he went out onto the landing, feeling ready to turn in. He tapped lightly on the middle door, but there was no response. He went to the top of the stairs and called down quietly, 'Good night,' but there was no reply. He returned to his room.

With the door closed, he changed into his pyjamas. He thought of Paula, who slept naked and had always made fun of his pyjamas. But, he had said to her, he felt the cold.

There were things he wanted to say to her. He had stationery in his suitcase, and while his hair dried he began a letter. *It was a shock*, he wrote, *I was really hurt*. He wrote a few lines but could go no further; he did not know how to continue. And he was tired. He put his letter aside and got into bed. The bedding was a little cold, and musty, perhaps unused for years, but he got himself settled. He had a book he'd been trying to get through but he didn't feel like reading; he could hardly keep his eyes open. The book, it occurred to him now, was one of Paula's. He supposed he ought to return it.

He switched off his bedside lamp, still listening out for Neville, as if Neville might come to his room like a father, a figure in the doorway, fix his covers, say *Sleep tight.*

He closed his eyes and turned over. He could smell the sweet vanilla clinging to his skin, wafting around him whenever he moved. He pushed his face into the pillow and smelt the dust on the pillowcase. But he was so tired and so comfortable, he was asleep in moments.

He woke to daylight in the strange bedroom, feeling the cold, feeling all over again the loss of Paula. It was later than he would have expected to wake; it was mid-morning, and, with alarm, he remembered the recovery service. He got out of bed and looked inside his little suitcase. Nothing was clean.

In yesterday's clothes, he went downstairs, carrying the suitcase and the tin of shortbread. There were blankets on the sofa, and Paul wondered if Neville had slept there; he wondered, when he found him in the kitchen, if he had slept in his clothes, if he had slept at all. He looked exhausted.

There was coffee brewing, and a pan simmering on the stove. 'You slept well,' said Neville, pouring out two coffees, handing one to Paul. 'You were sleeping like a baby when I looked in on you.'

'I slept so late,' said Paul.

'I waited for you,' said Neville, turning off the hob and spooning out baked beans.

'I take it they haven't been,' said Paul. He tapped at his phone. 'Nothing – no messages, no news. They said they'd be here first thing.'

'They've let you down,' said Neville. 'Forget about them. I've sorted it.'

'What do you mean, you've sorted it?'

'I'm getting your car fixed. Don't worry about it.'

Paul went to the front window and looked out at the driveway, at the space where his car had been. 'But I have to use an approved garage.'

'It's being done as a favour,' said Neville. 'It won't cost me a thing. We don't need to go through insurance at all. You'll get your car fixed without having to pay the excess, without losing your no-claims discount.'

'But they're on their way.'

'I've taken care of it,' said Neville. 'You'd waited long enough. You can forget about them now. You can stay here.'

Paul turned away from the window. There had still been no mention of culpability, no apology, but then again, Paul supposed this was it, this was Neville's way of making amends. He thought of his mother, waiting. 'Well, thank you,' he said, 'but how long will it take?'

'I don't know exactly,' said Neville. 'Come and eat your breakfast while it's hot.' He led the way back to the kitchen. 'Sit down.' He put a plate in front of Paul, who picked up his knife and fork. 'There's toast if you want it,' said Neville, 'and sloe jam, homemade.'

'You've gone to a lot of trouble.'

'It's the end of last year's batch,' said Neville.

'I mean everything,' said Paul. 'Taking me in.'

'We'll have to decide what to do with ourselves. Have you got walking boots?'

'No,' said Paul. He only had the town shoes he'd arrived in.

Neville asked his size and said, 'My wife's boots might fit you.'

'I should phone my mother,' said Paul. 'I should let her know what's happening.'

'You do that,' said Neville, as he refilled Paul's cup. 'Let her know you're staying.'

His mother picked up immediately. 'But who *is* this man?' she asked.

'His name's Neville.'

'But how long are you staying there?'

'I don't know,' said Paul. He told her she was not to worry, that he was being well looked after, that the car was being fixed, that he would call again soon.

Neville, meanwhile, had cleared the table and was washing up.

'How's your neck?' asked Paul.

'It's a bit stiff.'

'I'm a bit stiff too,' said Paul.

'A bit of exercise might do us good,' said Neville, peering out at the moor.

'Is someone going to phone about the car?'

'Not today,' said Neville. 'But don't worry, you'll stay as long as.'

'Do you think, while he's at it, he could take a look at the radio?'

'What's wrong with the radio?' asked Neville.

'It's just stopped working,' said Paul. 'Given up the ghost.'

'Fixing that will take a bit longer,' said Neville.

'Of course,' said Paul. He asked if Neville had a newspaper. There would be one somewhere, said Neville, and after a while he brought Paul a pile of old magazines, which Paul read at the kitchen table while Neville made pastry.

At lunchtime, there were sandwiches, cut into triangles, with homemade pickles. Paul wondered what Paula was doing. There was the time difference of course. *This isn't* . . . she had said, *I'm not* . . . He said to Neville, 'Have you heard of happy numbers?' but Neville wasn't sure.

'Maybe I did them at school,' said Neville. He asked why they were called happy numbers, what made them happy, but Paul didn't know.

He thought about having to tell his mother about Paula. She would relish the news of their break-up; she would enjoy telling him *I told you so.*

'You're thinking about her,' said Neville.

Paul nodded.

'You need to let her go.'

'It's hard,' said Paul.

'It is,' said Neville. 'I know.'

Neville left the table to rummage in a cupboard full of games. 'I have something for you,' he said, bringing out an Airfix box, passing it to Paul. 'You can make this if you want.'

'I haven't made one of these since I was a boy,' said Paul. He inspected the box. 'A Ford Mustang. I've never made one of *these.*'

'Go ahead,' said Neville.

While Neville made an apple pie, Paul opened the Airfix box, emptying the kit out onto the kitchen table. It was different from the ones he was used to, the ones that came with glue and paint. *No Glue*, said the box, *No Paint*. This pre-coloured kit was more like Lego. Paul followed the numbered instructions, snapping the pieces into place – the wheel arches, the seats, the roof – seeing the shape come together.

He attached the tyres to the wheels, the wheels to the axles, the axles to the car. He could lift the bonnet and see the little plastic engine underneath. He sat back and admired the finished Mustang. It had taken him twenty minutes, minus the stickers. He used to spend hours – entire rainy days – at this labour of love. It used to be messier.

He looked for Neville, wanting to show him the finished car. The apple pie was in the oven, and there was a new fire going in the living room. Paul looked into the garden, but Neville wasn't there. He might have gone to see the man about the car. Paul had no idea where he was, this man; he supposed he was somewhere in the village – not that there was a village. Perhaps Neville would bring his car back, all mended, as good as new, looking as if the collision had never happened. Paul imagined leaving, Neville standing on the pavement, waving. He could imagine glancing in his rear-view mirror and seeing nothing there, just the road behind him, and finding that no time at all had gone by, that he was still driving home for his six-o'clock meal. Or perhaps he would return sometime, looking for Neville's place, and find nothing there but the moor.

He could smell the apple pie. He remembered the chest freezer full of berries, out in the garage, and wondered if Neville was there. He went, in his socks, out of the back door and over the slabs to the back of the garage. 'Hello?' he called as he opened the door.

Inside the garage, beneath a bare bulb, was his car, not only not fixed but dismantled. Beneath the open bonnet was a gaping space. Was that his engine, lying on the concrete floor, in its own oil? Like a creature with its heart out. He stared at the gutted vehicle, at the displaced parts: the exhaust pipe here, the wheels over there, the body propped on blocks.

He closed the door again and returned to the house, the oven-warmed kitchen, the apple-pie smell. Standing at the foot of the stairs, he looked up at the empty landing, the closed doors. He climbed into the silence. There was no one in his bedroom and no one in the bathroom. He tapped gently on the third door and cautiously opened it.

The curtains were closed but still the light came in. There was a body in the bed, a head that wasn't Neville's on the pillow. Paul moved closer.

'Heart trouble,' said Neville from behind him.

There were pills on the bedside table.

'The heart kills one in four people.'

She looked peaceful, carefully laid out.

'One in eight,' he added, 'die in their sleep.'

'You need to tell someone,' said Paul.

'I will,' said Neville.

'Let's go downstairs,' said Paul.

'The apple pie will be done,' said Neville. They left the master bedroom and he closed the door behind them.

'Have you heard from your man about the car?' asked Paul as they went downstairs.

'It's likely to take a little longer,' said Neville.

He fetched the pie out of the oven, using a tea towel to protect his hands. The crust was perfect, golden.

'Shall we have some now?' asked Neville. 'Are you hungry?'

'Yes,' said Paul. 'Let's have some now.'

Neville brought the pie to the table and they sat down, facing one another. They had the pie with cream, and a glass of port. 'It's good,' said Paul. 'It's really good.'

'The rain's found us,' said Neville, turning to the window.

Paul nodded. 'I don't suppose we'll be going out anytime soon.'

'What shall we do with ourselves?'

'We'll keep ourselves busy.' When all this had gone down, thought Paul, they could open the shortbread.

CONTRIBUTOR BIOGRAPHIES

DAVID BEVAN is a graduate of the Manchester Writing School's Creative Writing MA programme. His first two published stories appeared as chapbooks from Nightjar Press - one of which, 'The Bull', was reprinted in *Best British Short Stories 2023*. A mini-collection of stories about birds, *Sightings*, featuring photography by Maya Sharp and part of Confingo Publishing's ongoing series of writer/artist collaborations, was published in May 2025. He lives in West Yorkshire.

ROSE BIGGIN is a writer and performer based in London. She is the author of two novels, punk fantasy *Wild Time* (Surface Press) and gothic thriller *The Belladonna Invitation* (Ghost Orchid Press), and short fiction collection *Make-Believe & Artifice* (Newcon Press).

CHRISTOPHER BURNS is the author of five novels and two collections of short stories. His most recent collection, *Mrs Pulaska and Other Stories* (Salt), includes stories first published by *Les Temps modernes*, *Prospect* and Nightjar Press. He lives in Cumbria.

IAN CRITCHLEY is a freelance editor and journalist. His fiction has been published in several journals and anthologies, including *Neonlit: Time Out Book of New Writing*, Volume 2, *The Mechanics Institute Review 15*, *Structo*, *The Fiction Desk*, *Lighthouse* and *Litro*. He has won both the Hammond House International Literary Prize and the HISSAC Short Story Prize. His story 'Removals' is published as a chapbook by Nightjar Press. His journalism has appeared in the *Sunday Times*, *Times Literary Supplement* and *Literary Review*.

PIPPA GOLDSCHMIDT lives in Edinburgh and Berlin. She has a PhD in astronomy and is an Honorary Fellow at the Science, Technology and Innovation Studies unit at the University of Edinburgh. Her most recent books are *Night Vision* (Broken Sleep Books), an essay about our social and cultural relationship with outer space, and *Schrödinger's Wife (and Other Possibilities)* (Goldsmiths Press/Gold SF), a short story collection mostly about women in science.

LINDEN HIBBERT runs a pop-up art gallery in rural Suffolk. She has a PhD in creative writing from UEA, and is currently researching the adaptation of Ovidian myths from poetry to sculpture. Her short stories have been published by the *Baltimore Review*, and the *Madrid Review*, among others.

HANNAH HOARE is a television producer, director and scriptwriter specialising in natural history programmes. Her short fiction has been published online by *The Molotov Cocktail*, *Flashback Fiction*, *The Cabinet of Heed* and *Thin Skin*. She lives in Wiltshire, in southern England.

CATRIN KEAN's debut novel, *Salt*, won the Wales Book of the Year Award in 2021 and her second novel, *Lace*, was published by Gwasg Honno in 2024. She lives in the Garw Valley in South Wales.

ROGER LUCKHURST has written cultural histories on the topics of JG Ballard, telepathy, science fiction, trauma, corridors, graveyards and the Gothic. He has also edited several classic Gothic writers for Oxford World's Classics, including HP Lovecraft, HG Wells, Robert Louis Stevenson and Bram Stoker. His edition of the *Ghost Club Minutes* will appear from Strange Attractor Press in 2026.

BARET MAGARIAN is a British-Armenian writer who is currently working on a novel about Artificial Intelligence and on a thriller set in the Mojave desert. His non-fiction has appeared in *World Literature Today* and *The Riveter*. He has written for the *Independent, Guardian, Observer, Times, New Statesman* and *The Florentine*. His multi-media monologue *The Manuscript* has been performed in English, Italian and French in Reykjavik, Florence and Paris respectively. He is also a composer of piano improvisations which draw on the tonalities of Armenian sacred music.

WYL MENMUIR is a multi-award-winning author based in Cornwall. His 2016 debut novel, *The Many*, was longlisted for the Man Booker Prize and was an Observer Best Fiction of the Year pick. His second novel, *Fox Fires*, was published in 2021 and his short fiction has been published by the BBC, Nightjar Press, Kneehigh Theatre and National Trust Books. His first full-length non fiction book, *The Draw of the Sea*, won the Roger Deakin Award from the Society of Authors and a Holyer an Gof Award. His second non fiction book, *The Heart of The Woods*, was released in 2024 and the final part in the trilogy, *The Spirit of Stones*, will be published in 2026. A former journalist, who has written for Radio 4, *Guardian* and *Observer*, he is a course leader for Curtis Brown Creative, co-creator of the Cornish writing centre, The Writers' Block, and a senior lecturer in creative writing at Falmouth University.

ALISON MOORE's first novel, *The Lighthouse*, was shortlisted for the Man Booker Prize and the National Book Awards (New Writer of the Year), winning the McKitterick Prize. Her most recent novel is *The Retreat*. Her short fiction has been included in *Best British Short Stories* and *Best British Horror* anthologies, broadcast on BBC Radio, and collected in *The Pre-War House and Other Stories* and *Eastmouth and Other Stories*. Born in Manchester in 1971, she lives near Nottingham with her husband Dan and son Arthur.

OKECHUKWU NZELU's debut novel, *The Private Joys of Nnenna Maloney*, won a Betty Trask Award and was shortlisted for the Betty Trask Prize, the Desmond Elliott Prize and the Polari First Book Prize. His second novel, *Here Again Now*, was published in 2022. He is a lecturer in creative writing at Lancaster University.

SIMON OKOTIE's novels *Whatever Happened to Harold Absalon?*, *In the Absence of Absalon* and *After Absalon* are published by Salt. *The Future of the Novel*, a book-length essay, is published by Melville House. He lives in London.

IMOGEN REID completed a practice-based PhD at Chelsea College of Arts, her practice being writing. Her thesis focused on the ways in which film has been used by novelists as a resource to transform their writing practice, and on how the nonconventional writing techniques generated by film could, in turn, produce alternative forms of readability. Her work has appeared in *gorse*, *Firmament*, *Mercurius*, *Overground Underground*, *3:AM Magazine*, Vanguard Editions, Nightjar, Gordian Projects, and Rossi Contemporary.

CD ROSE's work includes *We Live Here Now* and a collection of stories, *Walter Benjamin Stares at the Sea*, shortlisted for the Edge Hill Prize. He lives in West Yorkshire and is currently working on a paratopian gazetteer of the Upper Calder Valley.

IAIN SINCLAIR lives and writes in Hackney. His books include the novels *Downriver* and *Radon Daughters* and the short story collections *Slow Chocolate Autopsy* and *Agents of Oblivion*. He has also collaborated on films with Chris Petit, Andrew Kötting, Grant Gee and John Rogers. His archive is to be found at the Harry Ransom Centre, Austin, Texas.

ELIZABETH STOTT was born in Kent and has lived in the north of England for most of her life. Her fiction and poetry has been published in magazines and anthologies, also as a collection of stories - *Familiar Possessions*. Her poetry pamphlet - *The Undoing* - was published in 2023 by Maytree Press. Most recently, her stories have appeared in *Confingo Magazine* and *Mslexia* and featured at a *Liars' League* spoken-word event.

MARK VALENTINE is originally from Northampton but now lives in Yorkshire. He is the author of nine volumes of short stories and six shared volumes of stories (with John Howard). He has also written five books of essays, and studies of Arthur Machen and Sarban. His work is published by the independent presses Tartarus (UK), Swan River (Ireland), Sarob (France), Zagava (Germany) and others.

NAOMI WOOD is the bestselling author of *The Godless Boys*, *Mrs. Hemingway* and *The Hiding Game*. Her novels have won a Jerwood Award, the British Library Hay Festival Prize, and been shortlisted for the Walter Scott Prize, the Dylan Thomas Prize, and the Historical Writers Golden Crown. Her début story collection is *This is Why We Can't Have Nice Things*, which includes the 2023 BBC National Short Story Prize winner, 'Comorbidities'. Her interests are complicated femininity and transgressive motherhood, especially in the modern workplace. She is an Associate Professor of Creative Writing at the University of East Anglia.

ACKNOWLEDGEMENTS

'Helium', copyright © David Bevan 2024, was first published online in *Fictive Dream*, 31 May 2024, and is reprinted by permission of the author.

'The Ice Tigs', copyright © Rose Biggin 2024, was first published in *The Black Beacon Book of Ghosts* (Black Beacon Books) edited by Cameron Trost, and is reprinted by permission of the author.

'Junction', copyright © Christopher Burns 2024, was first published in *Mrs Pulaska and Other Stories* (Salt), and is reprinted by permission of the author.

'Ghost Walks', copyright © Ian Critchley 2024, was first published in *Inside Voices* (The Fiction Desk) edited by Rob Redman, and is reprinted by permission of the author.

'Lord of the Fruit Flies', copyright © Pippa Goldschmidt 2024, was originally commissioned by the BBC for Radio 4's Short Works and first broadcast on BBC Radio 4, and is reprinted by permission of the author.

'Torsos', copyright © Linden Hibbert 2024, was first published online at *The Brussels Review*, December 2024, and is reprinted by permission of the author.

'Flight of the Albatross', copyright © Hannah Hoare 2024, was first published online at *Thin Skin* issue 1, and is reprinted by permission of the author.

'Dŵr', copyright © Catrin Kean 2024, was originally commissioned by the BBC for Radio 4's Short Works and first broadcast on BBC Radio 4, and is reprinted by permission of the author.

'You', copyright © Roger Luckhurst 2024, was first published in *Supernatural Tales* issue 56, and is reprinted by permission of the author.

'The Portal in Lisbon', copyright © Baret Magarian 2024, was originally commissioned by the BBC for Radio 4's Short Works and first broadcast on BBC Radio 4, and is reprinted by permission of the author.

'The Incidents', copyright © Wyl Menmuir 2024, was first published in *Twelve Stories For Twelve Sections: An Anthology of Short Fiction Inspired by Cornwall's Protected Landscape* (Hermitage Press, in association with Cornwall National Landscape (AONB)), and is reprinted by permission of the author.

'The Junction', copyright © Alison Moore 2024, was first published in *The Junction* (Nightjar Press), and is reprinted by permission of the author.

'The Headteacher', copyright © Okechukwu Nzelu 2024, was first published in *The Book of Manchester* (Comma Press) edited by David Sue, and is reprinted by permission of the author.

'When Viewed From the Head Rather Than the Foot', copyright © Simon Okotie 2024, was first published in *Cybernetics, or Ghosts?* (Subtext Books) edited by Michael Salu, and is reprinted by permission of the author.

'Fabrication', copyright © Imogen Reid 2024, was first published in *Fabrication* (Nightjar Press), and is reprinted by permission of the author.

'I'm in Love With a German Film Star', copyright © CD Rose 2024, was first published in *Walter Benjamin Stares at the Sea* (Melville House), and is reprinted by permission of the author.

'Under the Flyover', copyright © Iain Sinclair 2024, was first published in *New Worlds* issue 224, and is reprinted by permission of the author.

'The Fictional Detective', copyright © Elizabeth Stott 2024, was first published in *Confingo Magazine* issue Autumn 2024, and is reprinted by permission of the author.

'Laughter Ever After', copyright © Mark Valentine 2024, was first published in *Lost Estates* (Swan River Press), and is reprinted by permission of the author.

'Flatten the Curve', copyright © Naomi Wood 2024, was first published in *This is Why We Can't Have Nice Things* (Phoenix Books), and is reprinted by permission of the author.

This book has been typeset by
SALT PUBLISHING LIMITED
using Neacademia, a font designed by Sergei Egorov for the
Rosetta Type Foundry in Czechia. It has been manufactured
using Holmen Book Cream 65gsm paper, and printed and
bound by Clays Limited in Bungay, Suffolk, Great Britain.

CROMER
GREAT BRITAIN
MMXXV